THEIR POSSESSION

DIAMOND TIES SERIES
BOOK 2

A.K ROSE

For all of us who crave not just a savage kind of hunger,
but the kind of devotion that never lets go.

This book doesn't ask. It takes.

Their Possession is a brutal descent into control, corruption, and sacred violence. It contains explicit scenes of psychological dominance, non-consensual power exchanges, emotional manipulation, voyeurism, and enforced submission. Expect possessive billionaires with no moral compass, and one girl caught in the crosshairs of legacy, lust, and a vengeance coded in blood.

This is not a romance.

It's a reckoning.

Cloe is no longer the girl who ran. She's the girl who gets owned—body, name, and soul—by the empire she thought she could escape. There is no safe word here. Only obedience, betrayal, and what it costs to belong to four men who don't share.

If Book One made you kneel—

Book Two will make you crawl.

1

———

CLOE

The light above the dryer flickered, once, then twice. My pulse boomed loudly in my ears and for a hopeful second I prayed it'd hold, until it didn't, plunging me headfirst into the dark. My pulse stuttered, my heart slamming against the insides of my ribs too fast to control. But I kept myself steady, exhaling hard as that ugly yellow glow from the bulb sparked back to life once more.

You can do this.

I squeezed my eyes closed.

You have to do this.

There was no choice anymore, was there? I made damn sure of that. There was no going back. No undoing what'd already been done. Not the lies or the betrayal or that desperate longing inside me. One that didn't belong anywhere near the Lawlor men, but somehow—like that fragile light overhead—it roared to life in the recesses of my heart and stayed there.

An ache tore down my knees from kneeling on the cold concrete. I winced and adjusted. Pain soaked through my jeans.

I deserved it all. My hands shook so hard it took effort just to keep the ledger from slipping out of my lap.

It felt like it weighed a hundred pounds.

I hadn't opened it since the night I ran. Since Wolfe looked away long enough for me to make the worst decision of my life. I took what was important to him—*loyalty*—and ripped it apart.

My fingers moved clumsily, tugging a thin shirt from the bottom of my bag—a soft, old thing I'd left behind once in Wolfe's apartment. My fingers trembled fighting the need to lift it to my face and inhale the scent of him. God, I missed the scent of him like cedar, smoke, and want.

So much fucking want.

It made my throat tighten. I wrapped the ledger in it. Slowly. Shamefully. Each fold a betrayal. My phone buzzed on the concrete beside me.

Selene: *We still meeting?*

My thumb hovered. Then I typed:

Me: *On my way.*

I didn't ask where. Or who. Or why it felt like my chest might cave in. Instead, I pressed my palm against the panel I'd already loosened behind the dryer. The drywall gave way with a reluctant crack. I'd used this space before—for rent money I couldn't explain, bills I couldn't face. But this wasn't that. This was the end of me. The end of the woman I'd become.

I pushed the book inside. It caught at first. The corner snagging on something sharp. I gritted my teeth and shoved harder. It slid in with a dull scrape. And then it was gone. Just a shadow behind the wall.

I stared at the hole, breathing like I'd run five miles. Then I sealed the panel. And whispered, "Stay safe."

I stared at the panel, breath caught in my throat.

Would he find it?

I imagined Wolfe standing in this room—silent, unmoving, eyes like storms. I saw him peeling back that drywall with steady hands. Saw the moment he realized I had touched what wasn't mine. What never was.

He once told me, *'If you lie, lie all the way. But don't think I won't know.'* But I hadn't lied all the way, had I? No. I wasn't even good at it. Just another failure in my life. Now that shit—failing—that I was good at.

Loser boyfriends.

Failing my friends.

Failing everyone really.

But only one who ever mattered.

Camille.

And now I was failing her all over again.

The shirt I wrapped the ledger in—it wasn't just old. It was his. One I used to wear when I stayed too long, laughed too loud, slept too close.

I closed the panel again, twisting the screws like I'd done so many times before and rose, wiping my hands on my jeans like it could somehow make them clean.

My voice cracked. My hands wouldn't stop shaking. I didn't move. Not yet. Instead, I reached for my phone again. Opened the camera, then snapped a photo of the panel. Slightly ajar. Crude. Unmistakable. I opened my messages. Scrolled to a number.

Wolfe.

My thumbs hovered. Then typed: *If you want it, come get it. Please.* I attached the photo. Paused. Then hit send. I didn't wait for the read receipt. Because if I did, I'd never leave this room, or this lie.

But I did. I turned and made my way out of the laundry, and the building taking my first real breath as I stepped outside. One call, I barely had to wait.

The cab smelled like cigarettes and old anger when I climbed in. I didn't look at the driver, just passed him a few of the last crumpled bills I had. What was left of Barron's envelope.

I hadn't touched the money until tonight. I'd clung to it like maybe I wouldn't fall all the way. But here I was. Spending it to finish what I started.

The driver asked if I was sure.

"Two blocks early," I murmured. "Thank you."

He didn't argue. Smart man.

I stared out of the window at nothing really. Still, his face filled my mind those piercing dark eyes that seemed to know every secret I'd ever kept. Only he didn't know this one.

The cab veered off, pulling up hard outside a darkened building. I muttered a, "thank you," and climbed out.

The sidewalk felt wrong under my boots. Wet in places. Too slick. Every step echoed like it might bring the past down on my head. The hoodie swallowed me. Too big. Too warm. Too him.

I pulled it tighter. It didn't help. The scent of Wolfe made my chest ache. Salt and smoke and command.

My phone buzzed again.

Selene: *You close?*

Me: *Here.*

I didn't stop walking. Didn't pause to breathe. The alley behind the café looked smaller than I remembered. Or maybe I was just bigger now—with all this fear stretching under my skin like wires pulled too tight.

The streetlamp buzzed once. Then again. Its light flickered like it didn't want to bear witness. Shadows spilled across brick and rusted fence. My fingers curled into fists inside the sleeves of Wolfe's hoodie. The fabric was soft. Familiar.

It made it worse.

I wasn't just walking toward a mistake. I was wearing the memory of everything I stood to lose. And I could already feel the bruises forming. I didn't see him at first. Not until the footsteps. Two sets. One too familiar. The other too silent. Then he stepped forward.

Callum.

His eyes were empty. Not guilt. Not anger. Just... vacancy. Like he'd already left the room. Left me. Again.

My feet stopped moving. The shadows shifted again. Another man stepped forward—broader, gloved, face hard enough to break stone. My stomach dropped.

"Where's Selene?" I asked, voice tight, barely audible.

Callum didn't answer.

The other man did. Scanned my hands, then shook his head.

"You were supposed to bring the book," he snarled.

Every part of me screamed to run, still I said nothing, straightened my spine instead. He stepped into my space.

"Well, did you bring it?"

My mouth dried. My hands twitched at my sides. I cut a frantic glance at the man I'd once given my heart and body to. But like always, Callum gave nothing. Just watched as the bully moved.

His grip came fast—fingers clamping around my wrist like a vice.

"Where. Is. It?"

I yanked back. Twisted hard.

Callum moved then, but not to help me. He was all shadows and control, grabbing my other arm.

"Don't," he muttered. Not to the man. To me. "Should've brought the book, Cloe. Should've bought the damn book."

His voice wasn't angry. It was tired. Like this was already done.

I kicked. Screamed. Fought like panic was the only thing left in my chest.

"I HAVE IT OKAY!"

That stopped everything.

My breath tore from my lungs, hot and sharp. Desperation roared inside me. But it wasn't desperation for me. It was to try to undo all I'd done—to protect the man I'd fallen for.

"I have it," I panted. "I'll give it to you. But you have to tell Selene—this is it."

They said nothing. I swallowed hard.

"She's to leave them alone. All of them. Barron included. I'll show you where it is, I swear, just—this is it. No more threats, no more blackmail...no more," I met his stare. "No more debts."

The man stared at me like I was nothing more than paper-work. Then, behind him—red and blue lights. A cruiser slowed at the end of the block.

The alley froze.

I stopped breathing. His grip on my jaw tightened. Callum dragged me back deeper into shadow, his fingers digging into my shoulder.

The enforcer shoved me to the wall, breath hot against my ear. "Make a fucking sound and you're dead, got it?"

I got it.

Real well.

We waited. My face smashed against the pitted brick wall so hard my teeth left indents in my mouth.

Red. Blue. Red. Blue.

The light strobed across the alley. The cop car paused. Engine low.

I wanted to scream. I tried. Bucked hard as I could, thrashing my head to work out of his grip. My jaw wouldn't open. Blood filled my throat. The car rolled on. Didn't stop. Didn't look. Didn't save. And when the light vanished—

They started.

My attacker yanked me forward by the hoodie, dragging me forward. Then he slammed my head into the wall. Once. Twice. The pain exploded behind my eyes. My cheekbone cracked against brick. Everything went white. I felt the alley. But I saw glass. Wolfe's office. His hands braced on either side of my hips. His breath behind my ear.

You know who you belong to?

Gone.

I was back in the alley. Back in my body. And my body was breaking. The man threw me down onto the concrete. I tried to roll, but his boot caught my side. Agony ripped through me. A crunch.

I screamed. The sound bounced between the walls like it didn't belong to me. He crouched beside me and drove his fist into my ribs. Again. Again. My body bucking under the blows. I curled. Tried to protect my stomach. My chest. My face.

He didn't care. He was methodical. Punishment, not rage.

"You think they care you bleed like this?" he muttered.

His fist slammed into my thigh.

"I told you," I sobbed. "I'd give it to you—I told you—"

He grabbed my ankle and dragged me across the pavement. Skin tore under my knees. My head snapped sideways, vision blurring.

"You should've stayed gone," he said. "Should've died with her."

Camille's name flared behind my ribs.

I saw her. Lipstick smeared on a coffee cup. Laughter from a rooftop. Her voice whispering, You're mine.

And then—

Pain ripped through my jaw as his boot connected again. My head snapped backwards. White was all I saw.

The world swayed. I screamed something. Maybe his name. Maybe hers. I kicked. My foot connected—barely.

He roared and grabbed me by the hair, forcing my head back until my neck screamed.

"You don't get to make demands." He slammed my back against the ground. Leaned close. "You get to bleed."

My phone buzzed in my hoodie pocket. A second of hope bloomed—sharp and stupid. The man paused. Pulled it out with a sneer.

The screen lit up.

Wolfe.

He tilted it toward me.

"Is this who you were waiting for?" he asked. "Your fucking knight?"

I said nothing.

Couldn't.

He pressed his thumb to the message. Read it silently. Then smashed the phone against the alley wall.

Once.

Twice.

Until it split open, plastic and glass exploding across the pavement.

"That's how much he cares."

Then came the next kick. It landed in the meat of my thigh, and I folded. He followed with another—to the back of my shoulder, then my ribs. I screamed, but it came out as a wheeze.

I tried to curl. He stomped on my hand. I felt the bones shift. Something roared white and hot. I begged without sound. Not for my life. Not for mercy. Just for it to end. My mouth filled with copper. I swallowed it.

Pain bloomed in bright pulses. My body was no longer

mine—it belonged to the concrete, to gravity, to him. To regret. And he made sure I did. Fist. Elbow. Knee. A shadow stood frozen, just feet away.

Callum.

He didn't move. Didn't help. Didn't look.

My lip split open. My eye swelled shut. My hoodie soaked in something warm and sticky and not just mine.

Still—

I whispered through the blood in my mouth, "Please. Just leave them alone."

He spat beside my face.

"Them?" He snarled. "Bitch, you think they give a fuck about you? You're already forgotten."

He hit me one last time. The lights dimmed. The pain stayed. He left me on the ground. Didn't check if I was breathing. Didn't care.

They both disappeared into the dark, Callum still refusing to look back. Footsteps echoed. Then nothing. The silence that followed felt thicker than the blood in my mouth.

I didn't pass out. I wanted to. Instead—I crawled. One elbow. One breath. One drag of a leg that wouldn't move. I curled my throbbing hand to my chest. The other I reached out, digging my nails against the asphalt and with trembling muscles inched my way forward.

I reached for my phone.

I tried to grab it. Missed.

Tried again.

My fingers barely worked. I pressed it to my chest. Couldn't lift it to my face. Red and black danced in front of my eyes.

I kept crawling. Out of the alley. Into the open. Somewhere between two dumpsters, I collapsed against a wall and vomited. Blood. Mucus. Bile. I couldn't even cry.

I pressed my cheek to the cold concrete. It was the only thing that didn't burn. My breath rattled. My ribs screamed. My leg wouldn't move properly. Just emptiness. Just numb.

I saw the stars above me, just barely. They didn't feel real. Nothing did. Except one thing. His name. It slipped past my lips like a prayer. Like a curse. "Wolfe."

Because he was the only thing I couldn't scrub from my skin. And the only thing I was still trying to protect. Then everything went still.

Darkness found me, curled around the fallen rubbish. It was the only thing that did. A fragment of thought pushed in. The book was still safe. And they didn't have the brothers. Not yet.

I lay there. I don't know how long. Minutes maybe. A lifetime. The alley was too quiet. Too still. Like the air didn't even want to touch me anymore. I rolled to my side, breath hitching. My arm dragged behind me uselessly, hand curled like it didn't remember how to be a hand.

I pulled myself forward. Elbow, then knee. Elbow again. Each inch felt stolen. My left leg cruel and unmoving. Couldn't feel anything but cold, shame, and the weight of the blood leaking through Wolfe's hoodie.

I saw headlights.

For a second, I thought—maybe.

Maybe he came. Maybe he got the message. Maybe he—

No.

The car turned the other way. Tires whispered down wet pavement. The silence closed around me again. I reached for something glinting under the dumpster. My phone. Or what was left of it. Shattered screen. Battery blinking red.

I pulled it to my chest like it was sacred. Like maybe he'd still read it. Maybe he'd still know I tried.

"I'm sorry," I whispered.

It wasn't enough. But it was all I had. My head dropped to the concrete. The stars above me blurred. My breath rasped in time with the pulse in my ribs.

"If I die here," I thought, "let it just be me. Not them."

Then, softly—

"Wolfe."

Not to summon him. Just to give him the last piece of me I hadn't already destroyed. And everything went quiet.

2

———

WOLFE

THE SCREEN WAS STILL LIT.

Her message waited, bright and raw. A photo of drywall—cracked at the edges, smeared faintly with dust. A panel. A hiding place. Something secret and small, made sacred by what it held.

If you want it, come get it. Please.

No punctuation. Just that word.

Please.

It sat like an open wound.

My thumb hovered over the screen, unmoving. A pulse ticked through my jaw—tight, sharp. It wasn't rage or grief. It was something older. *Deeper.* The tension I'd trained into silence. The kind you learn when you're taught softness gets you killed.

A twitch in the corner of my mouth tried to form something. It wasn't a smile. It was the barest flicker of something mechanical. The echo of violence. Of purpose. The memory of hands wrapped around throats that lied. Of knives held steady while a man begged and I didn't blink.

I zoomed in.

Not on the wall.

On the fibers.

The photo showed more than drywall. More than betrayal. It showed her. The shirt she'd used to wrap the ledger—mine. Black. Thick. Familiar. The same one I left draped over the back of the chair after my workout.

She didn't just take the book.

She wrapped it in me.

And that's when it hit. Not heat. Not fury. Not the fire that came later.

This was colder.

Steel-edged.

Final.

I stared at the screen and let the seconds bleed. Thirty-eight, exactly. Because I counted. Because that's how long it took to kill the version of her I kept alive in my head. The girl who came back with shaking hands and blood on her skin. Who looked at me like I was the only thing anchoring her to this world. Who slipped, because she was scared—but stayed because she loved me.

That girl was gone.

What she left behind was calculated. Cruel. Composed.

She didn't scream. Didn't rage. Didn't accuse me of anything I wasn't. She just left the ring on the dresser like it was a receipt. Like I was a transaction. And then she touched the only thing I told her never to go near.

Legacy.

She went back to the beginning.

To the place where everything that mattered was born in blood and bound by oath.

I blinked once. Let it settle. She sent this message not to be saved. She wanted to be punished. I gave her rules. She gave me blood. I gave her safety. She gave them war.

Now? She could have both.

Barron's name flashed across the screen. Calling. Not the first time. Probably not the last. I didn't answer. Royal's message followed like a demand wrapped in arrogance: *Where the fuck is she?*

I gripped my cell, thumb pressed against the button. I thought about turning the damn thing off...then thought better of it.

So I ignored the message.

Their noise didn't matter. Their rage didn't reach me. Because this wasn't about them anymore. This was about her.

The girl who ran without a scream. Who didn't leave a letter. Who didn't throw a tantrum or stage some final act of drama. No begging. No tears. Just silence—and the book she wasn't meant to touch.

I stood up, slow and steady. The air around me didn't move, but everything inside me did.

I walked to the drawer.

Opened it.

The ring was still there, tucked neatly in the darkness. Silver. Cold. Shaped by her fingers—narrow, delicate, deceitful. I stared at it like it could confess. Like it might tell me what part of her decided I wasn't worth the truth.

She used to twist it when she was nervous. Rub her thumb along the inside like it burned. It did. Because it belonged to me.

She wore it anyway. Until she didn't. Until she laid it down like it meant nothing. Like I meant nothing.

I didn't speak her name. Didn't break anything. Didn't bleed for her. The rage didn't look like rage. It looked like this.

Silence that hummed like electricity in my spine. A stillness that knew what to do.

No panic. No pain.

Just decisions.

Beep.

I snarled and looked down expecting a message from Loyal this time. But it wasn't. It wasn't even a damn text. No message. No call. Just a pin without a message, or even a timestamp.

But I knew it was her.

I knew it like I knew my own fucking blood. I stared at that pin like it had teeth. Like it might bite if I blinked.

The chill started in my chest. Spread slow, like ice cracking through bone. I didn't speak. Didn't think. I just moved.

Left the apartment. Left the discarded ring on the counter, catching the light like a curse. Pressed the elevator button with the heel of my hand and reached into my pocket, keys cold against my fingers.

By the time the elevator doors slid open, I'd checked the fucking location five times. Like maybe if I looked hard enough, she'd appear on the map. Breathing. Bleeding.

Alive.

I crossed the lobby fast. The glass doors hissed open, and I strode into the night like I'd been summoned.

The Audi waited at the curb—sleek, black, hungry. I unlocked it with a snap of my wrist, slid in, and punched the ignition.

The engine roared. Tires screamed as I peeled out, taking the corner hard, cutting through the city like a blade.

I didn't blink. Didn't breathe. Just followed her. Her pin. That fucking pin.

You better be there, Cloe.

You better still be breathing.

You better still be mine.

Downtown faded in the rearview. The neon. The noise. Gone. What was left was rot. Silence. The kind of quiet that said something bad had already happened—and worse was waiting.

I turned off the main road, following the blinking dot on the screen. It led me through cracked lanes and warehouse alleys, places even the rats had given up on.

My headlights carved through the dark—

Bouncing off broken chain-link fences. Catching in the glass eyes of trash-strewn gutters. Splashing against overflowing dumpsters sagging under their own stink.

I slowed when I reached the end of the pin. The alley was narrow. Filthy. Dead fucking silent. The car idled as I scanned the shadows. Nothing at first—just puddles reflecting the sky like oil-slicked mirrors. Then the beam of my headlights cut right.

And I saw it.

A foot.

Small.

Covered by a single white sock soaked through at the toe— grimy, wet, clinging to skin like it didn't belong there.

The other was missing. Just one sock. One foot. One horrifying moment of stillness. Half-hidden behind the dumpster. Pale against the alley floor.

I slammed the car into park. The door was open before the engine stopped ticking. I moved like I'd been shot—sharp, fast, all instinct.

Because I knew.

God, I knew.

One look. One fucking look and I knew.

It was her.

Even from here. Even twisted like that, half-curled in the

dark, my hoodie clinging to her like a second skin.

Cloe.

The blood had soaked into the sleeves. Smeared her legs. Matted her hair to her temple. Her cheek was pressed to the concrete. Her arm bent under her in a way that made my stomach twist.

I didn't breathe. Didn't blink. Didn't even whisper her name. I just dropped to my knees and reached for her. Because she didn't move.

Didn't flinch.

But her skin—

Still warm.

Faint. Fading.

Clinging to her like a secret she hadn't told anyone else.

"Cloe," I breathed, touching the side of her throat. Her pulse fluttered against my fingers. Shallow. Weak. "Baby…"

But there. She stirred—barely—and her mouth opened. Just a little. And then I heard it.

My name.

Barely audible.

"Wolfe…"

The sound cracked something in me I didn't know could still break. I gathered her into my arms, gentle as I could while rage churned beneath my skin like a storm begging to be free.

Her blood soaked into my hoodie—my blood now. She sent me a pin. Not because she had the strength to fight. Not because she thought she'd win. Because she knew I'd come. And now? Now someone was going to pay.

Didn't open her eyes. But her fingers moved. A fraction. A flicker. Recognition. I didn't speak either. There was nothing to say. No words could matter here. Felt the heat of her leaking through my coat as I stood.

I didn't look around. Didn't check who saw. Didn't care.

My arms were full of betrayal. And blood. And her. And that meant I had enough.

The book would have to wait.

I carried her to the car without speaking. The streets didn't stop me. The air didn't shift. No one asked what I was doing. They didn't need to. They saw my face. And they stepped back into their shadows.

The car door opened with the hush of leather and steel. I lowered her into the back seat like I was laying her into a tomb.

The hoodie clung to her—wet, twisted, red at the hem. The blood had seeped all the way through. Not just hers. Mine. Ours. It stained the places where we once touched, where she once leaned into me, asking nothing.

I covered her legs with my coat. Because if anyone looked into that car, they would not see her broken. They would not see her bruised. They would see a woman protected.

Owned.

Marked.

I drove. Didn't check the rearview mirror. Didn't look at her reflection. Didn't need to. I could feel it. She was still warm. And she was still mine.

The clinic knew better than to ask questions. No nurses. No waiting. No signing in. Just concrete and tile and silence.

I walked through the back, her body limp in my arms. She didn't stir. Not even a whimper. The receptionist looked up— then down, immediately. Her face went pale.

They had a room ready. I laid her on the bed. Her breath hitched once when her back hit the sheets, but her eyes stayed shut.

I didn't move. Just stood there. Watching. Her chest rose in shallow, stuttering pulls. Each breath like a cost she hadn't budgeted for.

The doctor entered a moment later, gloves already snapped

tight. He opened his mouth. I turned to him—slowly. He closed it.

I didn't need words. My silence said enough. You touch her wrong—you die. You ask the wrong question—you bleed. You breathe too loud—you get fucking replaced. *Got it?*

At first, my fingers refused to let her go. Even after the nurse said they needed to examine her.

Even after the blood started drying against my arms. Even after she was wheeled behind those fucking doors. I just stood there. Hands flexing at my sides like they didn't understand what not holding her felt like anymore.

I sat down eventually. Couldn't remember when. Couldn't feel the chair under me. Then I reached into my pocket and pulled out my phone. Thumb hovering. Not shaking. Just— deliberate.

I didn't send a voice note. Didn't call.

Just typed:

She sent me a pin. I found her in an alley. Broken. Breathing. Barely.

Saint Mercy Hospital. West Wing.

Come now.

I sent it to three people.

Barron.

Royal.

Loyal.

Then I dropped the phone face down on the chair beside me and leaned forward, elbows on my knees, fingers laced tight like prayer wasn't something I did but was doing me.

The door opened twenty minutes later.

Barron walked in first—

Like he owned the fucking building.

Just like he always did.

His coat was still half-buttoned, boots loud against the tile.

He didn't speak, didn't ask. Just scanned my face once and nodded. Royal followed close behind, jaw tight. Loyal came last, quiet as a blade.

None of them said they were sorry. None of them asked what happened. Because they knew. Barron didn't look at me. He looked at her. And stopped walking.

I saw it hit him. The bruises. The blood. The curve of her shoulder where the fabric stuck to her skin. He didn't speak right away. Didn't step forward. When he did, it wasn't to help. It was to witness. To remember. So he could bury whoever did this the right way.

"I told her this city would eat her alive," he muttered. Not to me. To her. Like she could still hear. "Maybe she'll listen now."

My hand clenched into a fist. Rage flared for a second. But it was long enough. He set something on the metal tray beside the bed.

A folded piece of silk. Pale. Soft.

Camille's scarf.

"She wore this the last time she felt safe."

I didn't look at it. I didn't need to. The weight of it settled over the room like a curse. The doctor returned. Cleared his throat.

Barron didn't move.

"She's not to be touched without gloves," he said flatly. "If she wakes up and finds strange hands on her again, you'll answer for it."

The doctor nodded.

Barron added without even looking at him, "You don't speak to her. You speak to me." He nodded at me, voice sharper. "Or him. If you're braver than you look."

The doctor froze. Didn't speak. Didn't breathe. Smart man. Barron folded his arms.

We both stood there, saying nothing. Watching her breathe. Like we were timing it. Like we weren't sure how many she had left. And if one more breath was stolen—someone would pay.

The doctor returned twenty minutes later. I hadn't moved. Neither had Barron. The room was too quiet. Too heavy. The kind of quiet that coats your teeth. That makes everything taste like metal and finality.

He stood just inside the door. Clipboard in hand. Hesitant. Like he knew there was a right way to speak—and a thousand ways to die. Cleared his throat once. Then again. The second time wasn't for volume. It was for courage.

"She's got three cracked ribs," the doctor said without looking up. "One of them's fully broken."

His voice was too calm. Too practiced. Like he was reading it off a chart instead of listing the damage done to her.

"Nasal fracture. Left shoulder dislocated. Four fingernails torn out."

A pause. A breath.

"Deep bruising along her spine, her left thigh... and her wrists."

Another pause.

"Where she was restrained."

My jaw clenched. Hard enough I felt something shift. I didn't speak. Didn't trust what would come out if I did. But the words found their way anyway.

"*Motherfuckers.*"

His voice thinned. "We'll monitor for internal bleeding."

Barron's jaw ticked, his arms crossed tighter.

Still, he didn't interrupt.

The doctor hesitated. "There's evidence of... repeated impact. Systemic trauma. We'll need to run a scan—"

"She conscious?" Barron asked.

A beat.

"In and out."

"When she's in—does she scream?"

The doctor flinched. Just a flicker.

"No. She... she doesn't speak. But she...hummed."

That part hit harder than anything else. The fractures were flesh. But this? This was soul-deep. She wasn't mute from shock. She was holding something. Or trying not to lose it.

She didn't scream. Screaming was a gift. They didn't want answers. They wanted a message. They didn't take the book. They took her silence. And for that? There would be consequences.

I didn't speak. Didn't need to. I stepped closer to the bed, slow enough that my coat whispered across the floor. Her hair was plastered to her cheek. A smear of dried blood at her temple. Her lip was cracked, split open like it had been chewed.

She didn't flinch. Didn't stir.

Just lay there, wrapped in my hoodie. Breathing like it cost her something she didn't have left to give.

I didn't touch her. Not yet. Touch would make it real. Touch would be too much. I stood at the foot of the bed and made a list. Not of names. Not of men. But of methods. Of bones that would break. Eyes that would never open again. Of the sound their kneecaps would make when they fell to the floor begging me for a mercy I'd never show them.

She gave them nothing. Not a name. Not a scream. Not a goddamn breath. So now? They would lose everything.

The room was dark now. No voices. No footsteps. No questions. Just machines. The monitors hummed low—too low. Her breathing stuttered between shallow pulls, each one like it had to claw its way out of her.

Barron had left an hour ago. Royal never came. Loyal didn't knock. He didn't have to. When the door opened, he was already inside—like he'd always been here. Sitting in the corner. One leg crossed over the other, arms folded. Silent. There was no lamp on his side of the room. No flicker of movement. Just shadow. Just him.

I didn't speak to him. He didn't speak to me. He knew why he was here. I stood at the foot of the bed, hands in my pockets, head slightly bowed—not in reverence.

In restraint.

The girl who once looked at me like I was both damnation and sanctuary lay there in a bloodstained hoodie, her fingers twitching through dreams I couldn't reach.

She moved once in her sleep. A flick of her ankle. A twitch in her hand. Her mouth parted. A sound caught there—but didn't escape.

I didn't reach for her. Didn't brush the hair from her cheek. Didn't kiss her temple like I used to in the moments between pain and surrender. I just stood there. Watched her. Breathed with her. Felt the war curling back through my ribs like it never left. This wasn't forgiveness. This was possession. She gave them blood. And I? I left her with Loyal.

He was already watching. Already waiting. His nod was enough. He wouldn't leave. Not until she woke. And even then —only if I told him to.

I parked three blocks from the apartment. The city didn't look the same anymore. The alleys were quieter. The streetlights more distant. Everything I touched tonight felt like it had already died.

I didn't hesitate. Just walked down the stairs, past the cold hum of the dryer still spinning in the corner, into the basement where she made her decision.

The panel in the wall was exactly where she said it would be. Cracked at the edge. Sealed, but rushed. Like regret had tried to cover its tracks.

I peeled it open with two fingers. There it was. Black cotton. Familiar weight. Still faintly warm. She hadn't just hidden it. She'd buried it. Inside something that used to belong to me. Inside something I gave her the night she told me the dark didn't scare her—only the silence after.

I unwrapped the bundle slowly.

The shirt folded tight around the ledger, like a body wrapped for burial. I pulled it free. The cover was smooth. Unopened since she took it.

She could've brought it to me. Could've placed it at my feet and asked for mercy. She didn't. She left it in a wall and sent me a message with the photo.

A map. A breadcrumb. A dare. She gave me silence. So now? I would give her what silence earns.

I took the book. Took the hoodie. Left the wall open. Let the space gape like a wound. Let anyone who passed see how she tried to hold both sides—and lost.

She gave them secrets. She gave me war. And now? She would get exactly what she earned. No leash. No forgiveness. Just me.

And the consequences.

3

———

CLOE

The first thing I heard was the monitor.

Beep.

Beep.

Beep.

Too clean. Too steady. The kind of sound that didn't belong to the living. It belonged to survivors. To ghosts still tethered by machines. To girls with blood under their nails and regret behind their eyes.

Girls like me.

My body ached. Like I'd been dropped into something cold and left there too long. My limbs didn't feel like mine anymore. They were weight and memory and consequence.

My mouth was dry. My tongue stuck to the roof of it, thick and useless. And my throat burned like I'd swallowed something sharp—metal, maybe. Regret. Rust.

I blinked once. Light flared overhead—low and sterile, too dim to be comforting and too bright to feel safe. It painted the world in sick tones, the kind of light that made even the living look like ghosts.

Ceiling tiles stared back at me. A faint hum from the wall behind my head buzzed against my skull. The air smelled too clean. Not like bleach. Not like medicine. Just... clinical.

This wasn't a hospital. It was something more private. More dangerous. A place where people didn't come to heal.

They came to be *kept*.

I turned my head. Slowly. Each movement came with its own threat of betrayal. My neck pulled. My ribs screamed. Even the muscles in my jaw felt tight.

There were no nurses. No doors opening down the hall. No carts squeaking or rubber soles scuffing tile. Just a room. A bed. A silence I recognized.

Then I saw him.

Loyal.

Sitting in the corner. Not moving. Not blinking. Like he'd been carved from the wall itself. Like shadow had decided it needed a guardian.

One leg crossed. Arms folded. Hands relaxed—not clenched. Not loose. Just... ready. Elbows resting on the chair arms like he had all the time in the world and none of it belonged to me.

He didn't look at the monitor. Didn't glance at the door. He just watched me. Still. Steady. Absolute.

His gaze wasn't angry. But it wasn't kind. There was no mercy in his eyes. Just verdict. Like my blood had already been weighed and the sentence had already fallen.

My lips parted. I wanted to speak. Wanted to explain. To apologize. To ask what day it was. What happened after—

But no words came. None felt right. I didn't know how to speak to the man who once laughed with me around a half-empty bottle and now sat like judgment itself.

So I whispered.

"Where..."

My voice cracked. It tasted like old pennies.

"Where am I?"

Loyal didn't answer. Didn't twitch. Didn't even blink. Like I was already in the ground and he was just waiting for the dirt to settle.

Tears pressed hot behind my eyes. Not grief.

Shame.

Burning, acidic shame that coated the back of my throat like bile. I looked away. Blinked them back. Closed my eyes again like I could undo this by slipping away.

But sleep didn't come. Only stillness. Only the quiet weight of being watched by someone who had nothing left to say.

It didn't feel like waking. It felt like being studied. Like surveillance disguised as mercy. I drifted. Pain softened to a dull ache.

My breathing leveled out. Shallow. But steady. I let myself blur. Let the world smudge at the corners. But before I slipped under again, I felt it—

A weight at my side.

Blankets.

Someone pulling them higher.

Slow.

Deliberate.

Fingers—not rough, not gentle—tucking the edge beneath my arm. Up to my collarbone. A gesture. A ritual. Not affection. But presence.

I didn't open my eyes. Didn't ask who it was. I already knew. I just lay there, letting the warmth wrap around my throat like a thread. And I let the shame settle in my chest like a stone I knew I'd never lift again.

When I woke again—

Loyal was gone.

But I wasn't alone.

I knew it before I opened my eyes. The room was different. Not louder. Not warmer. Just... heavier.

The air shifted. Bent around something larger than breath. I opened my eyes. And Wolfe was there. Standing at the foot of the bed. Still. Unmoving. Like he'd always been there. Like I was the one who had just arrived.

His gaze didn't roam my body. Didn't trail my bandages or trace the blood dried at the corner of my mouth. He wasn't checking me. He was *reading* me. Measuring what was left. Like he already knew what I gave them. And what it cost him.

I didn't speak. Couldn't. My throat closed. My lungs caught on the inhale. My ribs warned me against anything too sudden. But it wasn't the pain that kept me still. It was him. *Wolfe.*

His name rang in my chest like a memory wrapped in razors. He didn't speak. Didn't twitch. Didn't let me have even that small mercy.

His coat hung open. Dark. Heavy. His shirt beneath it matched—no tie, no buttons fastened high. Just black on black. His hair was slicked back, careless, like he'd done it hours ago and then forgotten to exist in the mirror afterward.

His hands were in his pockets. His shoulders were relaxed. Not because he was calm. Because he was *resolved.* He wasn't here for answers. He wasn't here to rescue me. He wasn't here to punish me.

He was here because I made a choice—and now I had to live inside it.

Or not.

He looked like silence. Like he wasn't angry. Like he was *finished.* And that was worse.

I opened my mouth. Closed it. Opened it again, even slower. The words gathered like splinters behind my teeth.

None of them right. None of them safe. But I said them anyway. "I didn't know what else to do."

It came out small. Fragile. The sound of someone already preparing to be disbelieved. Still, he said nothing. Not a blink. Not a nod. Just that stare. That fucking stare. Like I was nothing but an equation he'd already solved.

"I thought I could fix it—"

A twitch. His jaw shifted, sharp as a blade being drawn but not yet used. That was all I got. One flicker of tension. No words. No expression. Just the ghost of something deadly being buried again.

My stomach twisted. Shame rising like bile. "You don't understand what they have on me," I whispered. "I would've come to you—"

His voice cut through me like smoke sharpened into steel. "Would have."

Two words. They landed harder than fists. Colder than the night I ran. I blinked. My breath shook. "I tried—"

"No," he said. Crisp. Flat. Unshakeable. "You *chose*."

I flinched. There was no volume to his voice. He didn't need it. He stepped forward once. Slow. Intentional. Each footfall hit the tile like a closing door.

"You chose to lie." Another step. "You chose to run."

He was at the edge of the bed now. Close enough that I could feel his presence like a second skin. He didn't reach for me. Didn't need to. Just being there—looming over me—was enough to press all the air out of my lungs.

I pulled the blanket tighter around me, but it didn't help. Nothing helped.

"I left the ring behind because I thought I was protecting you," I said, barely able to push the words out. "Because I knew if you got involved—if you saw what they had—you'd burn everything down."

"No," he said again. But this time colder. Sharper. "You weren't protecting me." He leaned forward just a breath. "You were protecting *yourself.*"

That broke something. Something tight and buried. I wanted to cry. But I didn't. Because I knew better. Wolfe didn't assign value to tears. He assigned power to silence. And I had already spent mine.

He crouched—not all the way. Just low enough to make it personal. Intimate. I could see the shadows beneath his eyes. The tension in his throat. But not his mercy.

That was gone.

"You had your chance," he murmured. Then softer. "And you chose the leash."

I couldn't breathe. Not from the pain. Not from the bruises, or the ribs that felt like splintered glass beneath my skin.

But from him. From the way he looked at me like I had never been anything but this—*betrayal in skin.* Like I hadn't once stood in his kitchen barefoot, laughing. Like I hadn't touched his face after nightmares. Like I hadn't meant any of it.

"I'm sorry," I said. Even though I knew it didn't matter. Even though I could already feel the apology wither in the air between us.

It sounded small. Weak. Not enough. Nowhere near enough.

He rose slowly. Like gravity had simply changed its mind about him and he moved with it.

"You don't get to say that," he said.

No inflection.

Just a decree.

Something carved in stone.

My throat tightened. "Wolfe—"

"No."

One word.

Full stop.

A judge slamming the gavel before I even got to the defense.

He turned. Paced a single step. Came back. Not rushed. Not urgent.

Measured. He didn't look at me this time. Looked past me. Over me. Like I wasn't worth eye contact anymore.

"You don't get to cry. You don't get to beg. You don't get to ask me to understand."

I closed my eyes. But the silence didn't lift. If anything, it thickened.

"I gave you a chance to tell me the truth," he said.

A beat.

"And you gave it to strangers."

My stomach twisted. My fingernails dug into the blanket at my waist. "I didn't mean to—"

"But you did."

His voice didn't rise. Didn't bend.

It broke *me* instead.

He stepped closer. Just close enough that I could feel the space he took up. That I could feel the oxygen bending around him.

"You want mercy?" he asked.

I didn't answer. Couldn't. My tongue felt like ash.

His voice dropped again, almost gentle. "Then you shouldn't have made me choose between you and the truth."

That was what gutted me. Not the accusation. But the *truth* of it. I bit my lip until I tasted blood.

He didn't flinch. Didn't blink. Didn't stop me. He just stood there. The man I loved. The man I left. The man who never stopped knowing I was his.

Until I looked up again. And when I did—

He smiled.

Not soft. Not cruel. Just the quiet satisfaction of someone watching something he owned stop fighting its leash.

"You're not mine," I whispered. The words broke apart on my tongue. But I said them anyway.

He leaned forward. Not fast. Just enough to steal the space between us. Enough to make sure I couldn't pretend I didn't hear him. Couldn't pretend this wasn't what I wanted—what I feared.

His voice was low. Intimate. Coiled like silk over a blade. "And you never stopped being *mine*."

That's all he said. But it landed like a collar tightening. Like a hand closing over the back of my neck. Not violent. Not tender. Just... certain.

Then he turned. And walked away. No rush. No final look. He didn't slam the door. Didn't say goodbye. He just left. Because he didn't need to stay to be present. His absence still tasted like iron on my tongue.

They didn't keep me. That was the first surprise. No restraints. No security. No nurse entering the room to tell me I'd lost my rights. Just a doctor with too-neutral eyes, a clipboard, and Loyal.

He stood by the window, arms behind his back, posture perfect. Like a man attending a funeral. Not mine.

Theirs.

The doctor spoke without looking at me. He spoke to *him.*

"She's cleared. No signs of concussion. She can walk with assistance. No stairs. Limit strain. Avoid stress."

Loyal nodded once. No questions. No concern. No visible reaction.

"She's in your care now," the doctor said softly, as if Loyal was the mercy I'd been given.

But I didn't feel saved. I felt handed over. Signed off. Shifted from one kind of possession to another.

Loyal stepped forward with a voice like cool steel. "Right," he said. "Ready?"

I didn't speak. Didn't nod. Just stared into Wolfe's dark unflinching eyes as he said nothing. Then I just *moved*. Because I couldn't stay in that room any longer.

My legs felt thin under me. Fragile. Like they might collapse if I questioned anything out loud. So I didn't. I walked. Not because I was strong. Because I'd learned how to move when I was supposed to.

One foot in front of the other, resting against the railing before I pushed off, hedging to the front of the hospital.

Loyal opened the passenger door like this was just a favor he was doing for someone. Like this wasn't blood and bruises stitched into my skin. I climbed in without asking where we were going.

I folded myself into the seat. Pulled my knees in, arms tucked close. I didn't look up. Didn't ask. I felt him before I saw him.

Wolfe.

The heat of him behind me. The slow, calculated sound of his boots on pavement. The weight of his stare pressed into the back of my neck even after the car door shut.

He hadn't said a word since the doctor gave him the list of everything that had been done to me. Not one word. But I could *feel* it. The silence was worse than shouting. He didn't look away from me. Not once.

The car was silent. No engine hum. No music. No breath between us. He drove like a soldier returning from war. And I sat like the weapon they'd brought home to clean.

We turned left onto a street I hadn't driven down in years. The moment the tires turned, my body knew. My chest locked up. My stomach twisted.

No.

Not here.

Not—

The gates opened before we even reached them. Smooth. Silent. Like they knew I was coming. Like the house had been waiting.

Camille's townhouse rose behind the hedges like a specter dressed in glass and ivy. Elegant. Cold. Still too beautiful to feel like a place where something had ended.

I wanted to scream. Wanted to turn my face to the window and tell Loyal to drive somewhere else—anywhere else. But I didn't. Because my choices were gone. And my voice had stopped mattering.

He parked at the curb. Turned the engine off. Stepped out without a word. The front door opened like it had been unlocked this whole time. Not a creak. Not a groan. Just space parting for memory.

The air inside hit me first. Conditioned. Too cold. Sterile in a way Camille never was—but her scent lingered anyway. Flowers. Cinnamon. Something soft underneath it, like powdered sugar and jasmine.

She used to say cinnamon kept the shadows away. But the shadows were still here. They'd taken root. Everywhere.

Loyal didn't say a word as I stepped past him. Didn't gesture me inside. Didn't follow. He just stood there. A silent figure in the doorway. A gatekeeper. Not letting me in. *Returning me.*

My shoes echoed on the tile. The lights were already on. Warm, soft, timed to perfection—like someone had walked through minutes before I arrived and whispered, *Make it easy on her.*

But it wasn't.

The stillness wasn't welcoming.

It was curated.

Preserved.

Like I'd stepped into a museum made of grief.

A display of the life I let rot.

When I turned, the door was already shut. No key on the counter. No explanation. Just me. And Camille. And everything I'd buried under excuses.

I waited, barely inside the doorway, staring down the hallway like something might emerge from it—something still wearing Camille's perfume.

Nothing did. But her scent lingered. Faint. Faded. Like the memory of a touch that once meant something. Vanilla and cinnamon. Warmth. Repetition. Home.

I moved slowly, careful not to disturb anything. As if stepping too loudly might shatter her ghost.

Marble counters gleamed beneath soft lighting. Gold hardware glinted like jewelry. The wine rack was still full. I stopped in front of it. Her favorite bottle still sat center stage—red with the gold foil neck. The one she saved for *"when I need to feel expensive."*

I turned away before I could see the glasses. The living room was just as she left it. Cushions perfectly fluffed. Not a throw blanket out of place.

A scarf—hers—was folded on the arm of the couch. Not draped. Folded. Deliberate. Like someone else had done it. Like someone had come through after everything fell apart and tried to make it look untouched.

Preserved.

A still life of a woman no longer breathing.

The fireplace was cold and clean. But the scent of old smoke clung to the bricks. A candle sat melted near the base. Half-used. I knew that one. I'd teased her about it a hundred times.

You have twenty candles. Why always that one?

She'd smile and say, *Because it's the only one that smells like being held.*

I used to laugh.

Now?

I hated how much I understood that.

Her room was at the end of the hall. I knew it before I saw it. The air thickened with each step. Denser. Heavier. Like the house didn't want me to enter unless I understood what it meant to grieve someone properly.

The door creaked when I pushed it open. Her bed was made. Pillows perfectly fluffed. Crisp sheets tucked with military precision. Like she expected someone to inspect it even after death.

But someone had been here.

For me.

A nightgown lay folded at the edge of the mattress. Not hers. Mine. Fresh toothbrush in the holder—still packaged. A glass of water and a bottle of painkillers on the nightstand.

And at the center of the bed—

A note.

My name written across it in Camille's unmistakable slant.

Bre.

Only she called me that.

I sat slowly. Felt the bed dip beneath me like it had been waiting. I didn't open the letter. I couldn't. If I opened it, it would be real. If I read it, it would be goodbye. So I left it where it was—sealed and sacred.

I stood when the silence became unbearable. Crossed to the window and pulled the curtain back an inch. At first, there was nothing. Just trees. Branches motionless in the still air. Then—

Headlights.

Cutting through the dark at the far end of the driveway.

Slow.

Unhurried.

One car.

Black.

I didn't need to see his face. I already knew. My lungs forgot how to breathe. My fingers touched the glass like they could stop time.

The window was cold. He didn't park at the front. He stopped halfway up. Got out. Didn't pace. Didn't knock. Just leaned against the hood. Waiting. Like he already knew the ending. Like *I* did too.

I walked barefoot through Camille's house. Each step echoing like a countdown. The front door opened beneath my hand with no resistance. The porch light flickered above me.

I left it all behind. Not because I wanted to. But because my heart gave me no other choice. Wolfe didn't look up. Didn't move.

He was still.

Like stone.

Like inevitability.

I walked to the car. He opened the passenger door. Not with force. Not with ceremony. Just like it was already done.

I got in. The seat was warm. He closed the door. Walked around. Got in beside me. He didn't speak. Didn't look at me. Didn't touch the key. He didn't have to. The silence was enough.

It always had been.

The headlights lit up the gravel. And we left the house behind.

The letter still on the bed.

Unopened.

4

CLOE

THE CAR RIDE WAS QUIET. Not the kind that leaves space for thought or peace. The kind that builds behind glass in a sealed room, that hums beneath your skin until it replaces your heartbeat.

Not a single word passed between us. No sound except the low rumble of the engine, the occasional shift of gears, the distant sigh of tires against asphalt.

Wolfe didn't look at me. He didn't check the mirrors. He didn't even touch the radio. Still he was everywhere. In the static tension of the air. In the subtle flex of his fingers around the wheel. In the way his presence filled the entire cabin—thick, heavy, impossible to ignore.

I didn't ask where we were going. I already knew. And if I didn't? I wouldn't have dared to ask anyway. Instead I stared out the passenger window, watching the city blur into a smear of light and color—red neon bleeding into blue, high-rises reflected back at me through thick glass.

My reflection stared back like a stranger. Hollow eyes. Pale lips. A version of me that looked more ghost than girl.

The heat was off. The air in the car hovered just below comfort—cold enough to notice, but not enough to complain. Not enough to justify a word.

Wolfe wasn't the kind of man to fidget. There was no bounce of his knee or tap the wheel. But tension lived in his body like a second spine.

I saw it in the clench of his jaw. In the pale stretch of his knuckles as they tightened around the leather grip. In the fact that he hadn't blinked since the last turn.

We stopped at a red light. The world around us moved—crosswalks blinking, pedestrians darting—but we didn't. Not even breath disturbed the space between us.

He didn't glance over. But I did. His profile looked carved from cold stone. All lines and silence. His mouth in a perfect line, the tendon in his neck visible from where I sat.

He looked controlled. Contained. Like there was something under his skin he refused to let out—not because it wasn't ready, but because *I* wasn't.

I thought about speaking. A joke. A whisper. An apology. Something to bridge the space between us.

But I didn't know which version of him I was sitting beside. The man who once wrapped me in his hoodie and kissed the back of my neck before making me breakfast? Or the man who watched me bleed and said nothing.

I knew he wouldn't answer either way. So I stayed quiet. The closer we got, the colder I felt. Not on my skin. In my chest. Like something was unraveling beneath my ribs—quietly, thread by thread.

Wolfe turned onto his street without hesitation. No signal. No warning. My body didn't tense. It folded. My shoulders curved inward. My hands curled into my lap like they were trying to disappear.

I breathed through my mouth—shallow, tight—like that might stop the ache from climbing higher.

When the car pulled into the underground garage, I thought I might cry. Not because I was scared. But because I missed what this used to be. A sanctuary. A home. A place where silence once meant safety.

He killed the engine. Didn't move. Neither did I. We sat there for a full minute. Maybe two. The quiet between us had evolved into something else—something that hummed like a live wire between our spines. Then, without a word, he got out. Didn't open my door. Didn't wait for me. Just walked. Like I was a shadow he didn't need to check for.

I followed. Not because I knew what came next. But because I didn't know how not to. He didn't hold the door. He didn't even glance back. He just walked through it. Like this was a transaction, not a return.

The apartment was the same. But it wasn't. The air felt different now. Colder. Filtered. Like someone had replaced the oxygen with something sterile and quiet.

The scent of him was still there—clean, expensive, dominant. But mine? Gone. Scrubbed out. Erased. Everything was pristine. Immaculate. Like someone had come in and reset the entire scene—rewritten it to exclude the chapter where I ever lived here.

I stepped in and froze just past the threshold. The lights were on—dimmed low like someone had considered comfort, but only in theory. The living room was untouched.

No coffee ring on the glass table from mornings he let me curl up with his espresso. No hoodie draped over the back of the couch where I used to wrap myself in the scent of him.

No evidence that I'd ever breathed in this space.

No shoes in the hallway.

No perfume in the air.

No chaos.

No warmth.

It looked like a magazine spread. Perfect. Untouched. Unlived in. Like I had never existed here at all.

Wolfe moved through it like a man walking through a showroom. His body didn't brush anything. His feet didn't echo. He just glided from one room to the next without pause.

In the kitchen, he poured a glass of water and left it on the island. A gesture with no instructions. He didn't say it was mine. He didn't say it wasn't. Then he walked away.

Like I was a piece of mail someone had left unopened. I stood there for too long. Long enough for the silence to acknowledge me. Long enough to feel the shape of absence push against my chest.

I stepped out of my shoes. Slowly. Quietly. Like noise might make it worse. The floor was cold against my feet. Sharp. Clean. Sanitized.

Every surface was polished. Every reflection showed me a version of myself I didn't recognize anymore. I passed the main bedroom. Didn't stop. Didn't glance. That room didn't belong to me. Maybe it never did. He waited at the end of the hall. Not looking at me. Not calling me forward.

Just... standing there.

When he turned, he nodded toward the back of the apartment. A new room. I thought, *Maybe a guest room.* Something neutral. A couch. A blanket. A closed door and a chance to sleep.

But when he opened the door—

The hinges creaked.

The light flickered.

It wasn't a bedroom.

It was a box.

A low twin bed. One thin blanket. A chair in the corner.

Shelves half-filled with cardboard lids and a folded jacket. Storage.

He didn't hesitate.

"This is yours," he said. Then turned. And left.

Just like that. No explanation. No rules. Just... designation.

I didn't step inside right away. I stood in the doorway, staring at the space like I could make it reject me. Like maybe if I stayed still long enough, the walls would push me back out.

The boxes were neatly stacked along one side. The bed looked untouched. Hospital-cornered. Clinical. It wasn't a cell. It wasn't cruelty. It was something colder.

More precise. It was placement.

And somehow...

That was worse.

I backed away. Down the hall. Past the bedroom door I used to wake up in—warm, safe, wrapped in his scent and everything I thought we were becoming.

I didn't look inside. Couldn't. But my feet moved anyway. Back toward the space where everything used to feel like home.

The kitchen. The soft window light. The hum of something domestic and real. But now? Now it all felt like a museum of a life I was no longer allowed to touch.

That's when I saw it. Tucked into the alcove beside the liquor cabinet. Lit by a recessed bulb I knew hadn't been on earlier. Intentional. Isolating. A small black stand sat at the center.

Velvet square.

And on it—

The ring.

Wolfe's ring.

The one he gave me when I thought permanence came in the shape of gold. The one I had taken off with shaking fingers and left behind like it would somehow protect us both.

It hadn't. It had *marked* the moment I stopped belonging to him. But it hadn't moved. It had been placed. Polished. Centered. Lit. Displayed. Like a trophy. Or a headstone. Or a promise that had been cracked open and left bleeding under glass.

I stepped forward slowly. Each breath felt heavier. Each step closer to it a kind of collapse. I didn't reach for it at first.

Just looked.

Stared at the smooth arc of gold. The weight of it. The way it still looked like it belonged to me. Even though I didn't. I lifted my hand.

Fingers trembling like I was reaching for a live wire. And just as my fingertips brushed the edge—

"No."

The word snapped across the room like a whip.

I froze. Every muscle in my spine went rigid. His voice came from the hallway. Closer than I expected. I hadn't heard him move. Hadn't felt the air shift.

But suddenly—

He was there.

Wolfe stepped into the alcove light, not rushing, not glaring. Just *arriving*. Like judgment itself. He didn't look at the ring. His gaze pinned my hand. Then my face. Then my hand again.

"That doesn't belong to you," he said.

His voice was soft. Even. Cold in the way silk is cold when it slips down your back before it tightens into a knot.

"Not anymore."

The breath I'd been holding fractured in my chest.

I pulled my hand back like I'd touched flame. My mouth opened. I had nothing to offer. Not words. Not apology. Not even hope.

He didn't move closer. Didn't raise his voice. He just stood there like the god of some older myth.

And said, "You'll earn it back."

A pause.

A breath.

"If I let you."

Then he turned. And left me standing in the glow of something I used to call mine. Now? It was a symbol. Of failure. Of consequence. Of something too sacred to be given back without penance.

I stared at the ring for one more heartbeat. Then turned away. Back toward the room he'd assigned me. Every step stretched long.

Slow.

Painful.

The hallway felt longer than it should have, like I was walking further from something I'd never

I walked back to the room he gave me. The hallway felt longer now. Each footstep slower. The weight behind my ribs wasn't fear. It was gravity. Shame has a mass. And mine pulled me down with every step.

The door was still open. The light flickered once as I crossed the threshold—like it was warning me. Like it didn't want to light this space for me.

I didn't turn it off. I didn't touch the boxes. I didn't run my fingers along the shelf, or pretend this room had ever belonged to anyone real. I sat on the edge of the twin bed, the blanket still folded tight like no one was expected to use it.

Quakes ran through my body. I curled my shoulders and held on. I didn't cry. Because the crying had already happened —silently, somewhere between the car and the ring. What I felt now was different. It was a quiet collapse. A submission to stillness.

There was a water bottle on the nightstand. Unopened. Room temperature. No glass. No gesture of comfort. Just hydration. Because *survival wasn't the point.*

Endurance was.

I pulled the blanket back. Slid beneath it fully clothed. The fabric was stiff. Starched. It didn't drape—it *held.*

Every part of me ached. Not just the bruises. Not just the ribs or the shoulder or the deep throbbing in my thigh. But the pieces of me he hadn't touched. The places he'd carved open without ever laying a hand on my skin. This wasn't punishment. It was exile.

He hadn't screamed. He hadn't broken things. He hadn't locked the door or tied my hands or forced me to kneel. But I had never felt smaller.

The air in the room didn't want me. The silence felt *earned.* One of the boxes in the corner was slightly open. A photo frame peeked out—silver edge, the corner of a picture inside.

I didn't look closer. Didn't want to know what memory Wolfe thought belonged boxed up beside me. Whatever it was —It was more valuable than I was now.

I lay there for a long time. I don't know how long. Maybe minutes. Maybe an hour. Time didn't exist in a room like this. It just *waited.*

I don't know what time it was. The light in the hallway hadn't changed. The house was silent. Too silent. But the bed felt smaller now. The walls closer. The quiet louder. I couldn't stay in that room. Not another second.

Every step a whisper of pain when I moved. My thigh throbbed with every shift in weight. My ribs sent sharp warnings with each shallow breath. I braced one hand against the wall.

The bathroom looked the same. Too much the same. Marble floors that echoed beneath my feet. Polished chrome taps. A mirror that seemed too large, too cold. No towels out of place. No steam. No signs of anyone but me.

It looked untouched. Preserved. Like no one had been here since I left. Like *he* hadn't stepped into this space since the night I ran.

I turned on the shower with shaking fingers. Let the water run too hot. Steam poured from the glass before I even peeled off my clothes.

The hoodie was stiff. Still crusted with old blood. The dried part tugged at my shoulder when I lifted it over my head. The scab there cracked. I winced. Everything else came off slower.

Each movement a negotiation with pain. A bruise bloomed across my thigh—deep and dark and full of silent rage. I stepped into the shower and didn't look back. The heat hit like punishment.

I gasped, knees buckling, one hand smacking the tile to keep me upright. The water sluiced down my back. Too hot. Too sharp. But I didn't adjust it. I needed it to hurt.

My skin turned red. My breath hitched. The bruises pulsed. The cuts sang. But I welcomed it. Because it was mine. The first thing that touched me without taking anything.

I slid down the wall. Sat under the stream, arms wrapped around my knees, forehead pressed to wet tile.Tears didn't come. But it felt like I should have. Like my body was waiting for a release I no longer had access to.

Selene would come. I knew that. She wouldn't let me slip away—not without extracting everything left.

I was still a tool. Still a threat. Still a failure she hadn't forgiven. And Wolfe? He hadn't touched me. Not once. That scared me more than if he had.

I expected fire. Expected a slammed door. A thrown glass. A whispered command that made my knees hit the ground.

Instead?

I got a storage room.

A cold bed.

And the sound of my own breath in an empty house.

Barron had looked at me like I was fragile. Loyal had looked at me like I was already gone. And Wolfe? He hadn't looked at all.

I tilted my head back into the spray and let the water beat against my closed eyes. Tried to remember the last time I felt clean. Not washed. *Clean.* Like I hadn't lied. Like I hadn't touched something I wasn't meant to. Like I hadn't betrayed the only man who ever looked at me like I was his.

But I couldn't find it. That memory. That version of me. I wasn't sure she ever existed. I stood up slowly. Turned off the water. The silence in the room felt heavier now. Like the steam had stolen all the oxygen and replaced it with guilt.

The air chilled against my skin as soon as the water stopped. Goosebumps rippled over my shoulders. I reached for a towel. Wrapped it tight around my chest with hands that wouldn't stop shaking. Then I looked up. And saw myself in the mirror.

I froze. Not because of the bruises. Not because of the dried blood or the dark rings beneath my eyes. Not even because of the split lip. But because—for one awful, gut-wrenching moment—I didn't recognize my own face.

My eyes looked like mine. But empty. Like the girl behind them had packed up and left, and someone else was wearing her skin.

My hands twitched at my sides. A flicker of instinct. A memory. The phone. Where was it?

The last time I saw it, Wolfe had it in his hand. Broken. Cracked. Blood on the case. He hadn't given it back. Of course he hadn't. Was he reading my messages? Tracking Selene's calls? Did he know what I'd sent? What I hadn't?

I swallowed hard. The taste of metal lingered. I pulled the towel tighter around my chest and turned away. Didn't dry off. Didn't clean the mirror. Didn't try to fix what was already unrecognizable.

I pulled the hoodie back over damp skin. It stuck at the shoulders. Still stiff from dried blood. Still mine in the worst way. Still *his* in every way that mattered.

I walked back into the hallway. Barefoot. Quiet. The house was asleep. The lights low. Every door closed—except his. The main bedroom.

I didn't stop. Didn't knock. Didn't even brush the handle. But I paused. Just long enough to feel the weight of that door.

The quiet behind it. The fact that he was in there, breathing, alive, close enough to touch—

And I wasn't welcome.

I passed it. Like a ghost skimming past the heat of its old life. I returned to the box room. Slipped under the same blanket. Same bed. Same silence.

I sat there, knees pulled to my chest, hoodie damp against my skin. The light still on. The water bottle still unopened. I didn't lie down. Didn't close my eyes.

I just sat there. Waiting. Not for forgiveness. Not for sleep. For something I didn't have a name for.

Or someone I shouldn't still want.

But did.

Anyway.

5

______

CLOE

I woke before the sun. The blanket was tangled around my legs. My neck ached from sleeping too still. My back ached from sleeping at all. The apartment was silent. The kind of quiet that feels like being watched.

I sat up slowly. Every bruise protested. The hoodie clung to my back like a secret I hadn't earned. I stood. I didn't know why. There was nowhere to go. Nothing to do. But I moved anyway.

The kitchen was dim, lit only by the blue glow under the cabinets. The clock on the oven said 5:12. I filled a kettle. Slowly. Turned it on. I wasn't hungry. I just didn't know how to be still in this house anymore.

I cracked two eggs into the pan. The shell split wrong and one yolk bled out across the burner. I didn't clean it up. Just watched it sizzle. The oil hissed. Too hot. I didn't lower the flame. Didn't care.

The eggs burned before I could flip them. The pan smoked. I dumped them straight into the sink and ran the water until the steam blinded me.

There was a time Wolfe made me eggs. Three in the morning. My thighs still red from his hands. My lips still swollen from how he took my mouth without asking. He cracked them clean, like a man who didn't believe in mess. No wasted motion. No clumsy yolk.

He made me sit on the counter in his shirt—bare legs swinging while the pan hissed behind him. His hand never left me. A touch on my thigh. A thumb along my wrist. His body between me and the edge of the counter like he was the wall and the world all at once.

You get food when I say you do, he told me once—not cruel. Not cold.

Just *final.*

And then he kissed my throat.

I remembered the plate. The way he fed me the first bite like it was his name I was tasting. Now? Now I stood in his kitchen. Barefoot. Hollow. Starving. And I didn't know if I was allowed to eat.

The air smelled like clean linen and coffee beans. Neutral. Sterile. Like grief dressed in expensive clothes.

I reached for a mug from the cabinet—my hand shook so hard it knocked two others. I froze. Waited. No sound from the hall. No voice telling me to be quiet. No footsteps coming to see what I'd broken. Just silence again. The kind that made you ache.

When the water boiled, I poured it over the teabag with shaking hands. Held the coffee cup to my chest like it might settle the tremble in my bones. But I couldn't lift it to drink. Not yet.

I sat at the island. The chair was cold. The mug burned against my palms. I stared at the dark hallway and wondered if I should knock. Should ask if I was still welcome. But I already knew the answer. Because this wasn't welcome. This was consequence.

The tea went cold while I sat there. Then I stood. Put the cup in the sink. And breathed like it hurt. Because everything still did. And normal was never going to come back. I thought I was alone. Until I wasn't.

I stepped into the living room, barefoot, hoodie still damp at the cuffs, and stopped cold. Wolfe was already there. Sitting at the kitchen table. Phone in his hand. Sleeves rolled. Hair perfect in that way that looked unplanned but wasn't.

He didn't look up. Didn't say anything. But I felt it. That crackle in the air. Like lightning had been stored in the walls.

He was reading something on the screen. Completely still. One thumb moving slowly. Precisely. Like everything he touched mattered more than what breathed around him.

I opened my mouth. Nothing came out. I stood there too long like an idiot then sat. The chair across from him groaned slightly beneath my weight. The sound felt obscene in the silence.

I looked at him.

Really looked.

His sleeves were rolled. Shirt crisp. Collar open like he'd been dressed for hours. He looked like he'd stepped out of a boardroom, not the bedroom I used to sleep in.

The shirt he wore—navy, tailored, expensive—was one I picked out once. Casually. *I like you in darker blues,* I'd said. He'd bought five variations the next week.

He didn't seem to remember.

Or maybe he did—and just didn't care.

Now I watched his hand flex around the edge of the phone. Smooth, measured. Like everything in him had been trained to operate at a level below emotional.

He didn't look at me.

Not once.

Some part of me wanted him to yell.

To throw the glass. To growl. To crack open so I could *see* that something under all that silence still burned for me.

But he didn't give me that. He just sat there. Unmoved. Unreachable. Untouched.

I wanted to ask—

What are you thinking?

Do you hate me?

Do you still want me?

If I reached for you, would you recoil?

Or worse... would you let me?

But I didn't ask. Because if I opened my mouth, I was afraid the wrong thing would spill out. So I stayed still and stared at the man who used to command me with a whisper.

Now he didn't need to say anything at all. He didn't react. Didn't glance. Just kept scrolling.

The screen's glow flickered over his knuckles. I folded my hands in my lap. My pulse was too loud. I wanted to ask something. *Anything* really. But I couldn't find a question that didn't feel stupid. So I settled for the only thing that felt safe.

"Thank you... for letting me stay."

That was the moment he looked up. Just his eyes. Cold. Sharp. Final.

"I didn't."

One sentence.

Flat.

Like it didn't matter to him whether I heard it or not.

I swallowed hard. "Then why—"

He set the phone down.

Slow.

Precise.

Looked at me like I was something under glass.

"You're here," he said, "because you're unfinished."

I didn't understand. Not yet. But my stomach knew what it meant before my brain did. The shift. The power. The pressure.

He hadn't brought me home to comfort me. He'd brought me back to finish what I'd interrupted. To show me what it meant to stay. And what it cost to return.

"You don't get the same rules anymore."

His voice was quiet. Almost calm. Like he was reading something off a card he'd memorized days ago. Like this wasn't personal. But it was. Every word felt personal.

I didn't respond. I couldn't. He leaned back in the chair and looked at me like he was deciding whether to throw me out or feed me.

"I gave you choices," he said. "You wasted them."

My throat tightened.

He didn't wait.

"No more second chances. No more protection. No more comfort."

He said the last word like it disgusted him.

I wanted to argue. To say he didn't have to do this. But I knew better. And I knew him. So I just sat there, my hands knotted in my lap, the shame curling tighter around my spine.

"You want to stay here?" he asked.

I nodded, barely.

"Then you'll follow the rules."

My spine straightened. Not out of defiance. Out of instinct.

His voice was calm, but the tension beneath it pressed like a blade to the side of my throat. Wolfe never yelled. He didn't need to.

"You don't leave the apartment unless I tell you to," he said.

His tone never changed.

"You don't enter my room. You don't touch what isn't offered. You don't speak unless it matters."

I swallowed hard.

He didn't stop. "You don't use my name without permission."

That one made my chest cave in a little.

"Why?" I asked, before I could stop it.

He raised a brow. Not cruel. Just curious.

"You want to keep it?" he asked. *"Then earn it."*

I dropped my eyes. My hands trembled in my lap. This wasn't a conversation. It was a sentence being read aloud. And I couldn't breathe through it.

"I'm not asking for much," he added. "Just the truth. The whole of you. Nothing less."

The words hit like soft violence.

"I don't know who I am anymore," I whispered.

His eyes didn't flicker.

"I do."

Then he leaned in.

Close.

Low.

"This isn't about who *you* are, Cloe. This is about *what* you are."

I didn't ask. Didn't speak. Because deep down? I already knew. I was what he chose to keep. Or destroy. And he hadn't decided yet.

He said it like the rules were already written. Like they didn't need to be spoken aloud. But he kept going anyway.

"No lies. Not one. Not about what you feel. Not about what you've done. Not about what you want."

I swallowed. It burned.

"You don't get to use Camille as a shield. Not anymore."

That hit harder than anything else. I blinked fast. Once. Twice.

He kept going.

"You don't get to run to Barron. Or Loyal. Or anyone else when it gets hard. You ran to the world once, and it nearly got you killed." He paused. "Next time, it won't nearly."

I opened my mouth. "Wolfe—"

He raised a hand.

I froze.

He didn't have to say another word. Then he said one anyway. "You can go."

I stared at him. Heart stopped.

"You've proven you're good at that," he said. *"Leaving."* The air thinned. "I'm not going to chain you to the floor, Cloe." My name in his mouth was worse than silence. "I'm not going to chase you next time."

He stood. Walked around the table. Stopped behind me. His breath slid down the back of my neck like smoke. "If you want to stay, you stay on your knees." He leaned closer. Not touching. Not threatening. Just final. "Otherwise, the door's open."

I didn't move.

Because I couldn't tell the difference anymore—between staying and surrendering.

He turned back toward the hallway. I thought he was going to leave. Then I heard my voice break into the silence— uninvited.

"You don't have to do this. I'm not your responsibility."

He stopped. Just stood there, spine straight, arms loose at his sides like he was weighing the cost of breaking something.

His voice came quiet. Controlled. Precise. "You're not my responsibility." Then softer. *"You're my property."*

The words hollowed me. Not because they were new. But

because they weren't. Because I used to want that. Used to ache for it.

I'd once whispered *I belong to you* like a prayer between his hands—offered it like surrender, hoping it would be enough to keep him. And now that it was back etched in something colder, stripped of reverence and laced with warning.

He didn't wait for my reaction. Didn't smirk. Didn't soften. Just turned toward the hallway and started to walk. And then I did something stupid. Something I didn't mean to say aloud.

I whispered, "She wouldn't have let this happen."

He froze. Only for a breath. Then turned halfway. Not enough to face me. Just enough to *warn* me.

"Don't," he said. "You *don't* get to say her name like that."

I went still. Completely still. Because I knew I'd crossed something. Something invisible and final.

I thought about Camille. Her laugh. Her warmth. The way she made everything feel less sharp. I should've read the letter. I should've clung to what little of her I had left. Instead—I said something meant to wound.

And the worst part? It didn't even land. Because Wolfe had already buried that part of himself. And I wasn't allowed to dig it back up.

That one hit harder. Because it wasn't a threat. It was a correction. And he meant every word. He didn't wait for me to respond. Didn't ask if I understood. He just walked down the hall.

The silence that followed wasn't empty. It was loaded. And I sat there like someone waiting for the sentence to fall.

I didn't ask again.

Not until later. Not until I'd stared at the blank wall long enough to remember the way my phone had felt in my hand. The last thing that tethered me to anyone outside this place.

To Selene.

To fear.

To something I didn't control.

I turned toward the kitchen. Wolfe was pouring something into a glass. Ice clicked. I spoke before I could stop myself. "My phone... what happened to it?"

He didn't look up. Didn't pause. Just said, "Gone." Then he turned to face me fully. Set the glass down. "Broken. Smashed. You don't need it."

I swallowed. The way he said it—like it was obvious. Like it was handled. But something in me shifted. Because he didn't say it was lost. He said I didn't need it. And that wasn't the same thing.

I didn't ask again.

Because I was afraid of the answer. And afraid of what I might find if I went looking for it.

* * *

I didn't mean to look for it. Not at first. I told myself I was thirsty. That I just needed water. That the hallway didn't feel as dark as it used to. But my feet didn't go to the kitchen. They went to the study. To the drawer in the desk. The one Wolfe never used when I lived here. The one I'd seen him open earlier. Briefly. Barely. But I remembered.

The drawer smelled faintly like cedar and cologne.

His.

It wasn't just a place he kept things. It was a place he touched. And now I was touching it too.

The air felt thicker as I slid it open—like I was peeling back a wound he hadn't let scab yet. My fingers brushed the edge of the charger.

The phone lay face down, screen black, case cracked. There were smudges on the glass. *Mine.* A fingerprint over the camera lens. One that had pressed there during a message I never got to send.

I didn't touch it. Didn't even breathe. Beside it was another device. Identical. Newer. *His.* Unlocked. The screen was open to my messages. Every conversation. Every file. Every thread.

Selene.

Me.

Wolfe.

Like a map of everything I'd thought I'd hidden. Everything I'd ever tried to protect.

He hadn't smashed it. He hadn't thrown it away. He'd just taken it. Quietly. Effortlessly. And never given it back.

I closed the drawer. Not gently. Not with anger. Just finality. He hadn't lied when he said I didn't need it. He just hadn't told me why.

6

———

WOLFE

She was up before the sun. I heard her feet against the floor before the light shifted through the curtains. No sound from the shower. No cabinets opening. Just that slow, careful movement. Like she was trying not to make an impression.

I stayed in the hallway. Watched through the corner of the kitchen glass as she moved through the space.

She didn't open the fridge. Didn't pour coffee. Just stood near the window, arms wrapped around her chest, hoodie sleeves pulled over her hands like she thought the fabric could make her smaller.

It didn't.

She didn't look for me. Didn't ask where I was. Didn't try to speak. And that bothered me more than I wanted it to. Because Cloe never stayed quiet without an angle.

And this silence?

It felt like *strategy*.

I watched the way her shoulder dipped slightly—still sore. Her knee locked as she turned. She was favoring one leg. She hadn't taken the painkillers. She wasn't playing weak. She was surviving.

But I knew the difference between submission and patience. And this wasn't surrender. It was *waiting*.

She moved through the living room like a guest who used to be a lover. Her gaze flicked toward the alcove—at the ring— then snapped away too fast.

Let her see it.

Let her know it was still here.

Just *not for her*.

I watched her walk back toward the hallway, head down, breath shallow. She passed right by me. Didn't see me. Didn't know I was watching. But I was.

And I didn't stop. Because she wasn't asking questions anymore. Which meant she was learning.

Or planning.

Either way—

I'd be ready.

I woke at 5:04 a.m. Didn't check the clock. Didn't need to. My body didn't care about the time. It needed movement. Needed *purpose*.

I stripped off the black shirt I hadn't really slept in and pulled on my running gear—tight, efficient, black.

Everything was black today. Even my thoughts. The treadmill fired up beneath me like it had something to prove.

I didn't stretch. Didn't breathe deep. Just started. A full sprint. First stride like a hammer. Second like a blade. By the third, I was already sweating.

The room echoed with the pounding of my feet. Hard. Heavy. Intentional. I wasn't exercising. I was *breaking the floor* between what I wanted and what I couldn't let myself take.

She heard it. I knew she did. The rhythm bled through the walls like a warning no one had the guts to say aloud.

Let her hear it.

Let her know I was still here. Still moving. Still in control—even if she never saw me do a damn thing.

She came out once. Barefoot. Silent. I caught her in the reflection of the glass behind the weight rack. Her shape. Her stillness. Her curiosity.

I didn't turn. Didn't slow. Just kept running. Harder. *Faster.* Letting her see what I did *with the parts of myself that should've been used on her.*

I ran until the belt whined. Until the soles of my shoes smoked slightly from the friction. Until my lungs burned.

Then I stopped.

Breath even.

Face blank.

I walked straight to the shower.

The water was cold. Sharp. Didn't matter. I let it slice me. Let it ground me. Then I grabbed myself. Hard. Rough. Not for pleasure. Not to come. To remember. To *own.*

When it happened, it was fast. A grunt tore from my throat like the punchline to everything I hadn't said since she walked back into my life. I didn't clean up. Didn't shut the door. Just stepped out.

It wasn't release.

It was *refusal.*

I didn't come for pleasure—I came to keep myself from *taking her.* A warning. A leash only I could hold. Let the steam flood into the hallway. If she'd been listening?

Good.

Let her hear what it sounded like when control cracked—and I still refused to touch her.

The alert came at 2:13 a.m. I was in the study. Lights low. Whiskey untouched beside me. No music. Just silence humming against the windows. The phone buzzed once. Then again. Not hers. *Mine.*

The secondary device. The one synced to everything she used to own. I didn't move right away. Finished reading the paragraph on the screen in front of me. Then I reached for the phone.

UNKNOWN

"She's yours. But you still don't know why she came."

I blinked once.

Scrolled down.

There were attachments.

A photo of Camille. Not posed. Not soft. Surveillance grain.

A contract. Half-scanned. Cropped.

A message thread. Number blocked.

But the voice was clear.

Selene.

And Cloe.

I read it once. Top to bottom. Didn't react. Read it again. Slower. Not just the content. The *timestamps.* Her first message to Selene was sent two hours before the photo she forwarded to me. Two hours.

I stared at that gap like it might close if I looked hard enough. But it didn't. She reached for Selene first. She warned the woman who made her a weapon... before she warned the man who kept her breathing.

She could've come to me.

She didn't.

And that?

That was the truest part of the message.

She said *please.* But only after there was no one else left to call. I zoomed in on the message bubble. The punctuation. The phrasing.

If you want it, come get it.

No apology.

Just an offer. A test. And she knew exactly what I'd do with a test like that. She always had.

I watched the timestamps. Watched the language shift—from threat to instruction to *intimacy.*

You don't have to hurt her. Just keep her close.

He won't know until it's too late.

Deliver it when he's weakest. When he cares.

I set the phone down. Didn't smash it. Didn't speak. Just leaned back in the chair and closed my eyes for one breath.

I wasn't surprised. Not really. Not after the way she ran. Not after the silence. But I was *finished* pretending there was a version of her I hadn't already lost.

I stood. Picked up the ring from the alcove. Held it in my palm like a weight. Then walked it to the study desk. Set it beside the phone. And turned out the light.

Let her sleep. Let her dream she was still something worth saving. I had everything I needed now. And war never needed a reason. *Just a target.*

The phone was still on the desk. Still open. I should've shut it off. Instead, I scrolled. Deeper. Not looking for more. Just confirming what I already knew.

And then—

I found it.

The escort thread. Pulled from the message archive she thought I hadn't accessed. A thread from a blocked number. Weeks old.

I'll pay double if she doesn't speak.

I remembered that one. I remembered the night I almost asked. She'd come out of the shower, towel-wrapped, hair wet, eyes wrong.

She smiled at me. But it didn't reach her mouth. I saw

something on her thigh. A mark. Could've been a bruise. Could've been something else. She flinched when I touched it.

I didn't press. Didn't push. Didn't ask. Because she crawled into my lap after. Kissed me like she needed to be forgiven for something I hadn't uncovered yet.

And now I knew.

She hadn't wanted to lie. She just wanted to see if she could get away with it. And she had. Until now.

I hadn't asked her about it then. Because she was already shaking in my hands. Because I thought that was punishment enough. But now? There was a second message. Sent two nights ago.

Same number.

Still interested?

And beneath it—

Payment cleared.

The silence thickened around me.

I didn't blink. Didn't move. Then I tapped into the tracking app. The burner number bounced through VPN routes. Encrypted. Lazy. But not hidden. Not from me.

I stood. Walked to the closet behind the desk. Entered the code. The safe hissed open. Inside: a pistol. Matte black. Polished. I checked the magazine. Loaded. I didn't grab my phone. Didn't need a call. Didn't need a name. Just the *scent* of a target. And I had it now.

I walked to the window. Looked out over the city. Not for reflection. Not for breath. For *range.* They thought they could buy her. Claim her in silence. Use her body like it hadn't already been marked by something deeper.

I smiled.

Barely.

Because now—they'd learn what it meant to crawl toward something they *never* had a chance of owning.

I moved before the sun. Didn't need the treadmill. Didn't need to sweat it out of my system. I needed to act. The number was already tagged. Burner. Sloppy. Bounced through two fake proxies—cheap ones. He wasn't a professional. Just a man who wanted what he couldn't afford. Something that already belonged to me.

I traced the signal. He used a hotel Wi-Fi. Logged in twice. Fake name. Fake ID. The alias was familiar.

Camille's.

Stupid.

He left a trail because he didn't think anyone was following. But I don't follow. I end things. Twelve minutes later, I was out the door. Black coat. Gloves in the pocket. Not to protect myself. To keep what I took from staining anything that mattered.

The hotel staff didn't stop me. People rarely do. Room 1203. No knock. Keycard slipped into the reader. Door unlocked. He turned from the minibar. Stopped moving. He knew. Not who I was. What I was.

I closed the door. He opened his mouth. I shook my head once. Quiet. Clean. "You paid for silence." A beat. "I'm here to honor it."

I didn't enjoy it. I didn't rush it. It wasn't punishment. It was removal. One punch. Broken ribs. Shoulder out of socket.

Enough.

I crouched beside him. Whispered something just for him. Then left. No blood on my shirt. No mess on my hands. But when I came home—I felt it. She did too.

Through the walls. The floor. The silence I wore like a second skin. She didn't see me. But she felt me. The part of her that still believed I could touch her like a man—

Now understood what it meant to be owned by something far worse.

The man's phone was still warm in his pocket.

I didn't ask for the passcode.

Didn't need it.

The thumbprint worked fine—once the hand stopped shaking. I removed his passcode and entered one of my own. Simple really...now I had it all.

I sat on the edge of the hotel bed. Wiped the screen with a cloth from my pocket. Opened the gallery. Scrolled. The folder wasn't labeled *'Cloe.'*

That would've been too obvious.

It was labeled *'Sweet Camille.'*

That was the first insult.

I didn't blink. Just tapped it open. The images weren't graphic. They didn't need to be. They were worse for how *intimate* they were.

They weren't sent to me. That was the part that mattered. Not the lace. Not the bruise. Not the angle of her jaw or the slight turn of her head that made the picture look like an accident when it wasn't.

She'd taken them on purpose. *Sent them to someone else.* Let someone else see skin I hadn't touched since the night she left my bed in silence.

I imagined the light. The mirror. The way she probably held her breath while she took them. Not because she wanted to. But because she needed something. Attention. Leverage. Survival.

Maybe all three.

But none of it had been meant for me. And that was the final cut. Because she said she'd do anything to earn her place. But what she gave away? She didn't ask me first.

And now?

She wouldn't get to ask again.

A photo of her lying on a couch in a T-shirt—*my* T-shirt.

The hem hit mid-thigh. One leg curled. Her head turned just enough to hide her face.

A mirror shot from behind. Jeans pulled halfway down. The faintest curve of her hipbone exposed.

Another.

Her shirt lifted. Ribs bruised. Bra strap slipping off her shoulder.

I'd seen those bruises in person. But not like this. Not through someone else's lens. They didn't see what they were looking at.

They framed her in shadow.

I carved her into memory.

No nudity.

Just implication.

Just violation.

Just *theft.*

The last one was a screenshot.

Still interested?

Payment cleared. Full gallery on delivery.

I exhaled once. Quiet. Clicked through the phone. Found the backup folder. Downloaded it to a drive. Then deleted the originals. Encrypted the rest. Wiped the device. Set it on the counter.

The fire alarm triggered two minutes later. The phone melted in the sink basin. Smoke curled against the ceiling like it was mourning.

I walked out without speaking to the front desk. Got in the car. Pulled into traffic. Set the drive on the seat beside me.

I didn't look at it again. Didn't need to. Because those weren't just images. They were *evidence.* Of what she gave away. Of what someone else *saw.* Of what I hadn't been there to stop. That was the part I couldn't let go of. Not that she let someone look.

When I got home, I didn't go to her room. Didn't unlock the safe. I placed the drive in the drawer beside her ring. Next to the phone.

This wasn't a drawer. It was an altar. Not for forgiveness. Not for grief. But for the pieces of her she'd tried to keep from me. Evidence. Of what she gave away. Of what she still didn't understand was already *mine*.

Next to everything she'd left behind. Everything she'd kept from me. Everything she didn't know I already *owned*.

7

CLOE

I woke to silence. The box room looked the same. Still dim. Still cold. Still too clean for comfort. The blanket had slipped to the floor. My hair stuck to my jaw. My neck ached from sleeping without a pillow I trusted.

I sat up slowly and winced. My ribs pulled tight. My thigh burned. My shoulder ached like it remembered something my brain had tried to forget. I stood anyway. Because he hadn't told me not to. The apartment was awake. Not loud. Just... aware.

Cabinet doors shifting. A soft scrape of ceramic. Water running somewhere distant.

Wolfe was up.

And he hadn't come to get me.

I brushed my teeth with the spare brush in the bathroom drawer. Pulled my hair into something that looked less like panic. Found a clean T-shirt. An old one of mine folded on the chair.

I didn't know if he left it there. I didn't ask. I stepped out into the hall and didn't breathe until I saw the kitchen light.

He was there. At the island. Reading something on his

phone like he always did, keeping his focus on anywhere else while I was around. One hand resting on the countertop like he'd been standing there for hours.

The coffee machine was untouched. So was the second mug. I walked in. Careful. Barefoot. Every step quiet like it might be the one that made him look up.

He didn't. I waited. Not sure if I should sit. Speak. Bow. I just stood there. Until finally—he moved. Set the phone down. Lifted his eyes. And said—

"Wear something clean."

A pause.

"You have ten minutes."

I didn't ask where we were going. Didn't ask what he meant. Just nodded once and backed out of the room like I'd stepped into something I didn't know how to survive yet.

Back in the box room, I moved quickly. Not out of urgency. Out of fear. I peeled off the hoodie. My skin flinched where it stuck. The shirt beneath it was damp with sweat, sleep, shame.

I stripped in silence. Found a long black dress folded at the base of the bed. I hadn't put it there. Which meant he had.

It wasn't a threat. It was a reminder. That I still wore what he gave me. *And nothing else.*

I pulled the dress over my head. Winced as the fabric brushed my shoulder. The bruises were fading, but they still felt fresh. Like the memory hadn't moved on even if the skin had.

I stepped out into the hall. The lights were brighter now. Sunlight bleeding in through the living room windows. It made everything sharper. *Clearer.* Like the apartment was watching. Like it remembered who I used to be here. And who I wasn't anymore.

I hesitated when I passed his bedroom. The door was cracked. Just enough. I didn't mean to stop. But I did. There was no sound inside. No sign of movement. But I could feel him in the room. Not physically. Just... present. Like he'd left something in there that could still hurt me.

I kept walking. To the end of the hall. Where the door was open. The office. The study. The place I wasn't allowed to touch.

He was there. Sitting in the leather chair behind the desk. The screen of his tablet glowing faintly beside a glass of water. He didn't speak when I stepped inside. Just looked at me once. Then nodded at the chair in front of him.

I sat.

Slow.

Careful.

He waited.

And I knew—

This wasn't a conversation.

This was a sentence being handed down.

I just didn't know the name of the crime.

He didn't speak. Didn't look at me. Just opened the drawer beside him. Slow. Deliberate. Like he wasn't pulling out a weapon, but something worse.

The contents weren't hidden. They were arranged. My phone. My ring. A flash drive. All laid out like offerings. Like relics. *Like proof.*

My breath caught. He didn't need to say a word. I saw it. The glow of the screen. The lock pattern I used to trace without thinking.

The drive was matte black. Unlabeled. But I knew. I didn't know how. I just knew. He reached inside and pulled out the phone. Set it on the desk between us. Still cracked. Still familiar. And suddenly, I felt like I was watching a version of myself I hadn't met yet. The one who broke something and didn't remember how deep the crack ran.

He tapped the screen. The display lit. No sound. No drama. Just a photo. My photo. The mirror. The angle. The bruises I didn't cover because I hadn't thought he'd ever see them.

I didn't speak. Didn't blink. I couldn't. Because I remembered that moment. Not because I wanted to. Because I had to. Because no one else was looking at me. Because silence was worse than shame.

Because if I didn't show someone that I still had a body—

I was afraid I'd stop existing in it.

I remembered the way I held my breath. The way I didn't look at the camera. The way I thought—*this is what surviving looks like.* But Wolfe wasn't looking at the photo like it hurt him. He was looking at it like it belonged to him. And someone else touched it first.

He didn't show me the next photo. He didn't have to. I already felt it breaking under my ribs.

"You gave them this," he said.

Not loud.

Not cruel.

Just final.

"I know," I whispered.

It was the truth.

And it wasn't enough.

He didn't speak right away. Just looked at me. Long enough that I felt the shame crawl under my skin and settle there like it belonged. He turned the phone off. Set it beside the flash drive. Then reached for the ring. The same one I'd left behind in a panic. Polished. Still perfect.

He held it up between two fingers. Let it dangle. I stared at it like it might say something first. "You don't get to have everything," he said.

Not unkind. Just real. His voice stripped of decoration.

"You want this?" he asked, and nodded to the ring. *"Or this?"*

He tapped the phone once. The screen didn't light. But I didn't need it to. I swallowed. The room tilted. I didn't ask what the right answer was. Because I knew there wasn't one.

"I want—" My voice cracked. I stopped. Started again. "I want the chance to fix it."

He leaned back in the chair. No reaction. No grace. Just stillness. The kind that judged you harder than words ever could.

He set both down on the desk. And then he watched me like I was walking barefoot toward a noose of my own choosing. Not rushing. Not warning. Just waiting to see if I'd tighten it myself. Equal distance from my hands.

And said—

"Pick one."

I didn't reach. Not right away. Because I was afraid of what it meant. Choosing the phone meant I wanted to run again. Choosing the ring meant I wanted to stay—chained, claimed, owned.

Choosing neither?

Cowardice.

So I reached. Fingers shaking. And I took the ring. It was heavier than I remembered. The metal warm against my fingers, like it had been waiting. Like it knew.

I stared at it in my palm. Didn't put it on right away. Didn't speak. Just let it sit there like a verdict I hadn't earned. It still fit me. That was the worst part.

I hadn't been that girl in weeks. The one who wore this like it meant forever. The one who believed that if she stayed still long enough, the world would soften. Now it just felt like a brand.

I remembered the first time he gave it to me. Not in a box.

Not with a question. He'd slipped it onto my finger one morning while I was half-asleep on his chest. No smile. No ceremony.

Just—

"You'll wear this. No one else touches you now."

And that was it.

No vow.

Just *claim*.

And I nodded.

I whispered *"okay."*

Because some part of me had wanted to belong to someone powerful enough to end me. Now? I didn't even know if I'd survived that version of myself.

I looked up at him now. He hadn't moved. Hadn't blinked. He just watched me with that same unreadable focus.

Not pride or forgiveness. Just... stillness. Like he was letting me decide how to carry the chain this time. And I slid the ring back onto my finger. Slow. Like I was preparing for weight.

My fingers curled tighter around the ring. Waiting. For what, I didn't know. A word. A look. A nod that said I hadn't just thrown the last of myself at his feet.

Wolfe didn't give me any of that. He turned his back. Slow. Deliberate. Like I wasn't even worth the weight of his eyes anymore.

The drawer clicked shut with a sound so soft it felt like a slap. And that was it. No praise. No forgiveness. No permission to breathe.

I stayed frozen. The ring biting into my palm. The cold around me thick enough to drown in. Because I was. Not because I wanted mercy. Because I was tired of pretending I didn't already belong to him.

He said nothing. Just took the phone. Slid it back into the

drawer. Closed it. And that sound—the soft *click* of wood against metal—felt more final than any scream could've been.

Wolfe didn't say anything else. He just turned away. Left the study. Left me sitting there with the ring on my finger and the weight of it pressing into the space where my breath used to be.

I sat there for a long time. Didn't cry. Didn't move. The air in the room had gone stale. The light above the desk buzzed once.

I didn't flinch. Eventually, I stood. The chair creaked behind me. I walked back to the box room. Slow. Careful. Like the floor might give out beneath me if I stepped too hard.

The room looked the same. It always did. The boxes. The folded blanket. The empty space where comfort was supposed to be.

I didn't take the ring off. Didn't look at it again. I lay down on top of the blanket. Didn't pull it over me. Just stared at the ceiling. Eyes wide. Heart quiet. Hands folded over my stomach like I was waiting for something to be buried.

And when the first tear slid down my cheek, I didn't stop it. Didn't wipe it away. Didn't pretend I was stronger than this. Because I wasn't. Not anymore.

The light above me flickered. Once. Then stayed on. Too bright. Too quiet. And I lay there with the ring still on my finger. Not because I wanted it. But because it was all I had left.

Not freedom. Not absolution. Just the collar I chose to wear before he ever put it back on me.

8

———

WOLFE

She was sitting on the edge of the bed when I opened the door. The blanket swallowed her frame, too big, too heavy, pooling around her bare feet. Her knees tucked against her chest. Her head bowed low. Shoulders hunched in a way that made my teeth grind. She looked like she was trying to fold herself smaller. To take up less space. As if survival could be measured in square inches.

She didn't look up.

Didn't speak.

I closed the door behind me. Set the kit on the nightstand with a click that sounded louder than it should have.

No permission asked. No consent needed. She didn't flinch when I sat beside her. But she didn't lean into me either.

She stayed still. Tense. Waiting. Waiting for punishment. Waiting for mercy. She wasn't going to get either.

I unscrewed the lid of the salve. The scent hit first — clean, sterile, surgical. It didn't belong here. Neither did she.

"Show me." My voice didn't rise above the silence. It didn't need to.

Her hands trembled as she peeled the blanket down. Slow. Careful. Like every movement cost her more than she could afford.

The collarbone first. Purple-black and swollen. A bloom of violence painted on her skin. She turned slightly, wincing when her ribs protested. Her lip was split. Dried blood caked in the corner of her mouth. Her cheekbone carried a swelling bruise that would deepen before it faded.

I dipped two fingers into the salve. Pressed it against the wound. Not gentle. Not cruel. Just deliberate.

She sucked in a shallow breath, her body flinching under the contact. But she stayed still. I moved lower, hand braced against her shoulder to steady her. Faint fingerprint bruises marred her ribs — ugly reminders of hands that didn't belong. I pressed the ointment in slowly. Deliberate, circular motions that forced her to feel every second.

She didn't speak. Didn't cry. She breathed through it. Because mercy was never part of the deal. Shallow. Ragged. Like she knew even pain was a privilege now.

When I reached her thigh, I hesitated. A deep bruise. Dark, furious. Half-hidden beneath the fabric of her shorts. I looked up once. Waited. She nodded. No words. Because she knew better now. I pushed the fabric aside. Saw the wreckage of her skin. Saw the tremble in her muscles as I pressed the salve in.

Slow.

Measured.

Ownership written in each silent pass of my fingers.

"Breathe," I said.

She tried.

God, she tried.

The breath rattled out of her lungs like it hurt. Because it did.

When I finished, I wiped my hands clean. She looked up

once. Eyes wide. Mouth trembling with a question she didn't dare speak aloud.

I didn't wait for it.

"You don't talk while I'm healing you."

My voice was flat. Final. Not kindness. Not cruelty. Maintenance. Because no one else got to touch what was mine.

I rose. Left her sitting there, skin still raw, salve still slick against bruises that would never really fade. Left her holding the weight of a body that wasn't hers anymore.

She didn't follow when I left the room. She wasn't ready yet. I waited by the window. Watched the city breathe under clouds that looked too clean for the kind of rot crawling beneath them. When I heard her footsteps—barefoot, careful— I didn't turn.

I just spoke.

"Come here."

The floor creaked once under her weight.

Closer.

Slower.

I still didn't look. Because she wasn't a person anymore. She was a silence that belonged to me. When I turned, she was standing in front of me. Arms crossed tight across her bruised ribs. Hair tied back like it wasn't hers to touch. Eyes wide, but not defiant anymore. Just waiting.

I opened the top drawer of the desk. Pulled out the box. Black leather. Brushed steel clasp. No tag. No key. *No promises.*

I set it on the table between us.

Opened it.

Inside—the collar.

Simple.

Cold.

Undeniable.

I didn't touch it. Didn't hold it out. Didn't explain.

"You want to stay," I said.

Not a question.

A fact.

"Then wear it."

Her throat bobbed. The bruises along her jaw stood out against the rawness of her skin. She looked at the collar like it was alive. Like it might bite. Good. It should.

I didn't move. Didn't push the box closer. The air stretched thin between us. I let it. Let her feel the choice sink into her bones. Not because I wanted to break her. Because I already had.

And this?

This was just the funeral rites.

"I'm not giving you rules anymore," I said.

"I'm giving you expectations."

Her breath caught.

I stepped closer. Close enough to smell the blood dried beneath the clean scent of antiseptic.

"Obey without question. Without performance. Not because you're scared."

A beat.

A breath.

"Because you understand."

The collar gleamed under the low light. Softer on the inside. Not meant to hurt. That wasn't the point. The point was ownership. The point was belonging.

"One more lie, Cloe—*one more secret*—and you won't get a second chance to explain it."

She blinked once. Slow. Heavy. Tired. But still not broken the way she needed to be.

Not yet.

I didn't pick up the collar. Didn't fasten it for her. I stood there. Silent. Steady. Final. Like a grave marker. Like a gate closing.

"Wear it," I said again. *"Or walk."*

Her hands trembled as she reached out. Slow. So slow I could feel the moment she broke apart inside herself. Fingers curling around the collar like it weighed more than she did. She fumbled with the clasp. Slipped once. Twice. Tears prickled at the corners of her eyes, but she didn't let them fall.

Because she knew—*there was no forgiveness waiting for her on the other side of weakness.*

She wrapped the collar around her throat. Tightened it herself. Fastened the clasp. His fingers used to touch here. Pressed gently. Possessively. Now they didn't need to.

The metal said what his hands no longer would. The *click* was soft. Quiet. Final. She lowered her hands to her lap. Head bowed. Breathing shallow.

The collar sat perfectly against her bruised skin. A mark of survival. A mark of ownership. She didn't look at me. Good. Because there was nothing kind in my face. Only inevitability.

She stayed kneeling by the table. Hands resting lightly against her thighs. Shoulders tight with the effort of holding still.

The collar gleamed against the bruises at her throat. She was learning. Slowly. Painfully. The way all important lessons are learned.

I watched her breathe once. Twice. Measured. Shallow. Like every inhale scraped against cracked ribs. "Strip."

One word. Not barked. Not growled. Delivered with the same finality as a death sentence.

She flinched—*barely*. A flicker at the corners of her mouth. Then she moved. Slow. Mechanically. *Obedient.*

Her fingers shook as she peeled the black shirt over her

head. Exposing the bandages. The bruises. The broken pieces of the girl who thought survival meant escape.

The air hit her wounds hard. Her body flinched. But she didn't make a sound. The pants next. Trembling hands sliding down her thighs. Peeling away fabric that clung to scabbed knees and split skin.

She stepped out of them with a sharp inhale. Wobbled. Caught herself. Bare. Bruised. *Mine.*

I said nothing. Because there was nothing left to say. I let her stand there a moment longer. Shivering. Ashamed. Glorious. Then I stepped aside. Gestured to the center of the room.

The mat. The camera. The waiting silence.

"Kneel."

She walked slowly. Every step a sacrifice. Every breath a prayer. Her knees hit the mat with a soft, wet sound. The breath that left her chest was ragged. Pain blooming behind it.

She pressed her hands behind her back automatically. The way I taught her. The way she remembered even through the haze of bruises and shame. Head bowed. Spine straight. Exposed. Silent. Waiting.

I didn't move immediately. Let the silence coil around her. Let it tighten. Until her breathing turned shallow. Until the tension in her thighs started trembling.

I circled her once. Slow. Measured. Close enough that the heat of my body brushed her raw skin. Not touching. Never touching. Because touch was mercy. And she hadn't earned that. Not yet. Maybe not ever.

I sat down in the chair. Legs spread. Elbows braced against my knees. Eyes locked on her.

And said—

"Don't move."

The red light on the camera blinked once. Then held steady. Watching. Recording. Owning.

She stayed kneeling where I put her. Naked. Bruised. Silent. Her back was straight, but her shoulders trembled. A fine, visible tremor. From effort. From obedience.

The camera's red light blinked once above her head. Recording everything. Documenting every second of what she chose to become.

I didn't speak. Didn't move. Just watched her breathe. Slow. Measured. Pained. The door creaked open behind me. I didn't turn. Didn't need to. I knew who it was by the weight of their steps.

Royal entered first. Casual. Predatory. The scent of expensive cologne and quiet violence followed him into the room. His laugh was low. Amused. "Well, well. You do know how to break them, brother."

He circled her slowly. Boots whispering against the mat. Hands tucked loosely in his pockets. He didn't touch her. Not yet. But the heat of his body brushed too close.

I watched her flinch—small. Controlled. Still obedient.

Royal chuckled low in his throat. "Look at you," he murmured. "Pretty little pet. Not even bleeding anymore. Just breathing."

She stayed still. Perfect.

Loyal entered second. Slower. Heavier. The door clicked softly shut behind him. No words. No mocking smile. Just that deep, bruised silence Loyal carried like armor.

His gaze locked onto her the second he crossed the threshold. Wide. Pained. Almost reverent. He moved closer. Too close. I didn't stop him. Because sometimes the punishment wasn't in pain. It was *in being seen.*

My brother crouched. One knee on the mat beside her. His hand lifted. Hesitated. Trembled. Then he touched her. Not rough or possessive. Just—*gentle.*

His fingers traced the edge of her jaw. The skin there was

already bruised. He didn't flinch from it. Didn't linger either. Just a brush. A reminder.

She didn't resist. Didn't lean in. Just breathed through it. Silent. Obedient. Broken. Royal smirked from the shadows. "Careful, Loyal," he drawled. "She might think you're rescuing her."

Loyal said nothing. Just dropped his hand and stepped back like she burned him. Let them see it. The cost of ownership. The cost of weakness.

I stayed in the chair. Hands steepled loosely. Watching. Breathing. Waiting. Because this wasn't about pain anymore. It was about proof. Proof of what she would endure. Proof of what she would become. Proof of who she already was.

Mine.

Royal stepped back. Loyal retreated into the corner, chest heaving slightly, as if breathing the same air as her cost him something he didn't want to admit.

Let them feel the edges of it. Let them know what it meant to look at something broken and still want.

I rose from the chair. Moved slowly. Measured steps across the mat. She stayed kneeling. Stayed breathing. Didn't lift her head. Didn't speak. Didn't beg. Obedient. Exactly as I intended.

I stopped in front of her. Close enough that the scent of salve and sweat clung to her skin. She shivered once. Small. Involuntary. I didn't touch her. Touch would've been mercy.

I crouched instead. Leveling my body with hers. Her head bowed so low her curls brushed the mat.

She was trembling harder now. Not from fear. Not from pain. From restraint. Because every part of her was waiting for something—*some command, some punishment, some permission to survive.*

I leaned in. Close enough that my breath stirred the hair at her temple. Close enough that if she wanted, she could've pressed her forehead to my knee and begged.

She didn't.

That was better.

I let the silence drag a beat longer. One more breath. One more tremble. Then I spoke.

Low.

Quiet.

Deadly.

"You think this is the end."

A pause.

A breath.

Her body locked tighter.

"It's not."

Another pause.

Long enough for the words to sink into her bones.

"It's the beginning."

I didn't raise my voice. Didn't touch her. Didn't soothe. Just let the words settle into the empty places I had carved into her. Then—even softer, a whisper built for no one but her. *"You haven't even started bleeding for me yet."*

She shuddered. A full-body crack that she tried and failed to hide.

I stood. Looked down at her. At the bruises. At the trembling. At the stillness.

And knew...

She would never escape now.

Because she wouldn't want to.

Not really.

Not once she understood the cost of being seen.

I turned. Walked toward the door. Didn't look back. Because she would still be kneeling when I returned. Exactly where she belonged. Exactly where she asked to be. Even if she never said the words.

9

———

CLOE

THE MAT WAS cold under my knees. Not freezing. Just... *enough*. Enough to bite. Enough to remind me where I was. *What I was.*

The camera blinked red above me. Steady. Unforgiving. I didn't look at it. I didn't look anywhere. My head stayed bowed. My hands stayed locked behind my back. My breath stayed shallow. Because moving wasn't survival here. Stillness was. Obedience was.

I heard the door click shut. Not hard. Not loud. Just final. Wolfe was gone. And still—I stayed kneeling. Because I didn't know if moving would bring him back. Or worse—*bring him closer.*

The silence thickened. Pressed down against the bruises on my ribs. Sank into the raw places under my skin. Coiled around the base of my throat where the collar sat.

Tight.

Cool.

Unyielding.

I shifted once. A tremor. Not disobedience. Not yet. Just a breath too deep. A muscle clenching without permission.

The mat whispered under me. Footsteps. Soft. Measured. I didn't lift my head. But I knew.

Royal. His scent hit first—sharp, expensive cologne tangled with something meaner. Something hotter.

"Still breathing, sweetheart?"

The words brushed over my skin. Teasing. Mocking. I flinched inside myself. Tiny. Invisible. Not enough to break posture. Not enough to give him more.

Royal circled me once. Boots slow against the padded floor. The heat of him brushing against my bare shoulders. He didn't touch me. Not yet. Just watched. Waiting. For what—I didn't know.

Or maybe I did.

Maybe I always had.

"Bet you're wondering what comes next," he murmured.

I stayed still. My breath caught high in my throat. Because I was wondering. Because wondering was worse than knowing.

Royal stopped in front of me. Close. *Too close.*

I could feel the hem of his pants brush my knees when he shifted. A fingertip drifted along my collarbone. Not hard. Not cruel. Just a line of heat tracing the bruise there. A shudder ran down my spine. I swallowed it.

"You're pretty when you don't talk," he said.

Another pass of his hand. This time slower. He didn't grip. Didn't yank. He just—*brushed.* Like testing how much damage was already done.

I wanted to flinch. Wanted to move. Wanted—

I didn't even know.

The door creaked again. Another step. Heavier. Ragged.

Loyal.

He said nothing. Did nothing. Just stood there. Breathing too fast. Breathing like it hurt. Like watching *me* hurt.

I kept my head down. Kept breathing. Kept surviving. Because that's what obedience was now. It wasn't about pleasing them. It wasn't about forgiveness. It was about staying still enough to matter. Still enough to survive.

Royal's hand drifted higher. Paused just below the collar. One fingertip brushing the chain link. Not tugging. Not claiming. Just reminding me it was there. As if I could ever forget.

"Good girl," he whispered. Not mocking this time. Almost —*soft.*

He said it soft. Like comfort. And somehow that hurt more. Because part of me needed to hear it—*even if I hated that I did.* And somehow, that cut deeper than cruelty ever could.

I didn't react. Didn't thank him. Didn't breathe differently. Because Wolfe hadn't told me I could. And because even if he had—I didn't know if I could survive moving. Not now. Not with the leash wrapped so tight around my lungs.

The floor blurred under my knees. Heat rising through the mat. Sweat sticking my hair to the back of my neck. The collar felt heavier now. Like it grew tighter the longer I obeyed.

Royal circled again. Slow. Lazy. A king at a private viewing. "Look at her, Loyal," he said, voice all teeth and velvet. "Look how good she is."

Loyal didn't answer. I could feel his stare though. Heavy. *Hot.* Pinned between my shoulder blades. Seeping through my skin.

Royal crouched beside me. I smelled leather. Smoke. Felt his gaze skimming over my body. The bruises. The blood. The slow, breaking stillness.

"Bet you want to touch her again," Royal murmured. "Bet you want to see what sound she makes when someone's kind."

I swallowed. *Hard.* The motion made the collar dig into my

throat. *As it should be.* It was supposed to hurt. Royal didn't touch me. Not yet. He let his hand hover—a breath from my hip.

A sigh from my ribs. Waiting. Testing. Daring me to flinch.

I didn't. Couldn't. Because survival didn't live in motion anymore. It lived in stillness. It lived in breath.

Royal laughed low in his throat. "She's learning," he said. He stood. Stretched like a cat. Turned to Loyal. "Go ahead," he said, lazy. "She's yours too."

I couldn't stop the shiver that ran through me. Because those words—*those words felt like chains tightening.*

Loyal didn't move.

For a heartbeat.

Two.

Three.

Then—

He knelt.

Slow.

Painful.

Like gravity was stronger near me.

His hand hovered above my hair. Trembled. Dropped. The backs of his fingers brushed the shell of my ear. Down the curve of my neck. To the swell of my shoulder. Gentle. Terrible.

He was breathing hard. Too hard. Like looking at me—touching me—*was ripping something out of him.*

I stayed still. Breath catching. Body screaming. But I stayed. Because that's what Wolfe wanted. Even when he wasn't here. Especially then.

Loyal's hand paused at the hollow of my throat. Right above the collar. One fingertip tracing the line of metal. Soft. Worshipful.

I felt the breath catch in his chest. Felt it shudder through his fingertips. Then he pulled away. Sharp. Like it hurt him.

Royal laughed again. "Didn't even kiss her, Loyal," he teased. "You're getting soft."

He didn't defend himself. Didn't argue. Just stayed kneeling beside me, like something sacred had already broken inside him. And I hated that I wanted to touch it.

Loyal didn't rise immediately. He knelt there beside me. Breathing. Breaking.

And I—

I stayed kneeling.

Stayed breathing.

Stayed silent.

"Did someone tell her about the two galas she'll be attending?" Royal murmured, I could feel his icy stare fixed on my every reaction. "No? Hmm. I thought Wolfe would've told you. After all, you'll be the center attraction. The one they'll all want to see...even if you're on your knees." He crouched down, black slack pulled taught over his knees in front of me. I kept my gaze down even as my cheeks burned. "This is your test, Cloe. This is Wolfe's personal test for you. I've bet against you. Just wanted you to know."

He leaned closer.

"I've bet you'll break before the first one is over." That smarmy tone grew cold. "But fuck I'd love you to prove me wrong."

The door creaked again. A shadow sliced across the floor. He was back. *Wolfe.* I didn't lift my head. I didn't need to. The air tightened around us the second he entered.

Royal fell silent. Loyal rose stiffly. Stepped back.

The room rearranged itself without a word. Because it wasn't ours to hold. It was his. All of it. Even me. Especially me. The red light on the camera blinked once. Then burned steady. Still recording. Still witnessing. Still owning. The air in the room shifted. Tightened. Thickened. Wolfe crossed the mat in silence. Boots whispering against the padded floor. No rush. No threat. He didn't need either.

I stayed kneeling. Stayed breathing. Stayed still. Because anything else would've been worse.

Royal stepped back.Loyal disappeared into the corner. Only Wolfe remained. Close enough that I could feel the gravity of him.

The coldness that wrapped tighter around my skin than the bruises ever could. He didn't touch me. Didn't crouch. Didn't lower himself to meet me where I broke. He stood. Over me. Around me. Claiming the air. The silence. The shame.

I kept my head bowed. My knees ached. My ribs ached. My pride ached. But I didn't move. I couldn't.

Wolfe waited. Long enough that my breathing turned shallow. Long enough that my hands started trembling against my thighs. He let it happen. Let me shake. Let me bleed silence across the floor. Because breaking wasn't the goal.

Obedience was.

Finally—

finally—

he spoke.

Quiet.

Almost curious.

"You think you're surviving."

The words hit harder than any slap. I squeezed my eyes shut. Breathed through it. Held.

"You're not."

Another pause.

Soft.

Deadly.

"You're breathing because *I* allow it."

My throat locked. The collar bit harder. Because he wasn't wrong. Because somewhere in the hollowed-out places inside me—*the places that still bled grief and shame and ruined hope*—I already knew.

I wasn't kneeling to survive. I was kneeling because it was the only place left where the world made sense. Because survival here wasn't about strength. It was about belonging. It was about ownership.

His.

Not mine.

Never mine again.

Wolfe stepped closer. Boots brushing against my knees. I felt the heat of him. The violence buried under all that control.

I stayed still. Trembling. Breathing. Obedient. He crouched finally. A slow, deliberate folding of power. Brought his mouth close enough that his breath stirred the hair at my temple. Close enough that I could feel the heat of his skin against my bruised cheek.

He didn't touch me. Didn't comfort me. Just whispered. "You live because I let you."

I should've felt fear. But all I felt was relief. Because someone finally told me the truth I was built to kneel for.

A beat. A breath. The leash tightening around my ribs.

"And you'll stay because you were never built to run."

Tears burned at the back of my eyes. I didn't let them fall. I stayed kneeling. Because there was no survival outside his hands now. Only silence. Only breath. Only chains I asked for without ever speaking.

Wolfe rose. Left me kneeling. Left me trembling. Left me exactly where he wanted me. And I stayed. Because the truth wasn't that I couldn't run. It was that I didn't want to anymore. Not if it meant losing the only thing that still saw me—*even if it was just to own me.*

10

———

CLOE

The dress was black. Satin. Backless. High neckline. It whispered across my skin. Too soft against the bruises mottling my ribs. Too expensive for someone kneeling on the floor hours earlier.

Wolfe fastened the clasp at my nape himself. Silent. Efficient. The tiny brush of his knuckles against my hair sent a tremor down my spine I couldn't stop.

Not fear. Not anticipation. Something worse. Something that tasted like submission and regret all at once.

His fingers brushed the hidden chain under the fabric. The collar. Still there. Still tight. My breath caught when his thumb dragged briefly across the metal. A reminder. A warning.

His hand left it. But it stayed hot. Because the absence of his touch was just as commanding as the weight of it.

"Don't speak unless spoken to."

His voice was colder than the silk I wore. I nodded once. Tiny. Tight. Pain blooming along the strained muscles of my neck.

"Keep your eyes down."

Another leash looped around my spine. Another invisible knot tying me closer to the ground. I didn't dare lift my gaze. Didn't dare meet his eyes in the mirror. I saw enough without looking.

The reflection of him. Tall. Immovable. More force of nature than man.

And me.

A figure hollowed out in black silk. A thing dressed up to be paraded.

I adjusted the hem of the dress. My fingers brushed the fresh scabs on my thigh. The ache throbbed deeper with the contact.

Pain made it easier to remember who I was now.

Not Cloe Woods. Not Camille's best friend. Not even Wolfe's broken pet. Just obedience. Wrapped in satin. Breathing on command.

Wolfe turned away without another word. Without another glance. Because I didn't need approval. Only permission to exist.

"Come."

I followed. Silent. Shoes in hand. The walk to the elevator felt longer than it should have. Every step an exercise in remembering the rules.

Head down.

Mouth closed.

Breath shallow.

The ride down was silent. I watched the numbers blink by through my lashes. Not daring to lift my head. Not daring to breathe too loudly. At the lobby, a car was already waiting.

Black. Polished to a mirror shine. A beast crouched at the curb. Royal lounged in the backseat. Suit open at the collar. Smile already lazy and dangerous. His last words resounded in my head *this is Wolfe's test*. I lifted my gaze to him for a second catching the dangerous glint. He expected me to fail...*hoped I'd fail.* I swallowed hard. That wasn't going to happen. I didn't care if I had to bleed all over the goddamn floor. Loyal sat beside him. Hands folded. Posture too stiff. Tension bleeding off him in waves that prickled my bruised skin. Neither spoke as Wolfe guided me inside.

I slid into the backseat without needing to be told.

Royal's gaze dragged over me immediately. Slow. Calculating. The dress hid the bruises. The collar didn't. Not from them. Not from men who already knew what it cost to own me.

The air inside the car was too warm. Or maybe I was. Sweat clung to the backs of my knees. My ribs ached under the pressure of sitting upright. The collar chafed against the base of my throat when I swallowed.

I kept my eyes down. Focused on the carpeted floor. On the neat hem of Wolfe's trousers. On the faint scuff on Royal's expensive shoes. Anything but their faces. Anything but the look in their eyes.

The look that said:

You chose this.

The car pulled into traffic. I folded my hands in my lap. Tucked my elbows in. Made myself smaller.

Breath.

Hold.

Breath.

Hold.

Every inhale hurt.

Every exhale felt like surrender.

The car hit a bump and pain flared through my ribs. A gasp clawed up my throat. I swallowed it down. Because pain wasn't permission to speak. Because pain wasn't special here.

It was normal.

Expected.

Owned.

Wolfe said nothing. Royal chuckled low once. A private sound. I didn't ask why. Didn't dare. Because tonight wasn't about survival. It wasn't even about obedience. It was about proving what I was willing to bleed for. And Wolfe had already decided I would bleed beautifully. Whether anyone else saw it or not.

The car slowed. The brakes whispered. The tires crunched against the polished stone drive. I kept my eyes lowered. My hands folded tightly in my lap.

The collar pressed against the base of my throat. A pulse. A brand. A chain.

Wolfe stepped out first. I heard the hush of the door. The low murmur of event staff scrambling to greet him.

Royal followed. A soft laugh under his breath. Sin wrapped in expensive fabric. Loyal moved silently beside them.

Then—Wolfe's voice. "Out."

One word.

I obeyed. Not because I wanted to. Because I didn't know how not to anymore.

The air hit me like a slap. Cool night. Colder stares. The Lawlor building loomed over the city—glass and gold and legacy sharpened to a knife.

A carpet stretched ahead of me. Velvet. Blood red. Footsteps scuffed across it. Cameras flashed. Bright. Blind. I didn't look. I didn't blink. I kept my eyes down, the way Wolfe ordered.

The dress whispered against my thighs as I moved. Every step careful. Controlled. Every breath catching against bruised ribs. The collar chafed when I lifted my chin just enough to follow Wolfe. The diamonds at my ears and throat sparkled under the lights.

Hiding the leash.

Barely.

Because no matter how many jewels they draped me in—the collar would never be invisible to them. Not the men who already owned me. Not the women who would whisper behind raised glasses.

The marble foyer gleamed under soft golden chandeliers. People clustered in careful circles. Smiling. Sipping. Measuring.

I could feel the eyes starting. Dragging over my skin. Slipping over the silk. The hush that followed us wasn't reverence. It was calculation. Judgment. *Who is she? Why is she with them? Why does she walk like she's leashed?*

Wolfe didn't slow. Didn't acknowledge. He moved like the world rearranged itself around him. And I—I moved behind him.

Silent.

Invisible.

Until I wasn't.

A woman in a gold dress turned as we passed. Her gaze skimmed me. Sharp. Cool. She smiled at Wolfe. Tight. Polished. Then looked back at me. And smiled wider.

"Beautiful," she said.

I bowed my head lower. Because she wasn't admiring me. She was assessing me. Like women do before they take something they know they can ruin.

Because I knew she didn't mean the dress. She meant the collar. The bruises she couldn't see but could feel radiating off my skin. The ownership threaded into every step I took.

Royal caught the woman's eye and smirked. Lazy. Cruel. He knew. Of course he knew. Loyal said nothing. But I felt him behind me. The slow, weighted breath he dragged through his nose. As if the sight of me—silent, bruised, collared—cost him something he didn't have the strength to pay.

The ballroom doors opened ahead. And the world shifted again. Music. Low. Distant. Champagne glasses clinked. Laughter floated under the chandeliers like poisoned air.

Men in suits turned to look. Women in gowns glanced once. Twice. Measuring. Judging. I didn't lift my head. Not because I was scared. Because I was trained. Because Wolfe hadn't given permission to see anything beyond the carpet.

We crossed the marble. Past couples in whispered conversations. Past investors and executives and old bloodlines built on sharper sins. Every step I took, I felt the weight of the collar under the diamonds.

The rough edge of the chain hidden by silk. Every breath I drew felt borrowed. Every glance brushed against me like a blow. I didn't falter. Because shame wasn't weakness anymore. It was obedience. And obedience was survival.

Royal leaned down once—lips brushing the shell of my ear without touching. "Smile, sweetheart," he murmured. "They like it better when you pretend you want it."

My cheeks burned. But I didn't smile. Because Wolfe hadn't said to. Because Wolfe didn't need me to pretend.

He already owned every breath. He didn't need me to look like I loved it. Only to stay silent while it consumed me.

The ballroom pulsed around me. Laughter. Champagne. A hundred conversations stitched into the golden air. I stayed behind Wolfe. Eyes down. Hands at my sides. Steps measured. The collar sat heavy at my throat. Hidden under diamonds.

But I felt it. Every time I swallowed. Every time I breathed. The leash tightening. The silk whispering across bruised skin.

We moved through the crowd. Shadows parted for Wolfe. Bent themselves to the gravity he wore like a second skin. But they didn't part for me. They noticed me. They stared. Whispers drifted in low currents.

Soft.

Sharp.

"Looks young."

"New toy?"

"No ring."

The words slipped over my skin like knives drawn slow. I didn't lift my head. Didn't breathe too deeply. Just counted my steps. One. Two. Three. Each one a prayer for stillness.

Royal lingered behind me. A step too close. Close enough that when I stumbled once—just a hitch of breath against the pain in my ribs—his hand brushed the small of my back.

Not to steady me.

Not to help.

Just to remind me.

"Careful," he murmured, too low for anyone else to hear. "Pets don't stumble. It makes us look cheap."

Heat scorched the back of my neck. Not from his words. From the shame. Because he was right. I wasn't supposed to stumble. I wasn't supposed to bleed.

I was supposed to survive beautifully.

Silently.

Obediently.

His.

A server passed. Champagne flutes gleaming under the chandeliers. Wolfe took one. Didn't drink. Just held it like a king surveying a kingdom he didn't trust.

Royal took two. Handed one to Loyal with a smirk. "Drink up," he said lazily. "Might be the last party we get to enjoy."

Loyal didn't respond. He took the glass. Sipped. Didn't look at me. But I felt him. Felt the weight of his gaze dragging over the bruises hidden under silk. Felt the breath he dragged slow through his nose, like it cost him.

Another whisper floated past.

Closer.

Cruler.

"Is that the best they could buy?"

"Thought Barron had better taste."

"Maybe Wolfe's standards slipped."

My stomach twisted. The collar burned against my skin.

I wanted—God, I wanted—to disappear.

To sink into the marble. Into the walls. Into anything that wasn't the burning stare of the world. But I stayed standing. Breathing. Because Wolfe hadn't told me to stop. Because even humiliation was obedience. Because even shame was survival now.

Royal leaned down again. Closer this time. His breath stirred the loose strands of hair at my nape. "That's it, make it pretty," he whispered. "They're already deciding how much you're worth."

Wolfe shifted beside me. Subtle. Commanding. The small motion pushed me two steps closer to him. Under his shoulder. Under his shadow. I stayed there. Grateful. Broken. Invisible again—but only because he allowed it.

The whispers kept coming. They would never stop. Not tonight. Maybe not ever. Because no matter how many diamonds they draped me in—everyone here already knew. I didn't belong to the silk. I didn't belong to the ballroom. I didn't even belong to the brothers who stood beside me. I belonged to the leash. And they could all see it.

The ballroom blurred. Laughter. Clinking glasses. Silk swirling against marble. I kept my head down. Hands pressed to my sides. Breathing through the pain wrapped around my ribs. Breathing through the silk that clung to bruises not yet healed.

The collar chafed at my neck under the diamonds. Wolfe spoke low to someone near the entrance. Formal. Controlled. A titan conducting business under chandeliers.

Royal drifted closer to a group of investors. His lazy grin cutting sharper than any blade. Loyal lingered near the far wall. Silent. Watching me from under his lashes.

I stayed still. The obedient figure behind them. The breathing shame stitched into their shadows. More whispers floated past. Sharper now. Hungrier.

"Selene must be laughing herself sick."

"First the sister. Now the pet."

"Maybe the Lawlors like their toys broken."

I didn't flinch. Not outwardly. But inside—the leash twisted.

A slow, sharp knot pulled tight against my spine. The name stung more than I expected.

Selene.

A ghost that never really left. A knife still lodged in the cracks Camille left behind.

I swallowed hard. The collar bit deeper. .

The conversation shifted. New hands shook. New glasses clinked. But the chill didn't fade. It deepened. Spread. Across my shoulders. Down my spine. A wrongness blooming cold and thick in the back of my throat.

I kept my head bowed. I didn't search the crowd. Didn't dare. But the hairs along my arms lifted anyway.

The air changed. The way it used to when Camille walked into a room angry. Or when Wolfe stepped close enough to shatter. The crowd shifted, subtly.

A ripple.

A reaction.

And in the corner of my eye—a flash of gold.

Not the way Royal wore it. Not the way Wolfe's cufflinks caught light. Different. Rougher. Sharper than the silk and glass around it.

My throat locked. The mat burned against my knees in

memory. The cold leash tightened. I didn't move. I didn't breathe differently. Because Wolfe was standing only a few feet away. Because Royal was watching. Because Loyal was already bleeding guilt into the floorboards.

But I felt it. The prickle at the back of my neck. The weight of eyes that knew too much. A shadow stitched into gold satin and the scent of something sweet rotting underneath.

The bitch.

Not close enough to touch. Not close enough to speak. Just close enough to be seen. Or maybe—just close enough to make sure I knew she was always watching.

Always waiting.

And if Wolfe's leash slipped for even a second—she would rip my throat out with her teeth.

I stayed still. Breathing. Obedient. Because even if Selene dragged the past into the marble under my feet—it wouldn't matter.

Because Wolfe owned the present. Wolfe owned the leash. And if I obeyed well enough—maybe he would never let me go. Maybe that was the only kind of safety left. Not freedom. Not love. Just the comfort of a leash held by someone cruel enough to keep me alive.

11

———

CLOE

THE SILK of my dress clung to the heat gathering under my skin. Each pulse of my heart a bruise blooming deeper against my ribs. I was careful not to breathe too hard. Careful not to let the pain show. Because pain didn't excuse disobedience. Pain didn't make me special. It made me weaker.

The music swelled in the background—some string arrangement meant to sound expensive. I focused on the floor. Counted the flecks in the marble. The cracks in the grout. The way my heels barely touched the ground.

Until—

The first ripple.

Soft.

Subtle.

Wrong.

I felt it before I heard it. The way a ballroom full of predators shifts when fresh blood hits the water. A breath held too long. A conversation clipped too sharply. Then the first flash of light—too bright, too fast.

A phone lifted.

Then another.

Screens lighting up like fire catching on dry brush.

Quick.

Unstoppable.

The whispers started before I could even fully lift my head.

"Is that her?"

"No—no, it can't be—"

"Camille. *It's Camille.*"

The name cracked through the room like a whip. Soft enough to pretend it wasn't real. Sharp enough to leave bruises anyway.

I clenched my hands tighter against the silk at my sides. Fingernails digging into the fabric. Breathing through the sudden flare of heat behind my eyes.

Not now. Not here. I didn't look up. But I saw it anyway. Reflected in the gleaming surface of the polished floors. A screen. Bright. Brutal. A photo. Camille.

Not the soft, untouched image the world wanted to remember. Not the girl who wore crowns of glass and smiled for charity cameras.

This Camille—

Laughing.

Lips red from too much wine or too much sin.

She looked happy.

Unbroken.

And it hurt in ways I hadn't earned the right to feel. Because I wasn't mourning her anymore. I was mourning the part of me that used to believe we'd both survive.

She had an arm thrown around a man in a dark suit. A Lawlor contract tucked openly under one arm. Careless. Mocking. Alive in a way I didn't recognize anymore. Alive in a way that burned.

The caption was worse.

Short.

Final.

"Legacy built on loyalty. Loyalty built on secrets."

No hashtags. No accounts claiming it. Just those words. And the photo that shattered everything. The weight of it crushed the air out of my lungs. A slow, horrible compression.

The collar dug harder against my pulse. A perfect vice. I couldn't breathe. Couldn't think. Could only stay still. Because Wolfe hadn't given me permission to fall. And because falling wasn't obedience.

Not here.

Not now.

Royal's low chuckle sliced through the growing silence. Not kind. Not cruel. Just—*inevitable.*

Wolfe didn't move. Didn't flinch. I risked a glance up—*just once.* Wolfe's profile cut against the crystal light like something sculpted from darker things.

He sipped his champagne. Calm. Cold. Unbothered. Like the world collapsing around him wasn't new. Wasn't interesting. Wasn't worth blinking for.

I pulled my gaze down again. Faster than I should have. Sharp enough to make the collar dig into tender skin. Pain bloomed under my jaw. Hot and immediate.

I breathed through it. Felt the humiliation crack open wider inside my chest. Because this wasn't just Camille's death playing out again. This wasn't just another fall. This was a reminder:

I was never going to outrun the rot.

No matter how much silk they buried me under. No matter how still I stayed.

The ballroom shrank. Not literally. Not visibly. But it shrank all the same. The walls crept closer. The air thickened. The sounds folded in on themselves. The flashes of screens still sparked at the edges of the crowd. Bright. Hungry. Camille's laugh echoed inside them. Inside me. It scraped down the walls of my lungs like broken glass.

I kept my head down. Kept my hands still. The silk of my dress clung damp to my bruised spine. The collar chafed hotter against my throat with every shallow breath. My knees locked tight. A muscle in my jaw ticked from holding it clenched too hard. Because I knew if I opened my mouth—even to breathe too sharply—*the sound would splinter me open.*

I felt Wolfe shift beside me. Not much. Not even enough to call a movement. But I felt it. The ripple of gravity. The change in the air.

The leash pulling tighter.

And then—

He looked at me.

One glance.

One second.

It cut sharper than a thousand words ever could.

No fury.

No betrayal.

No forgiveness.

Just—*ownership.*

The kind that didn't need to be spoken. The kind that lived in the way my body locked tighter at the heat of his gaze. The way my lungs squeezed tighter against my ribs. The way my heart stuttered once against the cage of my chest—then settled into a slower, *steadier* beat.

One meant for survival. One meant for *his* survival. Because mine didn't matter anymore. Not really. Not when the only thing keeping me standing was the expectation of it.

Wolfe's stare didn't waver. It didn't soften. He didn't look at my bruises. He didn't look at the silk stretched too tight across broken ribs. He looked at the place where the collar sat. Where the diamonds glittered. Where the leash looped invisible through my skin.

It didn't hurt. Not really. It *settled*. Like I'd finally stopped fighting gravity.

And in that one glance—he told me everything.

Stay still.

Stay silent.

Stay breathing—only because I allow it.

A cold shudder worked its way through my muscles. I absorbed it. Held it. Turned it into stillness. Because moving now would be a betrayal. Not of him. Of myself. Of what he trained into me. Of what I begged for without words every time I obeyed without being told.

The music played on. The laughter returned. The ballroom rebuilt its careful, glittering lies around us. But I stayed exactly where I was. The shame weighing heavier than the silk. The obedience sinking deeper than the bruises. Because survival wasn't about strength anymore. It wasn't about hope. It was about surrender.

Silent.

Breathless.

Complete.

And I realized then—knees trembling under the weight of breath I didn't own—I didn't survive because I fought.

I survived because *I was allowed to.*

Because Wolfe decided I could. Because Wolfe decided I *should.*

And when the world shattered again—because it would, because it always did—I wouldn't fight it.

I would kneel in the wreckage.

Exactly the way he built me to.

The ballroom pulsed wrong. Too sharp. Too loud. Too slow. I stayed exactly where Wolfe's glance pinned me. Head down. Spine straight. Breath shallow. A figure wrapped in satin and shame.

The music kept playing. But it sounded off. Tilted. Like a record starting to crack. I didn't move. I didn't breathe deeper. Because Wolfe hadn't given me permission. Because Wolfe hadn't looked away yet.

I heard Royal first. Of course I did. His laugh split the heavy silence like a blade dragged slow across skin. Not loud enough to be noticed by the guests still pretending not to see. But loud enough for Wolfe. For Loyal. For me.

"Well," Royal drawled, voice rich with lazy cruelty, "it was never going to stay hidden forever."

I flinched inside. Not visibly. Not where anyone could see. But I felt it. The collar tightening against my throat. The bruises burning under silk.

Royal moved closer. Casual. Predatory. The kind of slow prowl that made the air thin in my lungs. He stepped into my peripheral vision. Close enough that his scent curled through the silk and sweat clinging to my skin.

Crisp cologne.

Smoke and sin.

"Still," he murmured, voice pitched for only me and Wolfe to hear, "I thought she'd hold out longer."

A beat. A smile I could feel without seeing.

"Guess loyalty runs thin when the leash gets too tight."

My throat locked. Not from anger. Not from shame. From knowing he wasn't wrong. Because even kneeling here—even collared and bleeding silence into the marble—a part of me wanted to scream. Wanted to run. Wanted to tear the diamonds from my neck and the leash from my skin.

But I didn't. Because Wolfe didn't need my love. He needed my obedience. And Royal? Royal wanted my cracks.

He wanted to see if I would bleed something different this time.

I didn't give him the satisfaction. I stayed still. Breathing shallowly. Because survival here wasn't about strength. It was about stillness. It was about showing them—showing him—*that I could carry shame like a crown if it meant staying leashed.*

Loyal shifted across the room. I heard his drink set down harder than it should have. A faint, sharp sound that cracked through the marble.

When I risked a glance—just a flicker under lowered lashes —I saw him. Standing stiff against the wall. Hands clenched at his sides. Eyes burning with something raw and broken.

Guilt.

Grief.

Something worse.

He didn't move toward me. He didn't call me away. Because he knew he couldn't. Because Wolfe was still watching. Still claiming. Still deciding. And Loyal—Loyal would rather bleed inside his suit than cross that silent line.

I locked my knees harder. Bit the inside of my cheek until I tasted blood. Because if Loyal reached for me—if he moved even a step—I didn't know if I would have the strength to stay still.

The music shifted again. Laughter tightened. Another server passed with champagne. No one took a glass this time. The world was tilting.

Breaking.

Waiting.

And then—*Barron.*

He reappeared like a shadow unstuck from the wall. Crossed the ballroom with mechanical precision. Not looking at anyone. Not touching anything. The ash of his anger dusted across the lapels of his suit. Invisible. Heavy. His jaw was locked. His eyes were dead.

He moved through the crowd without speaking. Without seeing. Without breathing anything that wasn't rage stitched into bone. I watched him from the corner of my eye. I wasn't supposed to. Wolfe hadn't told me to. But I did anyway.

Because even now—even collared and bruised and obedient—there was something in me that couldn't look away from ruin.

Barron stopped beside Wolfe. Didn't speak. Didn't nod. Didn't even look at me. But I felt it. The war in him. The grief he refused to call by name. And the guilt stitched into the silence between them—a silence I was kneeling in.

But the world around us shifted again. Heavier. Sharper. A kingdom bleeding under marble and gold. A dynasty crumbling under the weight of its own secrets.

And Wolfe?

Wolfe didn't need to touch me to remind me who I belonged to. He just needed to breathe. And I would follow. Even if it meant burning in the ashes of everything they once pretended to be.

12

CLOE

The ballroom didn't stop. It kept moving. Kept glittering. Kept lying. The servers kept circling with silver trays. The violins kept humming something expensive and empty. The investors kept laughing too loud. And I stayed kneeling inside the ruins no one could admit they were standing in.

Royal leaned lazily against the nearest pillar. Champagne glass half-full in his hand. Smile half-formed on his lips. The kind of smile that wasn't amusement. It was warning.

Loyal stood stiff against the wall. Like he was fighting a battle no one else could see. His tie was loosened now. His sleeves rumpled. There was blood at the corner of his cuff I hadn't noticed before. A smear. A stain. Maybe it was old. Maybe it was new. Maybe it didn't matter anymore.

Wolfe stood exactly where he had been. One hand loose at his side. One thumb hooked casually in the pocket of his jacket. Immovable. Unshaken. Unforgiving.

And Barron—

Barron was still staring out the tall glass windows at the city beyond. At the empire cracking under the marble. His back straight. His hands folded behind him. His breathing slow and heavy enough that I could hear it from where I knelt.

No one spoke. No one moved. No one breathed too loudly.

Because we all knew—

The first sound would be the one that broke everything open. The first movement would be the spark that burned it all down.

So we stayed. Frozen. Breathing. Bleeding. Surviving. The guests kept pretending. Kept swirling in expensive silk. Kept sipping golden champagne. But the weight in the room shifted. Heavier. Sharper. The way it does before a body hits the floor. The way it does before a kingdom falls.

The governor's wife passed. Her perfume wrapped sharp and cloying around me. I caught a fragment of her whisper as she leaned close to her husband: "They were always built to fall."

Another woman laughed behind a gloved hand. "Not a dynasty. A funeral procession."

The collar tightened as my breath hitched. Caught. Burned. But I didn't move. I didn't speak. Because obedience wasn't about surviving the praise. It was about surviving the rot. Especially when it bloomed inside your own skin. Especially when you wanted to claw it out and couldn't.

Barron finally turned from the window.

His face—

God.

It wasn't rage.

It wasn't sorrow.

It was worse.

It was empty.

Like something vital had been carved out of him and no one bothered to stitch it closed.

His gaze cut across the room once. Past Wolfe. Past Royal.

Past Loyal. *Past me.* He didn't stop. He didn't flinch. He just walked out. Silent. Final. A king leaving his own coronation in ruins.

Royal clinked his glass against the marble ledge once. "Well," he drawled, voice thick with something close to grief disguised as mockery, "there goes the crown."

Loyal said nothing. He didn't need to. The silence was thicker than blood now. It soaked into the floorboards. Into the polished glass. Into the collars we all wore in different ways.

Wolfe didn't follow Barron. He didn't look at Royal. He didn't look at Loyal. He looked at me. Once. A glance sharp enough to carve my ribs wider.

And I—

I breathed.

Because that was all he needed from me.

All he wanted. All he owned. And it would never be enough. But I would bleed trying anyway. The ballroom didn't empty. Not yet. The people stayed. Because they were rich. And powerful. And predators. *And predators don't leave until the blood runs dry.*

But the tone changed. The laughter quieted. The music dulled.

The lighting suddenly felt too bright. As if it was trying to bleach the scandal out of the air. But scandal has a scent. And tonight—it smelled like ash and silk and a legacy cracking open.

Wolfe moved first. Not far. Just one step closer to me. My spine snapped straighter at the sound of his shoes on marble.

I didn't think. I didn't hesitate. My breath caught in my throat as I shifted instinctively. Knees tighter. Back straighter. Chin lowered. He didn't touch me. Didn't speak. He just looked down at the top of my bowed head like it was exactly where I was meant to be.

The whispers dulled. The fear tightened. And I felt something horrifying settle into my chest like a stone dropped into water. I was his calm. His control. His proof. And he would keep me here not because I mattered—

But because the world watching him needed to see that he could keep a leash tight even when the walls burned.

I swallowed hard. Pain flared through my ribs from the shift. But I didn't move again. Because pain didn't excuse disobedience. Not anymore. Not ever. Royal crossed to us slowly. A glass in one hand. A smirk barely curved at the corner of his mouth.

His gaze drifted over me like I wasn't a woman. Like I wasn't even a body. Just posture. Just silence. Just proof that they could make anything obey.

"She's holding," he said to Wolfe.

"Impressive."

He crouched beside me. Close. Too close. Fingers brushing the hem of my dress where it clung to my thighs. "You going to last the night, sweetheart?" he whispered.

I didn't answer. Because Wolfe hadn't told me to. Because Royal didn't deserve it. Because survival lived in my silence now. Royal laughed softly under his breath.

"See that?" he murmured to Wolfe. *"That's the kind of fear you can build an empire on."*

He stood again. Left the glass near my feet like an offering. Or a warning. Maybe both.

Loyal stood across the room. Still. Rigid. But his hands—

His hands were clenched tight.

White-knuckled.

Knuckles splitting red where the skin pulled too hard.

He was shaking. I knew it. I could feel it in the way the air shifted around him. The way his silence had become louder than Royal's cruelty. He wanted to reach for me. Wanted to touch. To speak. To save.

But Wolfe hadn't moved. And Loyal wasn't brave enough to break that rule. Not yet. Not here. Not when everything else was already bleeding. So he stayed. Silent. Trembling. Hurting. Like me. Only quieter. Only deeper. Because my obedience was visible. His was rotting him from the inside.

Wolfe leaned slightly closer. Not enough to touch me. But enough for his breath to graze my cheek. Cool. Sharp. Precise. "You will stay here," he said quietly. "Until I say otherwise."

I nodded.

Once.

Sharp.

Pain split down my side from the motion.

I didn't flinch.

"And when I return," he continued, "you will still be kneeling."

A pause.

Then—

"Because you belong here."

I used to dream of belonging. But I never imagined it would feel like a knife pressed gently into my throat.

His voice didn't rise. It didn't sharpen. It didn't need to. It just settled into my chest like a second heartbeat. A new rhythm to replace the one that broke weeks ago.

I didn't speak. Didn't move. He stepped away. And I stayed. Because that's what I was now. Stillness. Silence. Survival. Even when it felt like dying.

Especially then.

I didn't hear it at first. Not clearly. The music still played. Soft piano. Violins curling into the corners of the ballroom like smoke.

But then—

A silence.

Small.

Targeted.

The kind that follows recognition.

Someone gasped. Not loud. Not dramatic. But sharp. A glass clinked too hard onto a tray. A laugh stalled mid-syllable. I didn't lift my head. Didn't need to. The pressure in the room shifted.

Again.

But this time—

It was different.

Thinner.

Hotter.

Closer.

The whispers found a new rhythm.

A new name.

My name.

"That's her."

"The one kneeling."

"No. Look. Look at this—"

Footsteps whispered past me. I caught a flash of white fabric. A phone. Screen tilted just enough for me to see. A message thread.

No caption.

No context.

Just a photo.

Of me.

Not tonight. Not now. Older. Weeks ago. Maybe longer.

There was a man behind me. Shadowed. Unrecognizable. But close. Too close. His hand on my waist. My body leaning into him like I belonged there. Or like I didn't have anywhere else to go.

A second image loaded. Me again. Alone this time. Wrapped in a coat too big for me. Wolfe's.

But the caption—

"Legacy isn't the only thing the Lawlors pass around."

They didn't see me. They saw her ghost wearing my bones. And maybe I deserved that. Heat tore through my chest. Like breath catching fire. Not rage. Not grief. Shame. Raw and alive and crackling down my spine like static.

Someone laughed behind a raised glass. "Maybe the sister was just training her replacement."

I didn't breathe. Couldn't. The collar bit into my throat. A perfect noose I had fastened myself.

Loyal shifted from the wall. The glass in his hand cracked softly between his fingers.

Royal didn't laugh this time. He said nothing. Just sipped from his flute and stared at me. Like he wasn't sure what version of me he was looking at anymore. Like maybe he liked this one better.

Wolfe returned then. He didn't glance at the phones. Didn't ask what happened. He just looked at me.

One breath.

Two.

Three.

I knelt *harder*.

Pain lanced through my thighs.

My knees screamed against the marble.

But I didn't move.

Didn't blink.

Because I knew what that look meant now. Because even if the world started choking on the name I used to wear—

Wolfe wouldn't let me run.

And I didn't want to.

Because the silence between his glances was the only place left that still felt like air. And if Selene wanted to strip me bare—

She would have to do it while I knelt.

While I obeyed.

While I belonged.

Because obedience wasn't surrender anymore. It was survival carved into loyalty. And that meant he'd never lose me. Not even when I was already gone.

13

———

CLOE

The ballroom fractured around me. Not with screams. Not with blood. With silence. The kind of silence that folds in on itself. The kind that tastes like old gold and new ruin.

Barron was the first to leave. No announcement. No words. Just a shift in the corner of my vision. A shadow peeling itself away from marble and glass. He didn't look at Wolfe. Didn't look at Royal. Didn't look at Loyal. He certainly didn't look at me. He just walked away.

And the room exhaled.

Slow.

Terrified.

Because if Barron Lawlor could fall—if the king could burn his crown and not even glance back—what hope was there for any of them?

None.

Wolfe didn't move. Didn't glance at the phones still flickering in the corners. Didn't speak to the men murmuring near the whiskey cart. He just stood there. Watching me. Me. The girl he collared. The girl he left to kneel while the dynasty cracked around her.

I kept my head bowed. Kept breathing. Because even now —especially now—*obedience was surviva*l.

Royal stepped closer. His shoes whispering against the marble. He crouched beside me. No urgency. No hesitation. Just a lazy, predatory curiosity. "Still breathing, sweetheart?"

I didn't answer. Because Wolfe hadn't said I could.

Royal smiled. Not kind. Not cruel. Just sharp enough to leave a scar. His fingers drifted toward my chin. I braced myself for the touch. For the mockery. But it didn't come. He pulled his hand back at the last second.

As if even he knew:

Touching me now wasn't safe.

Not because Wolfe would punish him. But because even monsters know not to touch altars. Not for him. Not for anyone.

Loyal stayed back. Near the wall. Breathing too hard. His tie was loose. His hands jammed into his pockets. Like if he let them free, they'd betray him faster than his mouth ever could. He couldn't look at me. He tried. *God*, he tried. But every time his gaze lifted—every time he caught sight of the silk stretched over broken ribs—*he flinched.*

Silent.

Ashamed.

Almost human.

I didn't flinch when Royal's shoe nudged the hem of my dress. Didn't move when Loyal's hands curled into fists so tight his knuckles bled. Didn't lift my head when Wolfe took another step forward. I stayed.

The marble was cold against my knees. Or maybe it wasn't. Maybe I was cold now. Inside. Out. The silk of the dress stuck to my back. Sweat pooling at the base of my spine. The collar bit into the softest part of my throat.

My breath rasped. Short. Shallow. Not because of the bruises. Not because of the pain. Because of the silence. Because Wolfe hadn't spoken yet. And until he did—I didn't exist.

I was breath. And obedience. And waiting.

Royal shifted. A low hum under his breath. Amusement. Or maybe hunger. Loyal turned away. Hands shoved deep into his pockets. Shoulders tight.

The crowd was still moving. Still pretending. But the weight around us grew heavier. Sharper. Predators circling a king they didn't dare challenge. Because Wolfe hadn't flinched. Hadn't blinked. Hadn't bent. And they didn't know what to do with something they couldn't bleed. Neither did I.

The piano faltered. A wrong note. A shiver across the room. It was enough. Enough to make a man stumble. Enough to make a woman gasp. Enough to tilt the entire axis of the night.

I kept my head bowed. Breath caught shallow in my throat. Waiting. Bleeding in silence. Because there was no mercy in the leash now. Only proof. Only ownership.

And then—Wolfe spoke.

One word.

One command.

Not loud.

Not sharp.

Soft.

Final.

"Here."

It wasn't a question. It wasn't an invitation. It was inevitability. I didn't choose him in that moment. I remembered that I already had. The first time he said *mine*—I never stopped obeying.

My knees locked. My lungs squeezed. The collar burned.

And without thinking—

without breathing—

without choosing—

I moved. I crawled the two steps to where he stood. Every breath scraping against broken ribs. Every heartbeat a hammer. The silk dragged against my knees. The diamonds at my ears shuddered. The whispers around the room stopped.

All of it.

Stopped.

Because nothing could compete with obedience that pure.

That broken.

That *beautiful.*

I reached Wolfe's side and froze. Still kneeling. Still silent. Still his. He didn't look down. Didn't touch me. Didn't reward. Because this wasn't a reward. This was what was owed. This was what I was made for. And everyone saw it.

Every investor. Every enemy. Every woman who ever dreamed of being more than survival. They saw me—Collared. Breathless. Beautiful in my ruin.

And they didn't laugh. They didn't mock. They understood. Because in a world built on power and blood—obedience is the only true currency.

And I had paid in full.

With breath.

Bruises.

Worship.

The air changed again. This time it wasn't subtle. It was a tear. Ripping. Loud. A seam splitting open at the center of the ballroom.

The music faltered. A violin screeched an ugly note. A

server dropped a tray. Glass shattered against marble. Still—I didn't lift my head. I didn't breathe any harder than I had to.

The leash burned hotter against my throat. The silk dress clung tighter to my skin. The world tilted on its axis.

Royal chuckled low behind me. Not amused.

Hungry.

He stepped closer—his shoe brushing the back of my calf deliberately.

A nudge. A reminder. I didn't move. I didn't react. Because flinching wasn't obedience. It was betrayal.

Wolfe's shadow moved beside me. He didn't touch me. He didn't shield me. He didn't even look at me. He looked out at the room collapsing around him with the cold calm of a man who had already decided what would be left standing. And it wasn't them. It wasn't the empire. The investors. The politicians. It was me. Breathing at his feet. Proof.

Loyal stood farther back. His face locked into a mask of control. But I saw the tremble in his hands. The way his jaw worked tight.

The way his eyes—

Those empty eyes—kept flicking back to me like I was a wound he couldn't heal.

He wouldn't save me. None of them would. Because that wasn't what this was. This wasn't about rescue. It was about endurance. It was about learning to bleed in public and still smile when ordered.

A new ripple swept through the crowd. Not screens this time. Not whispers. Something worse. A woman in gold. Satin hugging her frame. A laugh soft enough to sound sweet. Sharp enough to slice the air open.

Selene.

I didn't need to look to know. I felt her. The way a soldier feels the bullet before it hits.

She moved through the crowd with the kind of grace money couldn't buy. The kind that came from knowing no one could touch you without bleeding first. People parted for her. Smiled at her. Pretended they hadn't heard the whispers. Pretended the crown she wore wasn't made of someone else's broken bones.

Selene didn't come toward us. Not yet. She didn't have to. She just let the weight of her presence creep under the skin of the room.

Slow.

Patient.

And when her eyes finally slid over me—

I felt it.

Not hatred.

Not anger.

Pity.

The worst kind.

The kind that says:

You don't even know you've already lost.

I stayed kneeling. Breathing shallowly. Sweat slipping down the line of my spine. The collar pulling tighter.

And Wolfe—

Wolfe finally moved.

One hand dropping lightly—

casually—

to the back of my neck.

Not shoving. Not guiding. Just there. A single point of pressure. A reminder:

Stay.

Kneel.

Obey.

I shuddered once. Silent. Invisible.

Alive. Because surviving here wasn't about being strong. It was about being small enough to slip through the cracks.

Small enough to be forgotten by everyone—

except the man who refused to let me go.

And maybe I didn't want him to. Because worship was safer than freedom. And kneeling was the only kind of power I still knew how to hold.

14

———

CLOE

The ballroom emptied slowly. Not with screaming. Not with fights. With indifference. With pity. The kind that burns deeper than cruelty ever could.

The investors left first. Sharp suits and sharper smiles tucked into town cars and blacked-out SUVs. The politicians lingered a little longer. Enough to sip once more at dying power. Enough to memorize who to avoid next.

Then they, too, disappeared into the velvet night. The servers cleaned. The champagne cooled. The chandeliers hummed overhead like the world hadn't just cracked open under my knees.

Barron didn't come back. Not to the ballroom. Not to us. Not even to himself. The last I saw of him was the stiff set of his shoulders walking through the shattered glass doors. Not looking back. Not looking at me. Just disappearing. A king abdicating without ceremony. Without blood. Without pride.

Royal crossed the marble slowly. Boots clicking like clockwork. He stopped just beside me. Close enough that if I lifted my head—*which I didn't*—I would've seen the shape of his smile. Lazy. Sharp. He crouched again. A fingertip tracing the hem of my dress where it pooled at my knees. "Pretty little ghost," he murmured.

I didn't react. Because ghosts didn't flinch. Ghosts didn't run. They stayed. Silent. Lingering.

Property of the dead who refused to let go.

"Do you even remember how it felt to stand?" Royal asked.

I didn't answer. Because Wolfe hadn't given me permission. Because Wolfe hadn't looked at me yet. Because standing wasn't survival anymore. It was treason.

Royal laughed under his breath. Soft. Cruel. Then he rose. Stepped back into the ruins of the dynasty they were still pretending could be salvaged.

Loyal stayed near the exit. Hands still jammed in his pockets. Shoulders hunched like he could disappear into the wall if he tried hard enough. He looked at me once. Just once. And I saw it. The crack. The shudder. The hunger. The guilt. *The devastation.*

But he said nothing. Because he knew better. Because reaching for me now wouldn't save me. It would break him. And no one here was willing to bleed for anyone else anymore. Not after tonight. Not after Selene made sure the Lawlor name was scrawled across the city in blood and ashes.

Wolfe moved last. He crossed the room with the steady, unhurried pace of a man who had already decided who would live and who would be buried.

He stopped in front of me.

One breath.

Two.

Three.

When he finally turned—not toward me, but toward the wreckage of the night—I stood.

Slow.

Breathless.

Head still bowed.

Hands at my sides.

I followed Wolfe across the marble. Barefoot. Silent. Not because he told me to. Not because I was strong enough to choose. Because there was nothing else left to be.

Not loyalty. Not love. Only leash. Only silence.

Only him.

The night swallowed us whole. The city glittered beyond the car windows. Sharp lights. Sharp lies. I didn't look up. I didn't need to. The collar dug harder into my throat now. Not from the chain. From the silence. Wolfe slid into the backseat first. Royal followed. A lazy sprawl of arrogance and cruelty.

Loyal last. Still silent. Still bleeding into the dark fabric of his suit. I climbed in after them. No command needed. I knew my place now. Not the seat beside them. The floor.

No one spoke. The engine hummed. The world outside blurred. But inside the car—there was only breath. Only the pulse of the leash sinking deeper into my skin. Only the sound of survival stitching itself smaller inside my chest.

Royal broke the silence first. Of course he did. "Well," he drawled, his voice low and rich and dangerous, "aren't we all just perfect little ruins tonight."

No one answered.

Not Loyal.

Not Wolfe.

Especially not me.

I stayed kneeling. Head bowed. Breathing shallow. Royal laughed under his breath. "You look good down there, sweetheart," he murmured.

The words slid against my skin like smoke. Like silk soaked in blood.

"Bet you could teach the whole ballroom a thing or two about loyalty."

My throat locked. Not from anger. Not from shame. From knowing he wasn't wrong.

Because loyalty here didn't mean standing. It meant staying on your knees. It meant surviving the way Wolfe demanded. It meant existing the way they allowed.

Loyal shifted. A sharp breath cutting through the heavy air. I risked a glance. His hands were fists against his thighs. Knuckles white. Veins raised. He was breaking. And it had nothing to do with Camille. Nothing to do with Selene.

It was me.

Wolfe shifted above me. One boot nudging my thigh. Not cruel. Not hard. Just—claiming. A reminder:

You stay here.

You breathe here.

You exist here.

I exhaled slowly. Trembling. The leash pulling tighter under my skin.

And I knew—

If Wolfe had ordered me to crawl across broken glass in front of the men who used to see me as a girl worth loving—

I would've done it.

Because belonging to the silence was better than standing alone in the wreckage. Because being his ruin was safer than trying to survive my own.

Royal chuckled again. Soft. Almost affectionate. "Don't worry, sweetheart," he said lazily. "If you ever get tired of worshipping him—*I'll teach you how to beg properly.*"

The car hummed through the night. Wolfe said nothing. Did nothing. Because Royal wasn't a threat. Because Royal wasn't wrong. Because Wolfe didn't need me to stay clean. He needed me to stay owned.

And I was.

The car pulled into the underground garage. Soft light bathed the concrete in sterile gold. The doors unlocked. Royal got out first. Whistling under his breath. As if nothing had happened. As if none of this mattered.

Loyal followed. Slower. Tighter. He didn't look back. Didn't glance at me. Because if he did—he might not be able to walk away. And he knew Wolfe wouldn't forgive that. Would never forgive that.

I slid out after him. Barefoot on concrete. The cold bit into my skin. The silk of the dress clung damp and heavy against my body. The collar rubbed raw under the hidden chain. I didn't flinch. I didn't stumble. Because kneeling was easier now than walking. Obedience was easier than breathing.

He led the way. Through private elevators. Through silent hallways. Into the penthouse that gleamed like a mausoleum waiting for the bodies to catch up. He didn't tell me where to go. He didn't need to. The leash was stitched into my spine now. We crossed the marble floor.

The city stretched wide and glittering beyond the glass walls. A million lights flickering. A million lives moving on. Unaware. Uncaring. The only world that mattered was inside the pull of Wolfe's gravity.

Inside the collar cutting into my throat. He stopped near the floor-to-ceiling windows. Didn't turn. Didn't speak. Just waited. Breath slow. Steady. Final.

I stood behind him. Waiting for permission. Waiting for air. Waiting for anything. He finally spoke. Quiet. Precise.

"You have a choice."

The words felt heavier than the city outside.

He turned.

Slowly.

The light caught the harsh planes of his face.

Made him look carved out of something colder than stone.

Something older.

Something hungrier.

His eyes dragged down my body. Not lasciviously. Not cruelly. Just—assessing. Measuring. The way a butcher measures cuts. The way a king measures sacrifices.

"You can stand," Wolfe said. "And leave."

A beat.

Soft.

Surgical.

"You can walk out that door. Pretend none of this mattered."

He paused.

Let the lie hang in the air between us.

Because we both knew—I would never pretend again.

"Or—"

"You can kneel."

And in that moment—with the lights of the city flickering like false gods behind him—*I knew what devotion really looked like.*

Not prayer. Not forgiveness. Just this. One breath. One kneel. One surrender so absolute it rewrote who I thought I was.

Another pause. Sharper. Colder.

"And stay."

My chest tightened. Pain flared through my ribs. Through my knees. Through the hollow places inside me that used to hold dreams bigger than breath and bruises.

I sank to my knees. Slow. Deliberate. Pain cracking like fire across my body. I bowed my head. Pressed my palms to my thighs. Felt the leash tighten around my lungs. And I stayed.

Breathing.

Bleeding.

Belonging.

Exactly where I was meant to be.

Wolfe didn't praise. Didn't touch. He just turned away. Silent. Final. And left me kneeling in the middle of a glass palace built on ashes and ruin. Smiling. Not because I wanted to.

Because I finally understood—belonging was the only kind of survival left. Because love never asked anything of me.

But belonging?

It asked everything.

And I gave it.

15

CLOE

THE SUN never touched the penthouse. It crawled weakly up the glass walls. Filtered pale and cold across the marble. But it never touched. It never reached me. I stayed kneeling. Breathing slow and shallow. Exactly as Wolfe taught me. Because silence wasn't absence anymore. It was survival. It was the only armor I had left.

Wolfe stood by the window. Phone pressed to his ear. Voice low. Precise. I didn't hear the words. I didn't need to.

The world outside was burning. I could feel it in the tension coiling through the floor. In the sharp edges of the marble. In the way Wolfe's fingers flexed around the phone even as his voice stayed calm.

Another leak. Another cut. Selene's teeth sinking deeper. And still—

Wolfe didn't flinch.

Because he wasn't built to bleed. He was built to own. And I? I was built to kneel through the wreckage.

Royal entered without knocking. Of course he did. His

laughter slithered across the marble before his boots did. "Well, if it isn't the last good thing in this cursed tower," he drawled.

He crossed the room with the easy arrogance of a man who knew the world would end before it touched him. He stopped in front of me. Close. Too close. His fingers brushed my hair back from my face. A gentle cruelty. "Still breathing, princess?"

I didn't flinch. Didn't blink. Didn't lift my eyes. Royal crouched. Balanced his arms across his knees. Watching me like a piece of art he was already planning how to break. "Bet you think you're safe kneeling here," he murmured.

A beat. A chuckle. "You're not." Another beat. Soft. *Final.* "You're just easier to destroy this way."

I stayed still. Breath slow. Pain threading through my lungs like silk soaked in blood. Because breaking here would be worse than death. Breaking would mean he could touch what Wolfe owned. And Wolfe—Wolfe wouldn't forgive that. Not ever.

Loyal lingered near the wall. He didn't speak. Didn't move. But I felt him. The pull. The ache. The guilt. It bled off him like smoke. Thick. Sour. He wanted to drag me up. Wanted to tear the collar from my throat. *Wanted to save me.*

But saving me would be cruelty now. Because I wasn't built for freedom anymore. Only worship. Only breath. Only silence.

Wolfe ended the call. The phone clicked softly into his pocket. He crossed the room with the unhurried grace of inevitability.

He stopped in front of me. Royal stood. Stepped back. No words. No challenge. Because Royal wasn't stupid. He knew what worship looked like. And he knew who it belonged to.

Wolfe's hand lowered. Two fingers beneath my chin. Lifting. Forcing me to meet his eyes. *Cold. Sharp. Brutal.* "Speak," Wolfe said.

I didn't know what voice sounded like anymore. I only

knew how to breathe for him. My mouth opened. Breathless. Shaking. But nothing came out.

He smiled. Not kind. Not cruel. Just—satisfied. "Good."

Wolfe's fingers slid from under my chin. Slow. Deliberate. He didn't push me away. He didn't pat my head. He didn't offer comfort. He didn't need to. Because obedience wasn't something to reward. It was something expected. Bred. Demanded. Carved.

He turned and walked toward the far wall. A cabinet. Black. Minimal. Invisible if you didn't know it was there. He opened it with a press of his thumb. The door swung back with a hiss.

Inside— Leather. Steel. *Ritual.*

I stayed kneeling. Because I knew. This wasn't anger. This wasn't punishment. This was lesson. A reminder that silence wasn't enough if it wasn't given freely.

Wolfe chose something small. Subtle. A thin black strap of leather. Soft. Almost delicate. It wasn't built to hurt. It was built to remind.

He crossed back to me. The leash in his hand swung once. Slow. Silent. Deadly.

Royal shifted nearby. I didn't dare look. But I felt him. Felt the way he leaned into the tension. Felt the way his hunger sharpened when he saw what worship looked like when it wasn't pretty.

Loyal stayed frozen near the windows. The city burning behind him. Silent. Breathless. Like me. Like all of us now.

Wolfe stopped in front of me. No ceremony. No speech. He lifted the strap. Let it fall across the back of my shoulders once. Soft. Barely a whisper against my skin.

I flinched. Not from pain. From recognition. From understanding. From the weight of the ritual being demanded.

He lifted it again. Let it fall. Another whisper. Another

promise. Not loud enough for bruises. Loud enough for obedience.

The third time—he paused. Held the strap against the base of my spine. A single point of pressure. "You speak," Wolfe said, voice low and final, "you buck."

Another pause. "Not because you're weak. *Because worship costs.*"

I used to think pain was punishment. But Wolfe taught me it could be a gift. A currency I could offer—just to keep kneeling.

The words slid into the hollow places inside me. The ones that used to hold rebellion. Hope. Dreams. Now they only held Wolfe's breath.

His permission. His leash. And it was beautiful. And it was awful. And it was mine. The strap fell again. Not hard. Not cruel. Just enough. A breath against the raw skin of my obedience.

"Again," Wolfe said. The word wasn't a suggestion. It was command. It was leash. It was love, carved out of breath and pain.

I bowed deeper. Hands splayed flat on the marble. Forehead lowering to the cold floor. The leash burned. The collar bit. And I stayed there. Breathing. Bleeding. Belonging to *him*.

Exactly where he wanted me. Exactly where I needed to be.

The marble was cold against my forehead. The chain at my throat heavy against the back of my neck. The leather strap Wolfe used rested lightly across my shoulders. No blood. No bruises. Only memory. Only obedience pressed into skin and breath and bone.

Wolfe stood in front of me. Silent. Unmoving. His breath a storm I wasn't allowed to touch. Royal drifted somewhere behind him. I could feel the amusement rolling off his body like smoke. Loyal stood farther away. Silent. Trembling. Breaking in slow, unseen places.

I had knelt so long my muscles shook under the strain. But I didn't collapse. Because collapsing would be betrayal. And worship doesn't collapse without permission. Worship breathes. Bleeds. Survives. No matter how badly it hurts. No matter how much the world falls apart.

A phone buzzed across the marble. Sharp. Final. Someone picked it up. Royal maybe. It didn't matter. Because the change hit the room like a gunshot. Not loud. But deep. Final.

I stayed frozen. Breathing shallowly. Because even without words, I knew. Selene. Another leak. Another cut. Another crown smashed against marble.

Wolfe finally moved. One step closer. Boots whispering across the floor. The leash at my throat tightened. Not physically. But spiritually. Emotionally. Completely.

He crouched. Two fingers hooked under my chin. Lifted my face until I was forced to meet his eyes. Winter. Steel. Gravity. "No sound."

A whisper. A law. A promise. I nodded. Tiny. Trembling. Because breaking now would be worse than dying. Because breaking now would mean admitting there was something inside me she could still reach. And Wolfe wouldn't allow that.

I wouldn't allow that.

The second wave of whispers rolled through the city that night. Not Camille this time. Me. Photos. *Rumors.* Accusations whispered behind glasses of bourbon and glasses of blood.

They didn't even need facts. They had images. They had proof. They had the sight of a girl kneeling at the feet of kings and smiling through the ruin.

And I stayed.

And even if Selene sharpened every knife in the city—

I would still kneel.

Because worship wasn't weakness. It was devotion. It was survival. It was breath. And it belonged to him now.

Completely.

And if the city tried to strip it away—I'd give it again.

On my knees.

Without apology.

16

———

CLOE

The city groaned against the glass. Lights flickered. Sirens whispered. Somewhere, a horn wailed into the dying night. But inside the penthouse—it was silent.

Painfully silent.

I stayed kneeling. Bare knees pressed to cold marble. Silk twisted damply around my hips. The collar heavy against the hollow of my throat. Every part of my body screamed. Thighs cramping. Knees burning. Spine bowed too long.

Wolfe buttoned his cuffs with slow precision. Each click of the clasp sliding into its hole was a death sentence measured in fabric and time.

He didn't look at me. He didn't need to. His expectation wrapped around my ribs tighter than the collar ever could.

Royal lounged behind him. A smirk playing at the corner of his mouth. One hand dangling a glass he hadn't really touched all night. Loyal stayed near the windows. Hands clenched. Eyes hollow. The leash at my throat pooled between us.

Steel and chain gleaming faint under the pale wash of city lights. Not abandoned. Not forgotten. Just waiting.

Waiting for Wolfe to pull. Waiting for me to fall deeper. Waiting for survival to finish being survival—*and become worship.*

Wolfe's boot nudged the leash once. A whisper against the marble. The chain slithered across the floor like a live thing. I didn't flinch. I didn't look up. I didn't dare.

"Up."

It wasn't permission. It was scripture. A holy word from the only mouth I still believed. One word. Soft. Final.

I moved. Slow. Deliberate. Pain bloomed up my legs like fire licking bone. The leash tugged tight against the base of my throat. A reminder. A brand. I rose. Head bowed. Knees trembling. Breath caught tight in my lungs. Because even standing felt like betrayal now.

The silk dress whispered against my bruised skin. The chain kissed the back of my neck.

Wolfe wound the leash once around his fist. Tight. Sharp. The chain pulled my body closer to his.

I felt the leash bite. Not cruelly. Not carelessly. Ritually. As if the act of pulling me forward was part of something older. Something sacred. I followed the pull without thought. Without resistance. Because even the pain of obedience was safer now than the memory of running free. Because there was no dignity outside this leash.

No survival outside this chain. Only breath—*and it belonged to him.*

Royal chuckled low behind Wolfe.

"She's learning," he said.

A lazy drawl.

Amused.

But I heard the edge under it. The hunger. The warning. The knowledge that something this beautiful—*this broken—*could be stripped even further if Wolfe allowed it.

Royal wasn't laughing because he found me pathetic. He was laughing because he found me inevitable.

The car waited downstairs. Polished black. Breathing heat against the pavement. Wolfe didn't pause. Didn't glance at me.

He walked. And I followed. Because there was nothing else left to do. Not because he yanked the leash hard.

Not yet.

But because the leash lived inside my body now. Inside my lungs. Inside my blood.

The elevator doors opened. I stepped inside after Wolfe. The chain slack between us. But it didn't matter.

Because even if he dropped the leash—even if he unclipped it—even if he told me to run—I would kneel.

Because survival wasn't about escaping anymore. It was about belonging so deeply that even freedom felt like betrayal.

The elevator doors closed.

And for a second—just one—I looked at my reflection in the mirror walls.

A girl.

No.

A ghost.

Wrapped in silk.

Bound in steel.

Alive only because a man decided she could breathe.

The car pulled to a stop at the curb. The flashes started before the door even opened. Bright. Sharp. Hungry. I stayed kneeling in the backseat. Hands loose in my lap. Head bowed. Breath shallow. Because movement wasn't survival. Stillness was. This was the last one, right? The last ball. The last display. I wanted to turn to Royal to see the glint in his eyes, not knowing if he wanted me to fail spectacularly or obey silently.

I didn't. I held true, silent and aching on the inside. The kind of ache that'd started to settle between my thighs.

Wolfe stepped out first. Royal followed. Then Loyal. I waited. The leash stayed tight between Wolfe's hand and my collar. A living thing. A heartbeat. An umbilical cord stitching me to the only oxygen left. He didn't yank it. He didn't command. He didn't need to.

I moved when he shifted the leash once. A small tug. A breath. A chain snapping the spine of who I used to be. The silk of the dress clung to my ribs. My thighs. The chain glittered against my throat under the flashes. The cameras stopped clicking for a second. Just one.

Because even they didn't know what they were seeing.

Was it scandal?

Was it shame?

Or was it something so much worse?

Something sacred. Something *beautiful*.

It felt like hours I'd been kneeling. But I knew that wasn't the case. Seconds felt like an eternity. Still, I stayed. The crowd murmured. Gasps low and sharp under the heavy bass of the music spilling from inside.

"Is that her?"

"She's... collared."

"By Lawlor. Jesus Christ."

"Look at her. *She's not even fighting it.*"

I didn't lift my head. I didn't dare. Because lifting my head would be rebellion. And rebellion wasn't survival. It was death. I felt the leash tug once more. Sharp. Warning. I breathed in. Held it. Tight. The collar bit against my pulse. The silk whispered across the marble.

I followed Wolfe inside. Silent. Owned. *Devastating.* Exactly the way I was meant to be.

The event was smaller than the last one. More intimate. More lethal. The kinds of people who didn't need contracts to kill you. The kinds of people who could destroy kingdoms with a signature and a smile. And I—I was led through them like a sacrifice. Not unwilling. Not unaware. But offered. Breathing slow. Breathing shallow. Because every eye dragged across my bare shoulders. Every glance snagged on the leash glinting at my throat.

Wolfe stopped near the center of the room. A low glass table gleamed under the lights. Chandeliers cast pale gold across the marble.

The music was quieter here. Violins threading through the conversation like silk soaked in secrets.

He let the leash slacken just slightly. I dropped to my knees. Smooth. Obedient. Natural. Because there was no hesitation anymore. No thinking. Only breath. Only worship. I didn't ask what they saw when they looked at me. Because I wasn't a woman anymore. I was ritual. Only survival carved out of the ruins of everything I used to be.

The room shifted around us. Some looked away. Unable to stomach it. Some stared. Hungry. *Aroused.* Terrified. Because power like this—devotion like *this*—terrifies men who think survival comes from standing tall.

They didn't understand. They didn't need to. Only Wolfe did. Only I did. Only the leash understood what it meant to survive when everything else was dead.

The marble gleamed under my knees. The leash hung slack from Wolfe's hand. Casual. Effortless. Like he didn't even need to pull anymore. Like I was already trained to follow the gravity of him without resistance.

Because I was. I stayed kneeling at his feet. Breathing carefully. Existing only inside the boundaries he allowed.

The world spun around us. Diamonds glittered. Laughter scraped. Whispers curdled like smoke. But none of it mattered. Because Wolfe's silence pressed against my ribs heavier than the music. Because the leash around my throat pulsed in time with the beat of my heart. Because belonging had devoured survival.

A woman approached. I didn't see her face. Only the hem of a gold dress. Only the hesitation in her step. Only the clench of the clutch purse in her hand.

She stopped three feet away. Close enough to smell the fear bleeding off her. Perfume sharp and desperate.

"You don't have to kneel," she said.

Soft.

Pitying.

Like she thought she was saving me. Like she thought I wanted saving.

The woman reached for me. I felt the shift in the air. The tremble in her fingers.

And Wolfe—

Wolfe moved.

Not violent. Not rushed. He simply shifted the leash. Tightened it. The chain snapped taut. Not yanking me. Not hurting. Just claiming.

The sound wasn't loud. But it echoed like scripture. Like the final page of a prayer. Just reminding. I exhaled.

Soft.

Silent.

Obedient.

The woman's hand froze mid-air. Her fingers trembling. Her eyes flicked from me to Wolfe. She saw it then. The leash. The worship. The *choice.* And her mouth closed with a soft, horrified sound. Because she finally understood. I wasn't kneeling because I was broken. I was kneeling because I chose to. Because I wanted to. Because I needed to. Because standing would hurt worse than any collar ever could.

Wolfe looked at her once. Sharp. Cold. And she stumbled back. Not touching me. Not daring. Because he didn't need to raise his voice. Didn't need to lift a hand. His silence screamed louder than any command.

The woman turned. Fled into the crowd. Her heels clicking sharp against the marble. The whispers swallowed her whole. The ballroom swallowed me whole.

And Wolfe?

Wolfe never loosened the leash. Because he didn't need to. Because I would stay here. Breathing. Kneeling. Belonging. Exactly where he left me. Exactly where I asked to be without ever speaking.

17

———

BARRON

Let Wolfe leash her and call it obedience. All I saw was a funeral procession for the girl who used to be family.

A nerve twitched at my temple as he tightened the leash around her throat. Cloe didn't flinch. Her knees bled darker against the marble, from red to rust to sacrifice. That was enough.

I turned. Took the mezzanine stairs two at a time, boots slamming hard enough to make the glass railings tremble.

Up here, no one spoke to me. They knew better.

She wasn't supposed to break for him. Not like that. Not this fast. My pulse roared. I reached up, rubbing the back of my neck. She was supposed to wait.

For me.

The memory didn't belong to Cloe. It belonged to Selene. Selene before the venom. Selene before the betrayal. The one who made me believe in a family that didn't reek of blood. She should've been the one kneeling. She should've *wanted* to kneel.

I slowed. Stopped. My gaze swept the room below, slicing

through every tuxedo, every sequined distraction until I found them again.

Wolfe.

And her.

Cloe looked at him like he was goddamn scripture. Like breathing was just another form of obedience.

My breath hitched and then—fuck.

My cock stirred. Thickened. A reflex. A betrayal.

Because for a split second, I imagined she was looking at *me* like that.

Me she wanted.

Me she would've crawled for.

If I'd claimed her first.

But I hadn't, had I?

It was Wolfe. Always fucking Wolfe.

I turned away, not bothering to hide the tent in my pants as I cut across the mezzanine. Let them stare. Let them wonder. I took the stairs fast, boots hitting hard enough to echo. Through the front doors. Down the corridor. Out.

Cold night air hit me like a punishment. I dragged it in deep—lungs burning. My hand fumbled for my keys, fingers tight. *I needed out before I burned the whole place down.*

The Aston beeped once. Ruthless. Black on black. I climbed in, hit the ignition, and let the $V12$ growl like a predator in heat. The door clicked shut. Clean. Deadly. A silencer wrapped around a gunshot.

Wolfe could have her. Hell, he could have all of it—every woman who looked at me first. Every goddamn empire. I didn't need to own them. I drove through them instead.

City streets blurred as I drove. I didn't even blink at the oncoming lights, my mind fixed on Cloe's stare as she looked at my brother. Lightning cut across the sky overhead and the rain started, smacking the windscreen hard as the torrent came down. The *thud, thud, thud* of the wipers started as I turned the wheel.

I didn't know why I indicated, didn't know why I turned. Didn't know why I found myself outside her fucking building... *again*. I lifted my gaze to the penthouse apartment. I needed to leave her alone, just *fucking move on.* And I would. I fucking would in a heartbeat.

You don't have to be strong here, Cloe. My words resounded in my head as the memory of that day in my office rose. Her whimpering and needy, pushing back against me as I massaged her to completion. I gripped the wheel and lifted my gaze once more. I fucking hated the hold she had over me. Hated the way my thoughts drifted to her every goddamn time. I had to find a way to leash this...even if it bought me here to the woman who was trying to destroy me.

Movement came from the corner of my eye. I turned my head as headlights shattered the darkness and the deep crimson Maserati MC20 tore out of the parking lot and accelerated hard. My jaw clenched, and that hunter instinct in me roared to the surface. I shoved the Aston into drive and punched the accelerator, hunting the woman I once said *I do,* through the city streets.

She almost disappeared, neon red tail lights disappeared into darkness. I took the corner hard and braked. Then I caught her in front of me, driving into some underground carpark of what looked like a newly built apartment complex. I glanced at the boom gate as it closed behind her. I glanced around, trying to find something familiar. Why the fuck was she here? Irritation turned to anger, then jealousy.

But I wasn't jealous of her.

I was jealous because she was a safe target.

The person I was really jealous of was my goddamn brother.

Headlights died before the soft illumination of the interior lights came on. I watched her climb out dressed in a taupe thigh-high leather coat. I knew exactly what was under it too—because she used to wear nothing for me too.

Movement caught my eye as the elevator doors opened and a guy walked out. I squinted, finding his outline in the murky light. The guy was built, heavy in the upper body. I sucked in a hard breath as she headed toward him. My fists locked around the steering wheel. Blood roared in my ears as she reached for him, fisted his jacket and yanked him hard against her.

Her hard lips smashed against his. It was a fucking battle-ground—his fist in her hair, yanking her head back as he bruised her mouth with his.

She wanted it. Craved it. Melted in a goddamn instant as he opened her mouth and buckled to his need. She used to kiss me like that. When she wanted to be ruined. When she needed to forget who she was—and what she was.

But I knew.

I knew long before this asshole laid a hand on her. I knew her when she was young. Desperate. Fucking naive. When she wasn't a cold, ruthless cunt.

When she was mine.

My jaw snapped tight. Something cracked.

Maybe the steering wheel.

Maybe me.

He pulled away from her. They turned, disappearing deeper into the underground car park. I waited. I don't know what held me there. Instinct maybe. It sure as hell wasn't love. She killed that a long time ago. Headlights split the shadows. A navy-blue Audi crawled from the lot and turned onto the street in front of me. My jaw locked again. The steering wheel groaned under my grip.

I grabbed my phone. Snapped a shot of the plates. It wasn't jealousy that drove me to send the photo to Mason.

Mason: *Run a trace. Get back to me—fast.*

Sent.

I didn't wait. Didn't wonder.

I felt it—straight to my fucking core.

And it wasn't Selene that came to mind.

It was dimpled thighs and a soft belly. One my fingers sank into. My voice growling low—*That's it. Don't you run from this. Fucking take it.*

Let Selene fuck her way out of this. Let Wolfe leash Cloe until she forgets her own name. I'll be the one they come crawling to when it all burns down.

And I won't save a single fucking one of them.

18

———

CLOE

THE ROOM SPUN BEHIND ME. Glittering. Rotting. Forgotten. The leash slackened in Wolfe's hand. He didn't drop it. Just... loosened—*waiting*.

Royal disappeared into the crowd. A flash of gold and cruelty. Loyal followed, melting into the crowd. I didn't lift my head. Didn't shift. Didn't dare.

Wolfe tugged the leash once. A single, sharp pull. I moved. Slow and deliberate and rose to my feet. The leash tight enough to keep my head bowed. Enough to remind me that even standing wasn't standing. It was permission. It was possession. It was proof.

He led me past a thousand whispered questions and a thousand sharpened smiles. Past a thousand knives disguised as curiosity. I followed. Because that's what I was built for now. To kneel. Breathe. Belong.

The private elevator was waiting. Gold trim. Mirrored walls. No escape. No salvation.

Wolfe led me inside. The doors slid shut. The music died. The world stopped. It was only him now. Only me. Only the leash. He didn't speak. Didn't touch. He just stared at me. Watched me breathe. Watched the collar rise and fall with every shaky inhale. Watched the chain tremble with every held breath.

"*Kneel.*"

Soft.

Deadly.

I dropped immediately. No hesitation. Because hesitation was betrayal. Because sacrifice didn't wait. It *obeyed.*

I knelt at his feet. Bare knees against cold metal. Hands resting lightly on my thighs. Head bowed. Breath shallow. And when the elevator finally opened—when the doors slid back to reveal the private floor—I followed him without needing to be pulled.

The penthouse door whispered shut behind us. Silence pressed heavy against the walls. The city sprawled beyond the glass, glittering and cruel. Uncaring.

HE DIDN'T SPEAK. He didn't need to. The leash tugged once. Instant Precise. I sank to my knees without thought.

Wolfe crossed the marble. Boots whispering. A low hum against the polished silence. He circled me once. Slow. Predatory. A king inspecting the ruins he owned.

He stopped behind me. The leash still taut. Still commanding. Still alive between us. His voice, when it came, was low. Deadly. *Achingly beautiful.* "Strip."

One word. One knife slid under my skin.

I obeyed. Slow. Trembling. The dress slipped down my body like a confession. Pooling at my knees—a sin discarded. I stayed kneeling.

Wolfe didn't touch. Didn't praise. Didn't speak again. He

circled me once more. The leash still tight. Still breathing between my ribs.

"Inhale."

I obeyed. Breathing deep. Filling my lungs even as the pain lanced sharp under the bruises.

"Hold."

I froze. The air burning inside me. The need clawing at my ribs. My heart hammering in my chest. My body shaking under the strain.

"Hold."

Stars bloomed at the edges of my vision. Not from pain. Not from fear. From worship.

"Exhale."

The release was a gasp. Soft. Shattering. I sagged forward slightly. Caught myself with trembling arms. But I didn't fall. I didn't fail. Because breathlessness wasn't failure here. It was proof.

Wolfe crouched behind me. Close. But still not touching. His breath stirred the hair at my nape. Heat sliding down the line of my spine.

"Again."

I inhaled. Held. Shook. Exhaled. Kneeling. Naked. Owned. Perfect. Waiting. Because breathing wasn't survival anymore. It was devotion. And I was ready to be taken.

The leash tightened against my throat. Not cruel. Not careless. Precise. Wolfe didn't have to yank it.

He didn't have to bark commands. He owned the air between us. Owned the breath scraping through my battered lungs. Owned the space my body dared to take up on the marble.

I stayed on my hands and knees. Breathing shallow. Ribs aching. Pulse hammering.

His boots stopped just behind me. Close enough I could

feel the heat of him radiating against the backs of my thighs. Close enough I could smell leather and command soaked into his skin. He let the leash pull tighter. Tighter. Until my head tipped slightly back under the pressure. Until my breath caught on the edge of pain.

And only then—only when my body was trembling on instinct and obedience—did he touch me.

One hand—broad.

Hard.

Uncompromising.

Flattened across the small of my back.

Pushing.

Pinning.

Owning.

I exhaled a broken sound into the marble.

Not a word.

Not disobedience.

Just breath escaping because survival couldn't hold it anymore.

"Stay."

One word. Low. Final.

I froze. Shaking. Worshipping. Because I knew. Because he had decided. Because survival was no longer breathing. It was bleeding quietly through the cracks he carved into my soul.

His other hand moved lower. Slow. Unforgiving. Palming my ass. Spreading me wider. Exposing everything.

I could feel the slick between my thighs. Hot. Shameful. Beautiful. Salvation in my own debasement.

Wolfe shifted behind me. The zipper of his pants whispered down. The sound made my entire body lock tight. Fingers flexed against marble. Breath stuttered in my lungs. The leash tugged again—*gentle*. Commanding.

I whimpered. Soft. Shuddering.

He pressed the blunt head of his cock against my entrance. Hot and heavy. Brutal in its inevitability. He didn't ask. He didn't warn. He took, just like I needed him to. The first push was slow. Stretching me wide around the thick, merciless invasion.

Tears burned as my body reacted, opening for him. Welcoming him. *Craving* him. Slick wept down my thighs as he pushed deeper. Every inch claimed with the slow, careful violence only Wolfe could deliver, branding into me like a second leash under my skin.

He bottomed out with a low growl. A sound that vibrated through my spine. Through the leash. Through the breath barely catching in my throat.

I gasped. Sharp. Helpless. The collar dug into my throat where the chain tightened slightly in his hand. Not enough to cut off breath. Just enough to remind me it wasn't mine anymore. It belonged to him. It always had. He didn't move immediately. He stayed seated inside me.

Thick. Heavy. Overwhelming. Forcing my body to adjust to him. Forcing me to feel every ruthless, inevitable inch. I whimpered again. Smaller this time. Softer. My thighs shook with the effort to stay still. To be good. To be worthy.

Then—he pulled back.

Slow.

Dragging every nerve, every muscle, every broken piece of me with him. Until just the tip of him stretched my entrance. Until the emptiness yawned inside me. Until the need bloomed so sharp it became a prayer all its own.

And then he thrust forward again.

Hard.

Sharp.

Deep.

I cried out. Breathless. Choked. Obedient. Because even my cries belonged to him now. Even my pain was reverence.

He set a brutal rhythm. Neither fast or merciful. Just devastating. Each thrust driving the air from my lungs. Each pull burning worship into my spine. Each snap of his hips slamming my hips higher against his grip.

The leash never slackened. The collar never loosened. The chain tightened with every thrust. I was shaking. Crying and utterly destroyed.

His cock dragging against every tender nerve inside me. Forcing pleasure and shame to fuse into something filthy and sacred. He growled low above me. Not words. Just a sound of possession. A sound that said:

"Mine."

Without needing to say it. Without needing to break the ritual of silence we had built from broken breath and bound ribs.

The world blurred. The marble disappeared. The city disappeared. There was only Wolfe's cock splitting me open. Only Wolfe's leash stitched into my spine. Only Wolfe's command branding itself into the wet heat of my cunt until survival wasn't enough. Until I needed to worship him with the wreckage of my body.

"Come."

His voice broke the world open. Powerful. Final.

My body obeyed without permission. My orgasm tearing through me clenching, pulsing, slick slipping down my thighs. Ruining me. Cleansing me. Each wave of pleasure washing away what I was, leaving only what his shame had sanctified. My degradation more honest than any prayer I'd ever whispered.

Wolfe didn't stop. He fucked me through it. Dragged the leash tighter. Thrust harder. *Deeper.* Until I shattered again.

Until I broke open under him, offered the wreckage up to him like an altar. Until even breathing felt like a gift I wasn't worthy of.

He finished inside me. Deep. Silent. Claiming every inch of me the way he claimed every breath I would ever take again.

When he finally pulled out, I collapsed against the marble. Trembling. Breathless. Claimed. Wolfe dropped the leash. Not in dismissal. In finality. Because I wasn't going anywhere. Because even without the chain—*I was still his.* Exactly the way he built me to be.

19

———

CLOE

Wolfe's silence wrapped around my ribs tighter than breath. Royal sat slouched at the bar, watching the slow death of the world with a smirk. Loyal stood stiff by the windows, breathing like it hurt.

And Wolfe—

Wolfe was still. Too still. Like the earth before an earthquake. Like the sky before a storm.

The buzz of a phone sliced the silence.

Short.

Sharp.

A knife against the marble.

I didn't move. Didn't lift my head. Obedience lived in breath now—not curiosity, not fear. Only the ache.

I heard Wolfe pick up the phone, felt it ripple through the leash—tension coiling through the chain knotted to my survival. I stayed kneeling. Breathing. Moving would have been betrayal.

The silence stretched.

Thicker. Tighter. Deadlier.

Until it snapped across the room like a whip. Wolfe's fingers tightened on the leash—not yanking, not jerking. Just tightening. Claiming. Breath locked inside my lungs. Pain bloomed sweet and sacred across my throat. And I loved it. I loved it because it told me where I belonged, told me I was still breathing for him.

He spoke once.

Voice low.

Deadly.

Quiet enough that it shattered me harder than a scream would have.

"Us."

Two letters.

Spat like venom.

The leash jerked once. I gasped—silent, shameful, perfect.

Wolfe stepped closer. Boots whispering across the marble.

I bowed lower. Forehead brushing the cold stone.

I didn't flinch. The leash burned against my throat, Wolfe's breath pressed against my spine, survival demanded I stay exactly where he put me.

His voice brushed my ears.

Soft.

Final.

"Pick it up."

My hands trembled, fingers flexing against the marble. But I obeyed.

Obedience was breath now. Survival. Love. I picked up the phone—hands shaking, heart hammering, breath catching on the leash taut against my pulse. The screen glowed against my skin.

The message:

It doesn't have to be this way, Cloe.

Bring us the fucking book.

I shuddered.

Wolfe leaned closer. His voice a leash pulling breath straight from my lungs.

"Call him."

"Set up the meeting."

I nodded. Tears sliding silent down my cheeks. Worship offered to the marble. Breath offered to the chain. Heart offered to the man who owned every survival left in my body.

I called—hands trembling, voice steady.

Even in this, I chose Wolfe. I chose breath. I chose love. The phone shook in my hands. The leash burned against my throat. Wolfe said nothing. He didn't need to. His silence pressed heavier against my ribs than chains ever could.

Us.

The word tasted like ash, like a ghost clawing for breath that no longer belonged to it.

Us didn't exist anymore. I didn't exist anymore. Only worship. Only breath. Only Wolfe. I waited. Kneeling. Trembling. Phone glowing in my hand like a curse. Until Wolfe tugged the leash once.

A small, sharp pull. Permission. Command. Law.

I pressed the call button. The leash tightened immediately —not to choke me, but to keep me breathing, to remind me who I survived for now. The phone rang. Once. Twice. Three times. Every beat of the ringtone hammering against my ribs like a second leash.

Four.

Five.

Then—

he answered.

The ex.

The boy who once promised freedom if I ran fast enough. The boy who once taught me to lie louder than my breath.

The boy who would die at Wolfe's feet by the time this was over.

"Cloe?"

His voice broke through the line. Soft. Wounded. Desperate.

I didn't speak. Not at first. The leash stayed tight. Breath locked. Worship coiled. Waiting.

Wolfe crouched in front of me, boots creaking against the marble, hand wrapping the leash tighter. His free hand touched my chin. Lifted—not cruel, not rough. Just inevitable. He mouthed the words silently—not shouting, not forcing. Just offering survival.

I remembered his hands once. The ex. The way he kissed me like rescue. The way he promised that running would save me. And now? I would kneel to end him.

Not because I hated him. But because I had learned to love harder. And Wolfe never needed to promise me freedom—

He taught me to stop needing it.

"Set it up."

I breathed in once. Shuddering. Offered the breath to him silently.

Then spoke.

"Tomorrow."

My voice was barely a whisper. But it was enough.

"Alone."

Another breath. Another prayer.

"The old hotel."

A shiver ran through me—not from fear, but claim. Even setting my own trap for the boy who used to mean hope, I stayed kneeling, stayed breathing, stayed Wolfe's. The ex exhaled sharply. Relief flooding his voice.

"Tomorrow," he said. "We'll fix this, Cloe. You'll see."

I ended the call, let the phone fall to the marble with a soft clatter, lowered my forehead back to the stone. Breathing through the leash Wolfe pulled tighter against my throat—breathing because it was the only worship left to offer.

Wolfe stood. Silent. Towering. Immovable. Royal laughed somewhere behind him.

"Poor bastard."

"He still thinks she breathes for him."

Wolfe didn't answer. Didn't laugh. Didn't even smile. He just watched me. Kneeling. Silent. Breathing. Choosing him.

And I smiled—small, silent, holy.

Survival didn't live in freedom anymore. It lived here, at the end of his leash, at the altar of my own beautiful, ruinous devotion.

20

———

CLOE

THE OLD HOTEL hunched against the skyline like a broken tooth—dark, abandoned, windows shattered, marble cracked. The air leaking from the crumbling walls was cold enough to make me shiver.

It smelled like mildew and old velvet. A ghost place. A place built for breathing wreckage into bone.

I crossed the threshold. Boots scuffing against broken tile. The hallway stretched out before me. Flickering overhead lights buzzed low. Distant water dripped steadily. Somewhere, a door creaked on rusted hinges.

The city hummed beyond the walls. But inside? Silence. Thick. Waiting. Breathing.

I made it three steps in before I felt it—the shift, the weight, the world rearranging itself. He was here.

Wolfe stood at the end of the hall. Royal lounged against a cracked pillar nearby. Loyal leaned stiff against a broken radiator farther back. All three of them dressed like shadows. All three of them kings built for the ruins.

Royal wore dark jeans and a gray fitted sweater. Black boots scuffed and ready. A smirk bleeding lazy across his mouth. Casual. Cruel. Waiting for blood.

Loyal wore dark jeans, a black hoodie pulled low over his brow, hands flexing into fists and out again at his sides. Guilt dripped off him like sweat, regret crawled up the line of his spine. But he didn't move. Didn't reach. He wouldn't save me. Not now. Not anymore.

And Wolfe—

God, Wolfe.

Wolfe wore black tailored trousers. A black turtleneck that cut sharp against the line of his throat. The shoulder holster hugged his chest. A gun glinting under his jacket. Silent. Final.

My breath stuttered. He didn't look brutal or furious—he looked inevitable. A king not dressed for diplomacy, but for execution.

Wolfe's eyes locked onto mine—flat, cold, not angry, not cruel. Just certain, as if he already knew how this night would end, as if he'd already decided.

I felt the leash burn tight across my ribs—even without it around my throat, even without it wrapped visibly across my skin. Alive. Commanding. *Breathing for me.*

Wolfe's hand rested casually on the holster, thumb stroking slow over the black leather—not threatening, just patient. Waiting for me to finish remembering who I belonged to.

Royal chuckled low from the pillar. "She's going to survive this," he said lazily, smirk curving crueler. "One way or another."

Loyal didn't speak. Didn't lift his head. Just shook it once when Wolfe's phone buzzed briefly. A signal. A question.

Wolfe didn't even glance down. He looked at Loyal. Sharp. Demanding. Loyal shook his head again. A small, grim movement.

"Don't bother."

Barron wasn't coming. Barron wouldn't save anyone tonight.

A flicker of something cold slid down my spine—fear, maybe, or memory. But it died quickly.

Wolfe shifted—one step forward, one hand curling slow into a fist at his side. The gun didn't matter. The holster didn't matter. The world didn't matter.

The door to Room 305 creaked.

Callum.

My ex.

I heard his footsteps. Cocky. Confident. Hope bleeding off him like gasoline. He thought he could save me. He thought I still needed saving.

The door swung open wider. The ex stepped inside. Smirked. Wearing hope across his shoulders like a dying flag.

He didn't see the wreckage kneeling in front of him. He saw a girl he thought he could still save. And he was already dead for it.

He crossed the room with slow, careful steps, boots echoing hollow against broken tile. His eyes locked onto me—not Wolfe, not Royal, not Loyal. Me. He thought I was still his to save, still his to fix, still his to own.

I stayed kneeling, breath scraping raw against the leash burning invisible across my throat. I didn't look at Wolfe. Didn't look at anyone. Only stayed kneeling, breathing, praying to survive this the only way Wolfe taught me—by loving the chain, by worshipping the breath he owned.

Callum crouched down in front of me. Close enough that the heat of him burned wrong against my skin.

He smiled. Soft. Pitying. Pathetic.

"Come on, Cloe," he whispered.

"Let's get you out of here."

"This isn't you."

I didn't move. Didn't breathe harder. Didn't blink. Standing would be betrayal. Hope would be death. Survival meant kneeling even when shame ripped through my lungs like fire.

His hand touched my wrist. Gentle at first. Soft. The way memory remembered safety. The way ghosts whispered promises.

I flinched. Tiny. A tremble he mistook for longing.

He grabbed harder, yanked, dragged me against him. My breath snapped sharp, body locked, panic clawed up my spine. But I didn't scream. Didn't fight. Worship was survival now, and worship didn't flinch when the world tried to tear it free.

The ex's arm wrapped around my waist. Pinned me tight. Mauled my breast brutally through the silk. I gasped, tears stinging hot behind my eyes—not from pain, but rage, betrayal of the survival Wolfe built into me.

Royal moved, boots scraping sharp against the floor. Wolfe didn't move. Not yet.

Wolfe wasn't chaos—he was gravity, waiting for the right second to kill or save.

Callum leaned into my ear. Breath hot and cruel.

"You think you're his?"

A laugh.

Sharp.

Ugly.

"You were always mine."

He shoved me roughly. Hard enough to stagger me toward the broken stairwell.

The gun slid from under his jacket. Glinting. Sharp. Final. He pressed it against my temple. Breath rasping. Cocky. Terrified.

Loyal shouted once. *"Let her go!"*

Callum snarled. "She's not yours to save." A beat. A breath.

Then he hissed against my ear. "She was right, you know. You're just a Lawlor whore now. Just like their sister."

The leash snapped tighter in my lungs, vision blurred—not from fear, but survival, worship, love. Even here, even with a gun pressed to my skull, even with survival screaming to stand, I stayed kneeling inside myself. Breathing Wolfe. Choosing Wolfe.

Callum shoved me hard. Toward the stairs. Fired once wildly. The crack of the shot split the air.

Royal moved.

Loyal dove.

Wolfe—

He was already moving.

I stumbled. Hands catching air. Knees cracking against broken tile. The world tilted sideways. Breath vanished from my lungs.

I saw him—

Black-on-black.

Gun gleaming. Eyes dead and beautiful. And then—he moved past the shot. Past the danger. Past the kill. And caught me.

His arms locked around me. Hard. Brutal. Alive.

I broke there. Not like glass. Like prayer.

I didn't reach for him. I didn't need to. The leash never left —it just curled tighter inside me, pulling me home.

The gun clattered to the floor beside us. My ex-boyfriend ran. Footsteps pounding down the stairs. Gone.

I sobbed once—broken, breathless, beautiful. Wolfe didn't kill him. Not yet. He chose me instead. He chose breath. He chose leash. He chose survival. He chose love.

His hand fisted the back of my dress. Crushed me tighter to his chest.

The leash buried inside my ribs burned hotter.

Alive.

Sacred.

Silent.

Wolfe didn't speak. Didn't shout. He just held me. While the world burned around us. While Royal and Loyal closed ranks. While the hotel howled into the night.

Even ruined, even touched, even wrecked—I was still Wolfe's.

And he still chose me.

21

WOLFE

He came in like he owned the air.

Keys hit the counter.

Fridge opens.

A beer cracks.

He drinks.

Belches.

Turns.

I stand from the shadows—black-on-black. Legs steady. Breath slower than his heartbeat will ever be again.

He freezes mid-step. His eyes widen.

"What the—"

I cross the tile. Three steps. Grip his jaw. Slam the back of his skull into the drywall so hard plaster cracks behind his spine. He gags on breath. Eyes water.

"How the fuck did you find me?"

I don't answer. I drive my fist into his ribs hard enough to make him drop the beer can. It hits the floor with a wet thud, foam spraying his sneakers. Didn't matter. He was already dead.

I felt something give under my knuckles. A wet crunch.

"You touched her," I said. Not loud. Not angry. Just final.

I punched again. His cheekbone split under the blow. Teeth clacked together. Blood sprayed.

"You put your fucking hand on her."

Another punch. His head snapped sideways. Nose shattered under the pressure. My glove slick with him now.

I didn't stop. Didn't pause. Didn't need answers. This wasn't interrogation. This was prayer. This was the silence between her thighs turned into violence beneath my hands.

"You grabbed her breast."

My boot caught his shin. He dropped to one knee, blood pouring from his mouth, whimpering. Good. I wanted him to cry. I wanted him to beg. I wanted him to feel what it meant to make her cry.

"You made her flinch."

Another fist. Another crack.

"You used her. Pawned her things. Stole her breath. And I gave it back."

I gave her silence. I gave her worship. I gave her the leash so tight she could finally breathe again. I reached for the back of his neck. Drove his head down into the countertop. Wood splintered.

He crumpled. Didn't move. Didn't speak. Didn't scream.

I should've killed him then. But something caught my eye— something off, something wrong.

I stepped around the body. Dragged my bloodied glove along the back of the television. Nothing. Checked the wall. Nothing. Then—the back panel shifted. Loose. Taped. Careful. A file. Sealed. Flat. Hidden behind the screen.

I peeled the tape free. Opened it. Photos. Documents. Dates.

Selene's name at the top of every single fucking page.

She paid him.

She used him.

She owned this long before I ever stepped onto the field.

And Cloe?

Cloe was collateral.

Nothing more. Nothing less.

And now—she was mine.

I stepped back toward the ex—groaning, coughing blood, trying to crawl. I crouched beside him, leaned in close.

"She paid your debts, you know."

He froze.

"Not all of it. But enough. Enough to keep your lungs whole."

I grabbed his jaw. Pulled his bloody face toward mine.

He whimpered. I smiled. Dead. Sharp. Clean.

"And you fucking knew that."

His eyes rolled back. He collapsed. Not dead. Not yet. But small. Pathetic. Done.

I stood. Turned toward the door. File under one arm. Blood cooling across my gloves.

I didn't look back. I didn't need to. He wasn't mine. But she was. And now I had everything I needed. She wasn't waiting for rescue anymore. She was waiting for fire. And I would bring it—leash in one hand. Crown in the other.

22

BARRON

THE SOUND of the door didn't startle me. Not here. Not in the Lawlor Tower. Not in a room where surprises didn't exist. If someone crossed that threshold, they belonged—or they were about to die.

I didn't glance up. Didn't need to. I felt it. That stillness. That storm wrapped in skin. Wolfe's presence was always heavier than the space could hold.

So I sat—in the wide leather chair Camille used to mock, the one she said made me look like a villain in an antique painting—and stared into the bourbon. Deep. Amber. Neat. *Untouched.* The ice had already melted.

He moved like carved stone. All black. No coat. Shirt sleeves rolled. Collar stained at the edge. Knuckles bruised.

But his eyes—

Still.

Dead calm.

He didn't speak. Just crossed the room like gravity bent around him. In one hand, a folder. Slim. Closed. Didn't need to be heavy to hit like a brick.

I felt it before it hit the table. And when it did—paper to polished walnut—it echoed. Not loud. *Final.* I didn't look at him. Not yet. I looked past him.

Out the windows. Rain had started. Slicking the glass. The skyline blurred. Power turning to fog.

Camille used to hate this room. *Said it looked like a man who's never laughed.* She wasn't wrong.

Wolfe didn't sit. Didn't move. Didn't speak. Just stood there like a question no one had the courage to ask. Like silence was the only threat he needed.

I reached for the file. Slow. It was warm. Bent at the corner. Handled. I flipped the cover.

First page.

Case file.

Internal seal.

Ref: 17.3 – Sealed Witness Protocol.

Camille's name across the top like a stain.

My breath held itself.

Page two: account numbers.

Too many.

Spread across jurisdictions. Withdrawals sitting just beneath federal reporting thresholds. Patterned. Clean. Invisible to most. *But not to me.* I built this empire with hands that bled when necessary. I knew how poison moved—slow and silent.

Page three.

The handwriting stopped me.

Not typed.

Not printed.

Scrawled in that familiar, childlike loop:

The giraffes are quiet.

My stomach turned. Cold. Violent. I hadn't heard that phrase in years. Camille's code. Her signal.

A secret language from when monsters lived under beds, not in banks. She only used it when something was wrong. And she'd written it here—on a sealed government file.

On a ledger built to bury the dead. I turned the next page.

St. James.

London.

Flagged transfers.

Eight of the eleven linked to Lawlor Diamond Holdings. Two tied to shell corps I'd built myself. Only one bore my name. But that was enough.

My throat tightened.

Bottom corner—

Initials.

S.L.

Didn't need the full name.

Selene Lawlor.

My ex-wife.

The woman who loved Camille like a sister. And buried her with a signature. I blinked. Once. Then again. But the words didn't change. The file didn't vanish. And Camille stayed dead.

Wolfe still hadn't spoken.

The silence wasn't tense. It was tectonic. The kind that cracked empires when it finally broke.

I turned the last page. And stopped. At the bottom, printed in block caps: *If you ever want out of this, bring us the girl.*

That was it. No logo. No sender. Just that. Like blackmail was a grocery list. Like Camille had been a receipt. My jaw clenched.

I closed the file. Deliberate. Like a coffin lid. I sat still. Too still.

Then finally looked up. Wolfe's face didn't shift. Didn't

blink. Didn't breathe harder. Didn't need to. I asked, voice low, tight, controlled: "How long have you had this?"

His answer came without delay. "Does it matter?"

That landed.

I flinched. Not visibly. But something behind my sternum jolted.

I looked back down at the file. At my hands. Still. Steady. I forced a breath through clenched teeth. The bourbon was still untouched.

But the bottle beside it was half gone. Not my usual pour. Not my usual hour. Papers littered the table. Contracts. Memos. Redacted briefs.

I hadn't organized them. And that—more than anything—told me what Wolfe saw. Control. Slipping. Not all at once. But in small, deliberate fractures.

I looked up again. Wolfe's gaze flicked down. At the bourbon. At the mess. Then back to me.

And that silence? It wasn't silence anymore. It was judgment. A fucking mirror.

"You knew," I said.

It wasn't a question. He didn't answer. Didn't need to.

Because this—

Blood on his collar.

Bruised knuckles.

A file full of quiet giraffes—

This was the answer.

"It was always her."

Not an accident. Not a casualty. Not a name on the wrong list. Camille was the reason the silence cracked.

The girl who laughed too loud in rooms built for obedience. Who saw things we buried beneath gold. Who wrote secrets in children's code when she knew the walls were wired.

She was the beginning. The first threat. The first sacrifice.

The first truth we pretended didn't bleed. We thought we were protecting her. Turns out, we were making her a target.

And me? I didn't see it. Didn't want to. I loved her like legacy. Not like blood.

But she was always the center. Not me. Not Selene. Not this fucking empire. Her. And now she's dead. Because the rest of us let her carry the weight of our sins.

We thought she'd bend. She didn't. She broke. Quietly. Exactly the way they wanted.

I didn't nod. Didn't rage. Didn't slam fists on the desk.

I just exhaled. Long and quiet. Tasted like ghosts. Tasted like the last time Camille smiled without fear. Wolfe's gaze dropped. The papers weren't just financials and briefings.

Buried beneath an old file folder—

The corner of a page.

Typed header.

Three bold letters:

FBI.

Wolfe frowned. Reached out. Moved the folder aside with two fingers. More words. Black ink. Formal phrasing. Request for access. Sealed subpoenas. My blood froze. I hadn't told them. Hadn't told *anyone*. I was already at war. And losing.

Wolfe's voice went razor-sharp.

"Barron."

A pause.

"Do you have something you want to tell me?"

I didn't flinch.

Didn't snatch the paper back.

Just lifted my gaze—

Slow. Steady.

Old in a way he'd never seen me before.

"I'm handling it," I said.

But he heard it. The strain. That fucking strain. I didn't

sound like a man handling anything. I sounded like a man preparing to die standing up.

His chest locked. I saw it.

For the first time, he didn't see the brother who built this kingdom. He saw a reflection. What he would become. What we'd all become. If we stayed. If we fought. If we bled for ghosts that never bled for us.

I leaned back. Took a breath. Met Wolfe's stare. Didn't blink.

"You need to go home, Wolfe."

A pause.

"Take care of her."

I rose. Took the bourbon in hand. Swirled it once. Then drank it. All of it.

The glass hit the table with a quiet clink. I didn't speak. Didn't thank him. Didn't ask for time. Just turned toward the window. Let the rain blur the skyline. Let the silence speak the truth.

Behind me, Wolfe turned, boots whispering against the black marble—no ceremony, no parting shot. Just retreat. But not from defeat. From restraint. When the door clicked shut, I didn't move. I just stared through the glass at the city we'd built —on blood, on silence, on the lie that Camille's death was collateral.

But now I knew. She hadn't drowned in carelessness—she'd been sold. And we let her, let her carry our sins like she was made for it. It was easier than looking her in the eye and saying: *We'd trade you to keep breathing.*

And we did. Like diamonds. Like daughters.

And somewhere under all of it—

under the bourbon, under the rain—

something older stirred.

Sharper. Something that sounded a lot like *vengeance.*

23

CLOE

The apartment was dark.

And still.

The kind of stillness that lives in the air after a storm—before the damage settles.

I stood near the far end of the hallway, barefoot. The last of the moonlight filtered through the high windows, painting the hardwood in cold silver. The hem of my shirt brushed the backs of my thighs. My hands were tucked into the sleeves like a child, like I was still trying to shrink myself.

Wolfe hadn't come back bloody.

But he hadn't come back whole.

He'd said nothing when he entered. Didn't look at me. Just dropped his keys in the bowl near the door and walked straight down the hall, shoulders too straight, silence too loud.

The bathroom door clicked. Then running water.

And I stood there. Waiting.

Minutes passed. Ten, maybe more. Steam crept out from under the door. The kind that softened glass and skin.

Then it opened.

Wolfe stepped into the hall. Hair wet. Towel slung low. Eyes dark, unreadable. His chest rose once. Fell slower. Then his voice. Low. Not cold. Not commanding. Just a question wrapped in something that hurt worse than silence.

"Will you join me?"

I blinked. Nodded. Didn't trust my voice.

My hands shook as I pulled the shirt over my head. Stepped past him. Into the heat.

The mirror was fogged. Steam clung to the tile. The air was heavy, scented with soap and salt. Light pooled above the shower like confession. I stepped over the threshold, one hand on the cold marble edge, one heartbeat away from falling.

The water hit my skin like surrender. Too hot. Too clean. Too much.

Wolfe didn't speak. He stood behind me, just outside the spray. Close enough I could feel the heat of him without the touch.

I kept my back to him. The silence between us thickened. I felt the moment he moved. A ripple in the steam. A shift in the air. His hand brushed my lower back. Not possessive. Not demanding. Just—checking. Grounding.

I flinched anyway. Reflex. Memory. Not truth. His hand didn't move. But he didn't pull away either.

He exhaled. Slowly. "You're shaking."

I nodded. Once. He reached for the soap. The sound of the bottle opening was louder than it should've been. He worked the lather in his hands. Careful. Slow.

Then he touched me. Water streamed down my spine. His hands followed. Over my shoulders. Down the curve of my back. He washed me like I was made of something fragile. Not because I might break. But because he already had.

Fingers trailed down the outer edge of my arm. He turned me, slowly. I let him.

His eyes met mine. And for the first time in weeks, I saw it. Fear. Not for himself. For me.

His hands moved to my ribs. He paused where the bruises still lived. He washed me in silence. Every motion deliberate. Slow. He didn't speak until he reached my hips.

"They touched you."

I nodded. He nodded back. His jaw flexed. That single muscle, just beneath his cheek.

But he didn't growl. Didn't rage. Just ran his hands down my thighs like he was learning the map all over again.

"You're still mine," he said.

Not a threat. Not a claim. Just truth.

I whispered, "I know."

Then he stepped into the water. And pulled me with him.

He didn't press me to the tile. Didn't bend me. Didn't shove. He just kissed me.

Mouth to mouth. No demand. No force.

Like he was asking—

not for obedience,

not for worship,

but for proof I was still choosing him.

And I was.

Just his lips, warm and quiet, covering mine like he wasn't sure if I'd stay.

I did.

His hand found my jaw. Tilted it slightly. His thumb brushed the corner of my mouth, right where the bruise had bloomed. His breath stilled when I didn't pull away.

And that was all it took.

Wolfe kissed like ownership. Not brute force—not now. This wasn't about breaking. This was about confirmation.

About knowing the pieces still wanted to come back to him. His other hand slid around my waist. Flat against my lower back. He didn't push. He pulled. Slow. Until every inch of me was pressed to every inch of him.

I gasped softly. He swallowed it.

His mouth moved against mine. Down my jaw. My throat. He didn't stop at the collarbone—he lingered. Mouth on bruises. Breath on old chains.

Where he touched, I stayed. The hand at my back slid lower. Guiding me. Not taking. Leading.

I turned slowly. Pressed my hands to the tile. Not commanded. Just offered.

He moved behind me. One palm flattened against my lower back again. Steady. The other traced up my spine. Each vertebra. A vow.

I felt him behind me—not hard yet. But close. Then he bent slightly. Mouth to the back of my neck.

"Breathe," he said.

Just that.

And I did.

He slid his hand between my thighs.

Not urgent.

Not rough.

Just real.

His fingers found me already wet. He touched me like the world hadn't just come undone. Like my body still knew who it belonged to. And God, it did.

He whispered something I didn't catch. Too soft. Too close to prayer. And I rocked back against his hand. Needing him. Needing to prove I still knew how to be held. Not tamed. Not wrecked.

Just—

Held.

He pressed closer. Hard now. But he didn't enter me. Not yet.

Just kept breathing behind me. And I stayed where he placed me. Because that's where I belonged.

The sound he made when he slid into me wasn't a growl. It wasn't command. It was breath. A broken, guttural exhale. Like he'd been holding it for hours. Days. Weeks. Like this was the only way he could keep breathing.

He entered me slow.

Thick.

Careful.

Not because I was fragile. But because he needed it to last.

I pressed my palms harder against the tile. Felt him fill me inch by inch. Every line of my body stretched to meet his.

And still—*he didn't thrust.*

He stayed there. Inside me. Breathing. His hands on my hips. Not gripping. Just steady. Like I was the only thing holding him up.

"Say something," I whispered.

He leaned forward. Mouth beside my ear. "This isn't punishment."

A pause.

An exhale.

"It's *need.*"

He pulled back.

Slow.

Almost out.

Then slid back in.

My head dropped. My eyes closed. He did it again. And again. Still no words. Only breath. Only the sound of his hips meeting mine.

Each thrust built slower than the last. He fucked me like he was trying to memorize it. Like he knew it might be the last time. Like this moment had to hold all the ones we lost.

His fingers slid up my sides. Thumbs brushing beneath my ribs. I arched into the touch. Not from pleasure. From relief.

Because he was still touching me like I mattered. His mouth dropped to my shoulder. He bit down once. Not to hurt. To mark. To stay grounded.

I moaned softly. He exhaled harder.

Then his hand slid forward. Found the ache between my thighs. Worked it slow. Just like his hips. A rhythm. A ritual.

I breathed his name. He answered with a thrust. Harder. Deeper.

His mouth returned to my ear. "Don't go quiet on me."

I choked on a laugh. It cracked halfway out of my throat. "I'm here."

He groaned.

Like that was the only thing he needed to hear.

I came with a gasp. Soft. Raw. No scream. No collapse. Just breath. Given back to him. Because he asked.

He didn't pull out right away. He stayed inside me. His hands flattened over my hips. My back pressed to his chest.

The water beat down on our skin. Too hot now. Starting to burn. But neither of us moved. His chest rose behind me. Pressed into my spine. And then he spoke.

"I almost didn't make it in time."

It wasn't a confession. It was a wound.

I turned slowly. His body slid from mine. The loss a sharp, aching thing. He let me turn. Let me face him.

His eyes didn't look like stone now. They looked like aftermath. Like smoke rising after the collapse.

I touched his cheek. He leaned into it. Just slightly.

"But you did. You did make it," I whispered. "You found me, like I knew you would."

He shook his head.

"I shouldn't have had to."

I swallowed. The steam made everything blurry. Or maybe that was me.

He stepped back. Water slapping off his shoulders, hands dragging through his wet hair.

"Don't lie to me again."

It wasn't a threat. It was a plea. I nodded. "I won't."

He stepped forward. Took my face in his hands. Pressed his forehead to mine.

The water made it hard to hear. But I caught it. The breath. The tremble. The thing Wolfe never gave away. "Don't leave me quiet."

I froze. Because he didn't mean noise. He meant presence. He meant stay.

I wrapped my arms around his waist. Held him as tight as I could. Felt his hands flatten against my back.

The water cooled.

Still we stood there. No chains. No leash. No commands. Just breath.

And the man who once touched me like a sentence now held me like a prayer. And I would stay. Not because he pulled the leash—

But because I still remembered how to breathe when he touched me.

And nothing else had ever felt more like home.

24

———

BARRON

THE NEWS FEED was on mute.

I didn't need sound to cut.

The image was enough.

Selene, outside the federal building. Wrapped in winter silk and soft gold. A navy coat pulled tight around her waist. Hair perfect. Skin luminous. A crucifix at her throat like salvation had always been hers to wield.

She didn't flinch at the cameras. She smiled at them. The chyron at the bottom of the screen read:

SELENE LAWLOR: Whistleblower in Federal Probe of Diamond Empire

Whistleblower.

I leaned back in my chair.

Didn't blink.

Didn't breathe hard.

Just watched.

The office around me didn't move either. It was too quiet. The kind of stillness that makes noise feel like an insult. The air smelled like old paper, sharp ink, expensive leather. The windows were tinted, the light gray and indifferent.

The bourbon glass on the desk had gone untouched since last night, condensation trailing a single path toward a file I hadn't read.

The blinds were drawn, but light still bled through. Casting long, slatted shadows across the rug Selene picked out. The one she insisted tied the room together.

Every fucking thing in here she touched. Someone handed her a mic. She accepted it like a queen taking communion. The reporters swarmed. Then one voice rose—clear, firm. Female.

"You were married to Barron Lawlor for almost ten years. From the outside, you looked like the perfect couple. Is there anything you wish to say to him now?"

Selene paused. Turned. Tilted her head. Smiled. The kind that used to precede sex. *Or war.*

Then:

"Yes."

A pause.

"Thank you for giving me everything I needed to destroy you."

I didn't move.

She turned back to the cameras. Walked up the courthouse steps. Every click of her heels sounded like a countdown. I reached forward. Pressed the power button. The screen went black. The car was silent.

No music. No radio. No voice in my ear asking if I was okay. Because I wasn't. Because I hadn't been since the day she chose press over loyalty.

The drive was slow. Wipers dragging across glass that didn't need clearing. Even the city looked like it knew better than to ask questions. I turned down the street slowly.

The hedges were still trimmed. The mailbox still clean. The security system still blinking red like a pulse.

I pulled into the drive. The gate opened on cue. Like the house still thought I lived here. Maybe I did. Maybe some version of me never left.

The brick was clean. The lawn manicured. The path to the door lined with slate she handpicked. On a whim. The front door opened with the same code she once kissed into my jaw.

The foyer greeted me with polished tile. Scented candles. Ivory hydrangeas—always fake. It smelled like citrus and money. And her.

The chandelier above me glittered faintly in the filtered light. One of the bulbs was out. I hadn't noticed before.

I stepped inside. Silence. But not peace. Just design. Everything still in place.

The champagne flutes. The framed wedding photo that never made it to print. The couch she chose. The throw pillows she corrected. The mirror she hated until she saw her reflection in it at night.

The rugs were cream. No dust. No hair. No fingerprints. I walked through the house like a museum curator.

No.

Like a coroner.

I paused in the kitchen.

The wine rack was full. She never drank red.

The fruit bowl was wax. The lemons too perfect.

The counters wiped so many times they shone like guilt. Then upstairs. To the bedroom. The bed was made. Of course it was.

Egyptian cotton. Cream. A cashmere throw folded at the edge. Two pillows. One slightly indented. The other untouched.

I didn't sit. I didn't speak. I just stared at the place she used to fake sleep. And remembered the sound of her voice the last time she said:

"It just doesn't feel like ours anymore."

No. It never did.

It was always mine.

She never wanted a home—just something to decorate, something to own.

I walked to the garage. Pulled down the old ladder. Opened the locked trunk near the water heater. Pulled out the gas can. The weight of it was heavier than I remembered. Or maybe I was just tired. I moved slowly. Deliberately. Back through the bedroom.

I doused the sheets first. The pillows. The curtains. The rug that cost five grand and still made my skin itch. The walk-in closet where she left nothing but wire hangers.

Then the photo.

Of us.

The one she left on the mantle like a curse.

The frame cracked when it hit the floor. I poured gasoline over it anyway. I stood in the middle of the room. My shoes soaked in fuel. The air thick with promise.

I reached into my pocket. Pulled out the silver lighter Wolfe gave me for my thirty-fifth. I hadn't used it in years. But it sparked on the first flick. I dropped it into the rug. The fire caught fast. Like it had been waiting.

I walked out the front door without looking back. The porch lit behind me. Then the staircase. Then the room where she never slept.

I walked to the edge of the driveway. Lit a cigarette.

The neighbors didn't come out. Let them call. Let the fire department arrive. Let the city watch. Let Selene see it on the evening news.

When the first window exploded, I said it.

Soft.
Final.
"I made this for you."
A pause.
"Now you can have it."
Then I turned. And let it burn.

25

———

CLOE

I woke the next day.

The leash lay where he left it. Coiled neatly on the dresser. No note. No command. No lock around my throat. Freedom.

I sat up slowly.

Sheets cold against my bare skin. The apartment around me too still, too heavy. The air smelled like water and smoke and something older—something waiting.

The bedroom stretched wide and empty around me. The faint hum of the HVAC the only sound. Morning light broke against the edges of the blackout curtains, turning the room into a gray, muted box. Dust floated in the beams like it didn't want to land.

I touched my fingertips to the sheets beside me.

Still warm.

He hadn't left long ago. But he hadn't stayed either.

The bed still smelled like him. Leather. Rain. Something deeper—like ash. Like endings.

Wolfe was gone. The leash stayed. It wasn't folded with

ritual. It wasn't displayed like a threat. It was just... left. Quiet. Unmoving. As if it had a choice, and so did I.

I let the blanket fall. Stood slowly. Felt the stiffness in my thighs, in my ribs, in the bruises he hadn't kissed last night. He hadn't marked me. Not in the usual way.

He'd made love to me with a kind of desperation I didn't know how to name. A kind of stillness that made me ache more than any command he'd ever whispered.

And now he was gone. I padded barefoot across the wood floor. Let the cold ground bite.

My limbs still moved like memory—like submission wasn't just a position, it was a rhythm my body had learned to breathe in.

The bathroom mirror was fogged at the corners. I wiped a strip with the back of my wrist. Looked at myself. My eyes were hollow. Not tired. Just too wide.

My mouth was swollen from sleep—or from him. A faint shadow still ghosted along my collarbone. Proof. Not that he hurt me. That he stayed. That he touched without destroying.

I brushed my teeth. Washed my face. My reflection didn't change.

I walked back into the bedroom. Stared at the leash again. Still there. Still coiled. I remembered the way his voice sounded when he asked:

"Will you join me?"

Not a command. Not a test. An invitation. And I had. Now it was my turn.

I dressed slowly. Deliberately. Not soft. Not pretty. No silk. No heels. No ribbons.

I wore black slacks. A fitted turtleneck. Boots that hit my ankle and laced tight. No makeup. No perfume. Only a fresh wound I didn't cover. When I tied my hair back, my fingers trembled once. Only once.

I opened the closet. Saw the empty hangers. The shirts Wolfe no longer wore. The scarf Camille left here once that none of them ever threw out. I stared at it. Didn't touch. There was a note on the floor, from days ago. One of Barron's. Folded into perfect thirds.

I stepped over it. I didn't need words. Not anymore.

I picked up my bag. Slid my phone inside. Checked the screen. Two texts from Loyal. One from Royal. Nothing from Wolfe. Good. If this was a test, I wouldn't fail it by asking permission to breathe.

At the door, I paused. Looked back one last time. The leash was still there. Waiting. Not for obedience. For choice.

I walked out. And chose to stay. Not here. But with them. And whatever came next. The Tower loomed in the distance. It didn't shine the way it used to.

The morning light made the glass look grimy, almost bruised. Like the building itself was holding its breath. Like the weight of everything bleeding behind those windows was too much even for steel and stone to hold.

The city moved around it. Taxis honking. People hurrying past with coffee cups and clipped conversations.

But here? Here, time bent. The Lawlor name was still on the plaque by the door. But it looked smaller now. Less like a crown. More like a gravestone.

I adjusted the strap of my bag on my shoulder. My boots clicked against the curb as I crossed to the entrance. Every step felt heavier. Like the sidewalk could feel what I was carrying. Inside, the lobby was colder. Colder and emptier.

The chandelier overhead still glittered. But half the lights were dead. The marble floor—once buzzing with the scuff of heels and the low hum of power—was nearly silent.

The reception desk was manned by a temp. A young guy.

His tie crooked. His eyes wide with the kind of fear that didn't come from incompetence.

No one looked up when I passed. No one whispered. Security stood stiffer now. Their jackets bulkier. Guns not just allowed. Expected.

The air smelled faintly of ammonia and anxiety. A woman hurried across the lobby, heels sharp against the marble, clutching a cardboard box stacked with personal belongings. She didn't meet my eyes. Didn't look at anyone.

Another casualty. Another defector. I stepped toward the elevator. Pressed the button. I stepped inside. Pressed the button for the executive floor. The doors started to slide shut. Then a hand caught them. Barron.

He stepped inside. The air tightened. He didn't glance at me. Didn't acknowledge me. He didn't have to.

His suit was sharp. Dark gray. Impeccable. The cuffs crisp, but his tie hung loose, undone in a way that felt almost violent.

He smelled like smoke.

Leather.

Ashes.

The kind of scent you don't survive. The kind of scent you drown in willingly.

Barron Lawlor had always carried his authority like a blade. Today, it hung heavier. Deeper. Blunter.

He stood a step away. Hands loose at his sides. Chest rising slow and heavy like breathing cost him something.

The elevator rose. Soft hum. Soft breath. Soft ache.

I watched the numbers tick higher. Thirty-one. Thirty-two. Somewhere between thirty-three and thirty-four, I moved. Slow. Deliberate.

I reached out. Brushed my fingertips along the inside of his forearm. Just once. Barely a touch. Not even a graze. A question without a word.

He didn't flinch. He didn't pull away. He just—froze. For a breath. A heartbeat. A lifetime. Then the doors slid open.

Barron stepped out. His shoulders stiff. His fists clenched. He didn't look back. But his pulse thundered in the silence he left behind. And I knew. I still mattered. Even to him. Especially to him.

The executive floor wasn't empty. Not quite. But it had been stripped down to the bones.

No assistants lined the hallway. No interns scurried with coffees and files. No heels clattered across the polished marble. Just silence.

And war. The air was cold. Metallic.

The smell of old wealth and fresh blood.

I walked past Royal's office. Empty. A half-drunk whiskey glass tilted on its side. Past Loyal's door. Shut. Sharp. Uninviting.

My boots clicked too loud against the marble. Every step sounded like a vow. To stay. To breathe. To belong.

Wolfe's door was open. The room inside was a battlefield. Not of bodies. Not of blood. Of silence. Of choices.

Wolfe stood by the far windows. Hands tucked into his pockets.

The skyline blurred behind him in the morning haze. Royal sat half-slouched in a chair, staring at nothing. Loyal leaned against the desk, jaw tight, arms folded. Barron stood farther back. Near the bookshelves. Backlit. Dark.

When I stepped inside, no one spoke.

They looked at me.

Not with anger.

Not with pity.

Just—waiting.

I moved to the side. My legs didn't shake. My hands didn't tremble.

I picked up a manila folder. Opened it. Client lists. Damage reports. Threat analyses. Everything bleeding. Everything salvageable—if someone stayed to hold it together.

I pulled the laptop closer. Typed in the password. Opened the spreadsheet. Started working. Because that's what survival looked like now. Not kneeling. Not begging. Staying. Choosing. Fighting.

With bare hands and broken ribs and breath borrowed from the men who still stood. Minutes passed. The silence shifted. Not heavy. Not suffocating. Solid.

When Wolfe finally spoke, it wasn't to command. It was quieter. Almost proud.

"Good."

And for the first time since the leash fell silent, I breathed like I belonged.

26

———

BARRON

The office didn't look like power anymore.

It looked like war.

The carpet was shredded like old flesh. The walnut shelf split down the middle like a cracked ribcage. This wasn't an office anymore. It was a crime scene that hadn't decided who was the victim. Two chairs were overturned, one missing a leg entirely. The coffee table had gone sideways, reports scattered across the floor like bloodstains. The glass on the sideboard cabinet was cracked—spiderwebbed out from where someone threw a file like a weapon. The blinds hung half-drawn. The air reeked of paper, ink, and intrusion.

The Bureau had torn the room apart. And I hadn't put it back together. I stood at the window. Shirt unbuttoned halfway, no tie, sleeves rolled.

A glass of eighteen-year-old Scotch in my right hand. Not my first pour. Wouldn't be my last. Behind me, the Lawlor empire lay in fucking pieces.

My reflection stared back from the glass—older than I remembered. Lines etched deeper. Collarbone visible beneath the linen. Hair not quite right. I looked like a man fraying at the edges. I was.

They took the files. The backups. The offshore records.

But worse?

They took the illusion. The one that told me this place—this name—was untouchable.

I lifted the Scotch. Tasted nothing. Didn't care. The silence pressed against me. A scream with no air.

Then—

the elevator dinged.

I didn't turn. Didn't have to. I felt her before she stepped out. The shift. The chill. The silence holding its breath.

Selene.

She walked in like it wasn't a graveyard. Trench coat belted tight. Heels clicking across the marble. Lipstick perfect. Hair sculpted into armor. Perfume sharp enough to wound.

She didn't rush. Didn't flinch. Didn't act like she'd ever been thrown out of this room.

I stayed still. Facing the window.

"I always hated that painting," she said behind me. Light. Casual.

Like she hadn't gutted me.

I didn't answer. She took a few more steps. Stopped at the desk.

"It's impressive what the Bureau can do when they think they've cornered a legacy."

Still, I said nothing.

She perched on the edge of my desk. Crossed her legs. The coat parted. Black lace glinted underneath. A performance.

"You look tired," she said next.

My voice cracked when it came out, raw around the edges.

"Get to it."

Her smile curled. Like a blade finding skin. Like she tasted blood already.

"I can make it go away."

I turned then. Slowly. Just my head. She looked untouched. Unbothered. Like she hadn't fucked her way through the men trying to steal the Lawlor name.

I stared.

She smiled wider.

"The subpoenas. The press. The investigation. The fall-out," she said.

One finger drifted along the edge of the desk.

Deliberate. Light.

"I can bury it."

I blinked once.

"And what does that cost?"

She tilted her head. Unhooked the belt of the trench slowly. Let it hang open.

"You forgive me."

She waited. Then added:

"Publicly."

"You take me back. The way I was. Not as penance. As proof."

I didn't move. Didn't speak. She kept going.

Part of me wanted her to. Another part wanted her to never leave again. And that part? That's the one I've spent years trying to bury beneath bourbon and control.

"We rebuild the brand. The couple. The control."

"You hold my hand at charity events and let the papers spin their fairytales."

"And in return?" I asked, voice sharp as glass.

She leaned in. The lace visible now.

"You keep the empire."

A pause. Then quieter. Not soft. Not kind. Sharper.

"Do you want it?"

I looked at her. At the room. At what was left of everything I'd built—now held together with silence and pride.

I lifted the glass.

Drank.

And said nothing.

Answering her meant acknowledging the ache. And I wasn't ready to admit that some part of me still wanted her. Just not enough to bleed for her again.

The door clicked shut behind her. She didn't wait for an answer. Selene never did. She never needed permission to believe she'd already won.

I didn't finish the Scotch. Didn't pour another. Left the glass like everything else I couldn't fix—half-finished and reeking of what I used to need.

The elevator ride down was its own kind of hell.

Quiet. Suffocating.

The silence that settles into your bones and rots from the inside out.

I pressed the button with fingers still curled too tight—

From holding myself together While the woman who ruined me strutted across the wreckage like it was her goddamn runway.

She even smelled like manipulation. Amber. Powder. Victory. She'd come in perfect. Lips blood-red. Eyes starving.

And when she undid that belt,

Let the coat fall open—

Black lace. Skin. The scent of a woman who kissed me like a confession and stabbed me with the memory of it.

She touched me. Not gently. Not like she missed me. Like she owned the past. Like I should be grateful she survived the betrayal.

Her fingers grazed my chest. Nails tracing along my collarbone. Skin flinching under grief.

She leaned in. Pressed her mouth to my throat. Not a kiss. A warning.

That's the thing with Selene. She didn't love. She devoured. She fucked men to remind herself she could. Then came back like we were supposed to forget. Like I was supposed to pretend the blood on her mouth wasn't mine.

I gripped the wheel harder. Pulled out of the tower garage. Didn't turn on music. Didn't answer when the phone buzzed. Just drove.

City lights smeared across the windshield—concrete and glare and something sick underneath it all. My pulse didn't slow. Not when traffic thinned. Not when the roads quieted.

I didn't breathe right until I turned into the underground car park. The engine echoed in the concrete. Sharp. Empty. I eased into the spot. Let the car idle. And just stared at the elevator.

Felt her again—

Not her body. Not her scent. Her threat. Her voice, curling behind my ribs like smoke:

Do you want it?

And still...

I hadn't answered. I killed the engine. Got out. Didn't look back. The elevator waited. Still. Quiet. Watching.

Something older rose in me. Not grief. Not guilt. Something with teeth. And it wanted her to bleed.

27

CLOE

I could feel him watching me. Not with his eyes—not yet. With his silence.

Wolfe hadn't spoken since the shower. Hadn't touched me either. But I felt him. Every time I breathed, I felt the weight of his attention.

I stood at the kitchen counter in his robe, the fabric still damp at the collar. My hair clung to the back of my neck. My fingers wrapped around the handle of a mug I hadn't sipped from. The tea had gone cold. I didn't move.

The robe smelled like him. Like heat. Like control.

The silence pulsed.

Then—

the doorbell.

Sharp. Sudden. *Final.*

I flinched.

Wolfe looked up from where he sat in the chair across the room. No reaction. No tension. Just a shift. He stood slowly. Moved without sound. Opened the door. I couldn't see who it was. But I heard them.

A voice I knew better than my own.

Wolfe said it first.

Low. Measured.

"Want?"

Then silence.

Then—

Barron.

His voice was hoarse.

Ragged.

Almost broken.

"*Need.*"

I gripped the mug tighter. Wolfe stepped aside.

And Barron Lawlor walked in.

He looked different. Not in the way he dressed. Not in the way he moved. But in the way he didn't speak. His silence felt older than Wolfe's. Like it had been stitched into him instead of sharpened.

He didn't look at me right away. Didn't acknowledge the mug in my hand. The robe. The way my legs curled slightly inward like my body already knew something was coming.

He looked at Wolfe. Only Wolfe.

They didn't speak. But something passed between them. Something sharp. Something final. Then Wolfe turned to me.

"Go to the bedroom."

Just that.

Not a command.

A direction.

I didn't speak. Didn't ask. I set the mug down. Turned. Walked barefoot down the hallway. The robe brushed the backs of my knees with every step. My heart beat too loud to ignore.

I didn't close the door. I waited.

When they entered, neither man said a word.

Barron stepped in first. Stopped just inside. Wolfe followed. Didn't cross the threshold. Didn't sit. Didn't move. He stood against the doorframe like a verdict. And Barron finally looked at me.

My chest tightened. Not from shame. From the weight of it. His gaze didn't linger. Didn't wander. It dropped. To the robe. To the spot where the tie cinched just beneath my ribs.

And then—slowly—he walked to me.

Not rushed.

Not angry.

Just steady.

And when he reached me—

He didn't ask.

His fingers touched the knot.

And the robe fell open.

He stared at me like I was the last thing in the world worth touching.

The robe hit the floor. His hands didn't shake. But mine did. I stood there, bare, exposed. Wolfe behind him. Watching. Breathing. Silent.

Barron stepped forward, his hand rising to cup my cheek, then sliding down slowly to my collarbone. His thumb grazed the edge of a healing bruise, and his jaw flexed like the sight of it carved something open inside him.

"You're still soft," he murmured.

Not cruel.

Not mocking.

Just... surprised.

His palm spanned my chest, then drifted down the valley between my breasts. My nipples pebbled beneath the weight of his stare. My thighs clenched on instinct.

He looked down.

"She's wet already," he said. Not to me.

To Wolfe.

I didn't dare look back.

"Touch her," Wolfe said quietly.

That was all.

Barron groaned low in his throat. The sound rumbled through my chest before his mouth claimed mine.

It wasn't gentle.

It wasn't sweet.

It was desperate.

His tongue slid between my lips with a hunger I hadn't tasted from him before. Not in boardrooms. Not in stares. Not in war.

This wasn't power.

This was *need*.

His hands were everywhere. Spanning my hips. Squeezing my ass. Guiding me backward until my knees hit the bed.

He didn't ask. He didn't hesitate. He just lowered me. The mattress hit my spine. And Barron followed.

His body pressed into mine—hot, heavy, restrained only by the fabric of his undone shirt. His cock was hard beneath his pants, rubbing against my thigh with each shift.

I reached down to unfasten his belt.

He caught my wrist.

"No," he said.

"This is mine."

He didn't strip me like I was owed. He stripped me like I was sacred. Like worship had to be earned. *For him.*

He undressed for me like it meant something. Each button undone felt like a confession. Each breath he took before touching me again, a surrender.

His cock was thick. Heavy. Perfect. My body arched toward it before I could stop myself.

He positioned himself between my legs, dragging the blunt head along my slit until I cried out.

"You want this?" he rasped.

"Yes."

Wolfe didn't move. Didn't speak. But I felt his eyes. Watching me.

Watching what I became. Barron pushed inside me in one smooth, devastating thrust.

I gasped.

He groaned.

"Fuck," he whispered. "So fucking warm."

His thrusts weren't fast. They were anchored. Heavy. Intentional.

Every stroke said what his mouth wouldn't:

I need you to feel me.

I need this to mean something.

I need to exist here.

Tears stung the backs of my eyes. But I didn't cry. Because this wasn't shame. *This was permission.* To want him. To want *both* of them. To fall apart for the man who built the empire and the one still willing to burn for it.

His hands gripped my hips tighter. My legs locked around his waist. Wolfe stepped forward. Closer. Just enough. And Barron looked up at him. Then down at me. His pace stuttered.

"Say it," he breathed.

"You need me," I said.

His thrusts snapped harder.

"Say it again."

"You need me."

He came with a shudder. Groaning into my mouth like it was the only place left safe.

When he collapsed against me, I held him. And behind him, Wolfe stood still. Watching me. Breathing me. Choosing to stay. But he did.

Barron stayed. And *he meant it.*

He gathered his trousers, yanked the zipper.

He didn't speak right away. He didn't move. Just sat on the edge of the bed, his chest still heaving, his shirt half-open, the sweat on his skin cooling like surrender.

I sat with the blanket wrapped around my waist, legs curled beneath me, body still throbbing from the way he took me—not like he was entitled, but like he was starving. Like he had waited too long to be allowed to feel anything that wasn't grief.

Wolfe hadn't left the doorway. The room pulsed with heat, breath, and silence. Barron finally looked up. His voice wasn't broken. It was quiet. But it cut.

"She came to the office."

Wolfe didn't blink.

"Selene?"

Barron nodded.

"Tonight, after the raid. Place was torn apart. She walked in like it didn't matter. Like she still belonged."

He exhaled.

"Trench coat. Heels. Nothing underneath but black lace and audacity."

Something cracked in Wolfe's jaw.

"She offered a deal," Barron continued. "She said if I forgave her—if I took her back publicly—she'd make the investigation disappear. Said she had strings. Said she still owned the narrative."

Wolfe's voice came low.

Dead.

"She touched like the blood she spilled wasn't still on her hands."

Wolfe exhaled. The kind of breath that sounded too much like grief.

"It always was."

Barron didn't answer.

I watched them both. The tension between them wasn't sharp anymore. It was old.

Wolfe stepped farther into the room.

"Did you consider it?"

Barron turned his head. Met Wolfe's stare.

"Long enough to feel the bile rise."

My throat caught. My body tensed. Because when he looked at me—I saw it. He hadn't just chosen to walk away from Selene. He had crawled through the wreckage of his empire *to get to me*.

And I didn't breathe again until Wolfe nodded. Just once. Something passed between them. Not forgiveness. Not reconciliation. Just recognition.

Later. Wolfe stood in the kitchen with the bottle of Barron's untouched scotch. He poured four glasses. Didn't ask. Didn't explain. He just dialed two numbers.

"Get here. Now."

That was all. An hour later, the door opened. Royal entered first. Grinning like a man walking into a den he already knew how to burn.

Loyal followed. Quieter. Eyes scanning every inch of the room. Every bruise on my skin. Every breath between his brothers.

They didn't speak to each other. Not right away. But something shifted in the room when they stood there. All four of them. All Lawlors.

I felt it in the air. In the way the silence stopped feeling empty and started feeling loaded. It was like watching a crown rebuild itself out of fire and blood.

Wolfe handed out the glasses. Barron took his without hesitation. Loyal nodded once and accepted it. Royal raised his with a grin that didn't reach his eyes.

We stood in a room with no music, no laughter. Just breath. Just shadows. Just war. Wolfe lifted his glass.

"She came for us once."

Barron answered:

"She'll come again."

Royal clicked his glass softly against Wolfe's.

"Let her."

Loyal was the last to speak. His voice was quiet. But it carried.

"We don't fracture this time."

Wolfe stared into the amber liquid like it was prophecy.

"Then we bury her."

There was a pause. Not cold. Not hostile. Just full. Of memory. Of betrayal. Of something older than power.

Loyal stepped forward first. Raised his glass again.

"To the ones who remain."

This time, when they drank, it wasn't just strategy. It was blood.

I stood in the doorway, robe clutched tight around my body, and watched it happen. Not just the forming of a plan. The reformation of a kingdom.

Barron glanced over his shoulder at me. His expression unreadable. But his presence was loud.

You were worth staying for.

Royal looked me up and down. But for once, he didn't speak. Loyal just gave me a nod. One I didn't understand, but felt in my ribs.

And Wolfe? He didn't look away. He let me see it. His fury. His promise. And something new. Not possession. But allegiance.

This wasn't the end. It was the beginning. Of something brutal. Of something righteous. Of war. And I would stay.

Not to survive.

But to build it with them.

A kingdom forged in silence.

And ruled in ruin.

28

———

CLOE

I was still sore from Barron.

Every step through the apartment reminded me of what it meant to be wanted by a man who had been holding himself back too long. My thighs ached. My hips throbbed. The bruises were fresh, worshipped, earned. And still—I knew what Wolfe needed from me now had nothing to do with comfort.

It had to do with control.

He stood at the far end of the room, sleeves rolled, shirt black, eyes darker. The others were gone. Royal, Loyal, Barron —they'd left hours ago. After the plan was drafted. After the war was agreed on. After Wolfe had poured one last drink and handed it to Barron like a truce.

And now? Now he watched me. No words. No movement. Just that stare.

I dropped to my knees.

The floor was cold.

Perfect.

My hands folded behind my back. My knees spread. My eyes on the floor. My breath quickening.

He didn't tell me to do it. He didn't have to.

Wolfe moved slowly. The sound of his steps deliberate. Each one heavier than breath.

He stopped in front of me. Close enough that I could smell the leather of his belt. Close enough that my pulse jumped. And still he said nothing.

Silence stretched between us like a leash. I breathed through it. I knew the rules. This wasn't foreplay. This was obedience. And I was already wet.

His hand moved. Fingers brushing my chin. Not lifting it. Just resting there. Testing.

I held still.

He stepped to the side. Walked around me in a slow circle. Inspection. One hand behind his back. One at his side.

My heart beat harder the longer he stayed quiet.

Finally—

His voice.

Low.

Final.

"Open your mouth."

I obeyed. No hesitation. No sound. Just surrender. And Wolfe stepped in front of me again. Unbuckled his belt. Undid the button. Zipper slow. Deliberate.

His cock was already hard. Thick. Dark. Heavy with what he hadn't said. He gripped the base. Ran the tip over my lower lip. Not to tease. To mark.

Then—

He slid inside.

He didn't move fast.

He moved like time answered to him.

His cock filled my mouth inch by inch, stretching my jaw until my throat fluttered around the weight of him. My lips stretched wide. My eyes watered. Still, I didn't pull back. Pain in worship wasn't weakness. It was proof.

His fingers tangled in my hair. Not yanking. Just holding. Anchoring.

"Breathe," he said. Low. Controlled.

I tried.

His hips pressed forward. My throat opened for him—just barely. Just enough. The burn was sharp. Tears welled. Drool slid from the corner of my lips.

He didn't praise me. Didn't groan. He held still.

Deep.

And I held him.

The heat of his breath hit the crown of my head. His hand tightened. My scalp tingled under the pressure.

He pulled back slowly—just far enough for air.

"Again."

I opened wider. Took him deeper. My throat fought. My eyes stung. My fingers dug into my thighs, nails biting skin. But I didn't stop. Wolfe didn't fuck for praise.

He fucked for possession.

And I needed to be owned.

His other hand wrapped lightly around my throat. Not choking. Not yet. Just there. A reminder. Of who held my air.

He pushed in deeper. My nose touched his skin. My throat spasmed. He didn't flinch. I choked—soft, quiet, beautiful. His cock twitched. His breath caught. Still, he didn't come. This wasn't about him. It was about me breaking, bleeding obedience into the spaces between breath and silence. He pulled back again. My lips red. Raw. My chin slick.

"Keep it open," he said.

And I did. Pain was part of worship. Worship was survival. He didn't speak. Didn't tell me I was good. Didn't ask if I could take it. He just held my head still and fucked into my mouth like it was owed to him.

My knees dug harder into the floor with each thrust. The ache had long since set in, but the pain wasn't a deterrent. It was a direction.

He didn't hold my hair. He held my skull. One hand curled tight against the base of my neck. The other braced against his thigh.

He moved like a rhythm carved into marble—

Deep.

Hard.

Relentless.

Every thrust stole my breath. And I let him take it. My eyes blurred. My jaw throbbed.

Saliva dripped from my chin to my chest. The wet slap of his cock against the back of my throat filled the room.

Still, he said nothing.

Because this wasn't about words. This was about silence. And Wolfe had always known how to weaponize it.

He angled his hips, changing the depth. My shoulders jolted forward. My stomach tightened. I gagged around him. But I didn't pull away.

My nails curled into my thighs. My eyes locked on his abdomen. His breath was shallow now. His pace brutal.

My body shook. Not from pain. From need.

He held himself deeper than before.

Paused.

Let me feel it—all of him, thick and pulsing, taking space I didn't have. I blinked hard, tears falling freely now.

He slid out.

I gasped. Air flooded in. My chest burned.

"Look at me," he said.

I lifted my head. His cock glistened. His eyes were dark. But not cold. Just absolute. He slid back in. Faster. Harder.

My head rocked with each movement. My spine locked. My thighs trembled. And still I stayed. I stayed because he needed this.

Because I needed this.

The silence broke on a groan. Low. Ragged. Ripped from somewhere behind his teeth. His hand clamped at the back of my head, holding me in place as his cock jerked deep in my throat. Heat filled my mouth. Pulse after pulse.

He didn't pull out. Didn't give me warning. He finished inside me like he owned the right. He did.

I swallowed.

Choked.

Tears rolled down my cheeks.

And Wolfe exhaled above me.

Still.

Powerful.

Mine.

I stayed on my knees. My lips were swollen. My throat ached. His cum still coated the back of my tongue. I didn't wipe my mouth. Didn't move.

Wolfe zipped his pants slowly. Every motion deliberate. Every breath still measured. But his silence wasn't cold now. It was reverent.

He looked down at me. I looked up. My knees burned. My shoulders shook. He reached out. Fingers gentle. Thumb brushing the corner of my mouth.

He wiped the mess he left there. But not in disgust. Not in shame. In ritual. Then he cupped my jaw. Both hands. Held my face like it was something sacred. His thumb swept across my cheekbone.

Slow.

Like he could trace his ownership there. His fingers tightened just slightly—enough to remind me I was still his. Even after the violence. Especially after it.

He didn't kiss me. He didn't praise me. He just held me. And I didn't cry. But I wanted to. It wasn't just the pain that broke me. It was the way he stayed.

Wolfe dropped to one knee. His eyes never left mine. Then he leaned in. And kissed the top of my head.

Just once.

Soft.

Final.

Like he was sealing something. Something already written. Something he didn't plan on giving back. He didn't stand right away. Neither did I.

I knelt between his knees, throat raw, skin flushed. His hands still framed my jaw like he wasn't ready to let me go.

I watched his eyes. Dark. Unreadable. But not empty.

Never empty.

His thumbs brushed under my cheekbones.

Slow.

Measured.

And then—

He spoke.

Quiet.

Final.

"You were always mine."

I swallowed. The words hit harder than his cock. Harder than his silence.

"Before Royal flirted." He tilted my chin higher. "Before Loyal softened." His voice dropped lower. "Before Barron touched."

The air went still. My pulse thundered in my throat.

His fingers tightened, just slightly. Just enough.

"You were mine first."

I didn't nod. Didn't answer. I didn't need to.

He leaned in. Nose brushing mine. Breath hot. "And if they ever forget it..." His lips brushed my ear. "I'll remind them."

He stood. Fastened his belt. Ran a hand through his hair. Then looked down at me one last time. His mouth didn't move.

But his eyes said everything:

You don't kneel for them the way you kneel for me.

And he was right. I never would.

Worship has a memory.

And Wolfe wrote his name on mine first.

29

———

BARRON

IT WAS the kind of office that hadn't changed since the 1980s. Fluorescent lights buzzed overhead. Carpet the color of dried blood. One desk. One man. No secretary. No computer. Just a file cabinet with rusted handles and a coffee machine that hadn't been cleaned in a decade.

I didn't knock. I opened the door and stepped inside like I still belonged there.

Once, a long time ago, I had.

He didn't look up. Didn't need to. The kind of men who came to him didn't wait for permission. They walked in like ghosts. Like debts come to collect.

He was older now. More than I remembered. Thick hands, liver spots, that scar across his jaw still cutting clean through skin like it didn't believe in healing. He looked like a man who still knew the exact weight of a corpse under his boots.

He took one last drag of his cigarette, then set it down in the ashtray and met my eyes.

"How deep is the cut this time?"

I didn't sit. Not yet. I looked around the room. At the silence. The grime. The weight of a thousand secrets soaked into the walls.

"Deep enough to kill her."

He nodded once. Slow. Like he'd already read this script. He gestured to the chair across from him. I sat.

"You have a name?"

"Selene."

He exhaled through his nose, pulled a yellow legal pad from the drawer, and grabbed a pen that looked older than God.

"Then you're going to need more than leverage. You're going to need blood."

I didn't flinch. Didn't breathe.

"Then draw me a map."

He started writing. Didn't ask questions. Didn't ask for payment. Because some men still understood what a Lawlor promise was worth.

Royal

I didn't need a gun for this. Didn't need a knife, or a leash, or Wolfe standing behind me like a threat in a suit.

I had the file.

And that was enough.

He was already sweating before I sat down. Tapped the cigarette against the table even though I didn't light it. Just the sound made him twitch.

Selene's old contact. Some finance fuck with bad Botox and a bigger ego than common sense. He still thought he had options. Still thought this wasn't war.

That made it fun.

I leaned back, let him look at the folder I set between us. Thicker than it needed to be, heavy enough to hurt if I slammed it shut across his fingers. I didn't. Not yet.

His eyes didn't lift.

"I told her I was out."

His voice cracked. I smiled.

"Sure you did."

I tapped the cigarette again. Slow. Measured. I liked the sound. The rhythm of it. I'd watched Loyal play piano when we were kids—he made it a prayer. I made it a weapon.

"You think I give a fuck what you told her?" I asked.

He didn't answer. He didn't need to.

I opened the folder. Slid one photo across the table. His signature. Her signature. Wire transfers that didn't go where they were supposed to. Then I hit play on the voice memo. Selene's voice filled the room.

"You do your part, and if the Lawlors fall, I make sure your name comes out clean. That's the deal. You keep quiet, and I keep your daughter out of it."

He turned gray.

I smiled again.

"You thought she'd protect you," I said. "She won't. She never planned to."

He shook his head.

"You can't—"

I leaned in, let my smile sharpen.

"But I will."

I pushed another photo toward him. And another. Flight logs. Off-the-record meetings. One blurry picture of him holding hands with someone half his age at a hotel Selene owned.

His mouth opened. Nothing came out.

"You're going to tell the press Selene orchestrated the audit to sabotage us and take our board seats."

"That isn't true," he whispered.

"It doesn't need to be true," I said. "It needs to be loud."

He was still staring at the pictures. I knew what he saw. Not the evidence. Not the damage. His reflection. A man who thought he could lie to a Lawlor and walk away.

I tapped the cigarette once more. And exhaled war.

Loyal

I DIDN'T TURN on music. Didn't light a candle. Didn't pour a drink.

The silence was sharper than any of those comforts could have softened. I liked it that way. I liked the stillness, the hush that came just before collapse.

I wasn't here to be soft. I was here to ruin her.

The glow of the screen was the only light in the apartment. It flickered over the glass in my hand, untouched. Half-melted ice floated like the last remains of mercy.

The numbers on the screen didn't blur. They never did.

I ran my fingertip across the audit reports, tracing the patterns I knew better than her own lawyers. Selene had built her empire like a fortress. Tidy. Polished. Pretty. But even fortresses rot when the bricks don't match the foundation.

She forgot I knew what was under the floorboards.

She forgot who kept her secrets clean in the early days. Who sanitized her shell companies. Who caught the first three wire errors she pretended didn't matter.

She forgot me.

So now I was going to remind her.

I opened a cloned copy of her real estate filings. Cross-referenced the digital timestamp with the private entry she thought I'd never find. The one registered under an alias we used to joke about.

She had a sense of humor back then. It was one of the first things she buried when she decided power looked better in red lipstick. A flick of a key. One date altered. Another keystroke. A discrepancy introduced.

A signature I copied from a perfectly legal agreement, inserted onto one that should have never seen daylight. Just enough. Just a crack.

The kind of mistake that gets flagged by junior auditors. The kind that makes boards nervous. The kind that ends empires quietly. I zipped the file. Attached it to a burner account.

Drafted the email to a journalist I knew from the charity circuit. The kind who still believed in stories that made people bleed.

No name signed. No return address. Just the facts. Just the noise. I hit send. Then I leaned back. Closed my eyes. And breathed.

Because she wouldn't know it was me. Not yet. But she would feel it. When the accounts froze. When her investors pulled out. When her board demanded answers.

She would feel it. And she would remember. Because I don't need to put my hands on a person to hurt them. All I have to do is touch their name. And let the silence do the rest.

Wolfe

I DIDN'T TURN the lights on.

The apartment pulsed around me—still, black, watching.

Somewhere in the distance, the city kept breathing, but in here, the air didn't move.

I stood at the edge of the counter with my hands pressed flat to the marble, sleeves rolled up, the veins in my forearms twitching beneath skin that hadn't rested in forty hours.

The phone sat beside me. I stared at it for a long time. Not because I didn't know what came next. Because I did. Calling them was easy. Standing still afterward was harder. Royal answered on the second ring.

"We're done waiting."

That was all I said. He didn't ask for more. Because he didn't need it. Loyal picked up without a word.

"Bring everything. It's time."

He grunted once. That was his version of yes.

I didn't call Barron. He was already moving. I could feel it. The room buzzed. Not with noise. With inevitability.

I stood in the dark for a while longer. The silence in my chest felt wrong. Too quiet. Like something had been removed. Or ripped out. Or never belonged there in the first place.

Cloe stood in the hallway. She didn't speak. She wore my shirt—oversized, sleeves hanging down to her fingertips, the hem brushing the tops of her thighs. Her hair was pulled back in that half-tied way she did when she didn't want to look like she was trying.

But she was always trying. Trying to breathe. Trying to stay. Trying to be mine. I looked at her. She didn't look away. And when the knock came, neither of us flinched.

I opened the door. Royal stepped in first. All teeth and chaos, leather jacket slung over one shoulder like he hadn't just helped blackmail a man into breaking.

Loyal followed. Face cut from stone. Laptop under one arm, violence under the other.

Barron didn't walk in. He arrived. He filled the space like

judgment. Shoulders squared. Shirt open at the collar. Sleeves cuffed. No tie. No mask. Just weight. They didn't greet each other. Didn't need to.

I turned away and walked to the table. Everything was already laid out. Floor plans. Names. Photos. The fixer's notes. The last name Camille had written in her ledger.

Selene's. I didn't say her name. Didn't have to.

I lifted a photo. Set it down. Drew my finger across the inked line from one dockyard to one apartment to one faceless man whose silence had cost us too much.

"We end it," I said.

Royal nodded. No smile now. Just fire. Loyal sat. Opened the laptop. Pulled up schematics he'd hacked from three federal channels.

Barron leaned over the table. Picked up a pen. Circled the location.

"She'll be there," he said.

I felt the leash curl tighter inside me—

Not as fear. But as purpose.

I wasn't just standing here as their survival. I was their silence. And they were ready to kill for it.

Cloe stepped into the room. No one told her to leave. No one asked her to stay. She stood beside me. I felt the way her body pulled toward mine. Not for protection. For proof.

The brothers didn't look at her. They looked at me. And I didn't look away. We weren't fractured anymore. We were fire. And war had already started breathing our names.

Barron

I FOUND her exactly where I knew she would be.

In the center of Wolfe's bed. Wrapped in his shirt. Hair

damp, legs folded beneath her like she hadn't moved since the last time I touched her. She didn't hear me come in. Or if she did, she didn't flinch.

She just breathed.

Slow.

Even.

I stood in the doorway for a long time. Too long.

It felt like something sacred had grown in the space between us. Something that wasn't quite silence. Wasn't quite shame. Just weight. Just waiting.

She looked over her shoulder then. Like she felt it.

The heat of me. The tension. The pull.

Her eyes met mine.

Wide.

Open.

Wrecked.

And still—

Mine.

I didn't speak.

Didn't need to.

I walked to the bed. My shirt still open. My belt still undone from the last time I'd sat at that goddamn war table with my brothers and mapped out how we were going to bury Selene.

I hadn't meant to come back to her. I meant to burn through every lead we had until she was ashes in my hands.

But Cloe wasn't a detour. She was gravity. And she pulled me back. She shifted as I reached the bed. Her breath caught.

That sound. God. That sound.

I climbed onto the mattress slowly. Not to be gentle—to savor it.

I moved toward her like I had all the time in the world. Like the rage inside me wasn't blistering under my skin. Like I wasn't one more memory of her lips away from forgetting who the fuck I was supposed to be.

She didn't lean back. Didn't run. She just tilted her chin up. Like she was waiting for it.

For me.

My fingers reached for the buttons of the shirt. Her breath hitched. I slid each one open. One at a time. One for every reason I should have stayed away from her and didn't.

The shirt fell open. Her chest rose. Tight. Bare. Her nipples already hard. Her skin flushed.

I dragged my fingers over her collarbone. She didn't move. Didn't speak.

But her eyes—

They fucking begged.

I pushed the shirt off her shoulders. Let it slide down her arms. She sat there naked in front of me, spine straight, legs folded, thighs trembling.

I didn't kiss her.

Not yet.

I pushed her back onto the bed. Watched her elbows give. Watched her breath punch out of her lungs as her back hit the mattress.

Her hair fanned around her face. And I looked at her like she was the fucking end of me. Because she was.

I grabbed her knees. Pulled them apart. Her thighs fell open. She was soaked. Dripping.

I growled. Loud. Raw. My hands clutched her thighs so tight she gasped. But she didn't say no. She never said no to me. Because she knew I wouldn't break her. I'd rebuild her.

One thrust at a time.

I dropped my mouth to the inside of her knee. Bit. She cried out.

I kissed my way up her thigh.

Slow.

Torturous.

She arched.

Begged.

"Please."

I didn't answer.

I just slid two fingers inside her.

She choked on a moan.

"You missed me," I said. Low. Sharp.

She nodded. Eyes wide. Lips trembling.

"Say it."

"*I missed you,*" she breathed.

I slid deeper. My palm pressed against her clit. She shuddered.

"Say it again."

"*I missed you.*"

I leaned over her. My body hovered over hers. My fingers never stopped moving.

"Say you're mine."

"I'm yours."

"Say it louder."

"*I'm yours.*"

I ripped my belt off. Undid my pants. Freed my cock. And thrust into her in one brutal, breath-stealing movement. Her scream wasn't pain. It was coming home.

I fucked her like I didn't care if the world burned down around us. Because I didn't. Because I would burn it myself.

Her hands clawed at my shoulders. My back. My hair. Her legs wrapped around me.

She took every thrust like it was survival. And I gave her every inch like it was salvation.

I didn't stop. Not when she started to tremble. Not when she begged. Not when she came.

I chased it.

Mine.

Mine.

Mine.

Until the word didn't feel like a claim. It felt like a vow. And when I came inside her, I buried my face in her neck and breathed her name like a confession.

30

CLOE

It started with a memory.

Not loud. Not clear. Just a flicker. A scent.

Warm dust. Cedarwood. Velvet.

Camille's voice didn't come back all at once.

It slipped in like fog. Like the moment between sleep and waking where nothing is sharp yet, and everything hurts just a little too much.

I was still in Wolfe's bed. Barron's fingerprints carved into my thighs. The sheets smelled like everything I couldn't name. Sex. Shame. Worship.

Wolfe stood near the window, shirtless, jaw tight, his pen scratching something across the surface of a notepad. The war plan. The next blow.

But I wasn't looking at him.

I was looking at the shadows. At the space beside the bed where a sliver of moonlight caught the edge of the floorboard, and something in me began to shake.

I closed my eyes.

And Camille whispered.

Keep it. Just in case. She'd said it like a joke. But Camille never meant anything lightly. *If they come for me, you'll know.*

I sat up too fast. My breath hitched. My ribs ached.

Wolfe turned immediately.

"What is it?"

I shook my head.

He was halfway across the room before I could form the words.

"I think I still have something."

He stopped. His eyes darkened. Not in anger. In hope.

I climbed out of the bed. My legs trembled. I didn't wait for his permission. I didn't need it. This wasn't about disobedience. This was about resurrection. Camille had left me something. And I was going to get it back.

Wolfe was behind the wheel, engine idling low, one hand on the gearshift, the other resting on his thigh. His head turned slightly toward me, but his eyes didn't leave the building.

The apartment complex looked smaller than I remembered. Grayer. The corners eaten by water damage. The windows clouded over with grime that no one had cleaned in years.

I had lived in this building like a ghost. Forgotten by neighbors. Feared by landlords. My mail never lasted more than a week before being stolen or shredded. It was the last place I knew before Wolfe made me his.

He stared at it now like it was harmless. Like it was just a building. That was his mistake.

"I'll only be a second," I said.

He didn't speak

then.

"I don't like this."

"No one knows I'm here. You'll see anyone coming a mile away anyway. Beep the horn and I'm out of there."

His hand tightened on the steering wheel, leather creaking beneath his palm.

Then, finally:

"Be quick."

His jaw clenched hard enough I thought he might crack a tooth.

"You don't come out in sixty seconds, I'm tearing that door off its hinges."

I believed him.

I nodded. Reached for the door handle. He didn't look at me. That was the part that stuck. Not the silence. The trust. I closed the door gently. The latch clicked shut.

The air outside hit colder than I expected. The wind tugged at the hem of my coat. My boots scuffed the pavement as I crossed the lot. Broken glass glinted between the cracks in the concrete.

I knew this was stupid. I knew Camille wouldn't have wanted me to come alone. But I wasn't doing it for her. I was doing it for the part of me she left behind.

The building loomed above me like it had been waiting. I didn't look back. I couldn't.

I made it to the door. Key still worked. The metal stuck in the lock for a breath before it gave.

I slipped inside.

The hallway was darker than it should have been. One of the bulbs overhead flickered. Someone had sprayed graffiti across the elevator. I didn't take it. I never trusted that thing.

I climbed the stairs.

Two flights.

The same scent still lingered in the walls. Mold. Rot. Cheap detergent. The door to my old unit was exactly as I left it. Peeling paint. A dent near the knob from when I kicked it once in a fight I don't remember starting.

I opened it slowly. The apartment hadn't changed. Not the mess. Not the silence. The mattress was still on the floor. The curtains hung limp and stained. The light from the street outside bled through the slats in gray strips. But it was still mine. Or had been.

I crossed the room. The floor creaked under my weight. I knelt beside the vent in the wall. Fingers trembling.

I unscrewed it slowly.

There.

Wrapped in black cloth. Tucked into the space behind the grate. I pulled it free. A flash drive. A book. And beneath it, a folded photo.

I didn't open it. Not yet. I already knew what it was. Her smile. My shadow. The last proof that Camille never forgot me —even when I stopped remembering myself.

I tucked both into my coat pocket. Turned. And froze. The door behind me hadn't moved. But the air had. My breath stalled. Footsteps in the hall. Slow. Deliberate. *Wolfe.*

My fingers moved for my phone. But it was too late.

The floor groaned outside the apartment. And someone knocked. Once. Then silence. The kind of silence that tells you it's already too late to run.

THE KNOCK DIDN'T COME like a threat.

It came like breath. Like punctuation.

Soft.

Measured.

Wrong.

I was still crouched in front of the vent, knees aching from the cold floor, breath caught behind my ribs like it was trying to hide. My fingers were tight around the flash drive and the journal. The photo folded and crumpled in my coat pocket. I hadn't looked at it yet. I didn't want to. The weight of the drive was enough.

I slid the journal back into the vent, the metal covering left askew.

The knock came again.

Not louder.

Not urgent.

Just there.

Three taps.

Then silence.

Wolfe doesn't knock.

That was the first thought.

The first fracture.

I turned toward the door slowly, every part of me screaming to move faster. But I didn't. Something about the stillness on the other side told me everything I needed to know.

He wasn't there.

And whatever was—

It didn't want me to run. It wanted me to hesitate. My heartbeat thundered. My throat locked. I reached for something—anything.

My fingers found the rusted pipe from the radiator near the wall. I gripped it tight. It was heavier than it looked. Cold. Filthy. Another knock.

I rose slowly. I wanted to scream. Not from fear. From the weight of knowing this was already too late. The doorknob twitched. I froze. No voice. No sound.

Just the subtle squeal of the metal under pressure. The lock clicked. And the door creaked open. Not fast. Not like force. Like invitation.

I didn't move. My breath came in short, sharp bursts. The pipe shook in my hands. Then he stepped inside. He wasn't tall. He wasn't masked. And somehow—that made it worse.

His hair was shaved close to the scalp. His face pockmarked. His eyes empty. He looked like someone who'd never been caught. Like someone who never had to run.

He smiled when he saw me. Not wide. Not cruel. Just sure. Like I was already his. I raised the pipe. He tilted his head, as if amused.

"Easy now," he said, voice low, calm.

I swung. He ducked. Fast. Too fast. His hand caught my wrist. Pain bloomed up my arm as he twisted.

I screamed. *"Wolfe!"*

He didn't flinch. He slammed me back into the wall, pipe clattering to the ground. His breath hit my face. Hot. Sour.

I fought.

Kicked. Scratched. *Wild.*

I caught the side of his face with my nails. Skin tore. He grunted. He pushed his weight against me. Crushing against the wall.

I tried to buck.

Tried to draw breath.

"Wolfe! WOLFE!"

My phone.

I reached down. Drawing it free. Before an elbow to the stomach. Hard enough to tear the wind from my lungs. My phone slipped. Clattering to the floor.

Then his hand went to his pocket. I saw it too late. The cloth. The bottle. The rag. I thrashed harder.

His arm locked around my throat. Not choking—just holding.

"Don't make this worse than it has to be," he hissed.

He pressed the rag to my face.

The scent hit instantly.

Sweet.

Rotten.

Wrong.

Chemical.

My lungs locked. I held my breath. But it was too late. The edges of my vision began to ripple. Black pressed in from all sides.

I twisted. *"Nooo."*

The word warped and slow. My nails scraped his forearm. Blood.

He growled. Pressed harder. The cloth soaked through my skin. My knees buckled. My grip loosened. The room spun.

I thought of Wolfe. Of his mouth against my ear the night before. Don't disappear on me. And then I did. The last thing I saw was the ceiling. And the way the light from the hallway never reached me.

Thud.

I came back like something drowning its way to the surface with fists, not hands.

Everything hurt. My head. My throat. My wrists. Every inch of my skin buzzed like I'd been stitched back into a body I didn't ask to return to.

The dark was pure. Not quiet. Not gentle.

It pressed in from all sides. Trapped heat under my spine, cold sweat down my back. My legs were folded, crushed against each other, my arms bent painfully behind me, wrists lashed tight with something plastic and unyielding.

I shifted. Pain flared.

A scream ripped out of me before I knew I was making it.

But it caught.

"NO!"

My throat burned. My mouth was dry. The chemical taste still sat on my tongue like spoiled sugar. And the car kept moving. Not fast. Not reckless. Just steady. A rhythm built from apathy.

I pressed my shoulder into the trunk lid and pushed. Nothing. The walls stayed silent. I kicked. Twice. Three times. The heel of my boot caught something metal. It rattled. I kicked again. *Harder.*

The trunk didn't give. But the men did. Voices. Muffled. Shouted. Angry.

The car swerved. My body rolled. They were yelling at each other now.

"She's fucking awake."

"Hold her down next stop."

"You should've dosed her again."

"I told you to bring a second one."

Panic bloomed fast and vicious. I curled my legs in, turned sideways, braced myself against the tire well and screamed. Raw. Shaking.

I screamed until my lungs burned. I screamed Wolfe's name. And the car stopped. Slammed to a halt like it had hit a wall.

Doors opened.

Footsteps.

Then—

The trunk clicked. And I exploded. The lid opened. I came out swinging.

I launched myself like an animal. Caught one of them in the throat with my shoulder. Heard him grunt. Felt the satisfying crack of bone. The other grabbed me by the waist. I thrashed. Elbowed him in the nose. Felt the cartilage snap. Blood sprayed. He cursed.

I screamed again. Louder. Higher. He clamped a hand over my mouth. I bit. *Hard.*

He screamed.

"Fucking bitch!"

His fist caught my jaw. My head snapped sideways.

Stars exploded behind my eyes.

I staggered, spit blood. Didn't stop.

I turned, kicked the inside of his knee. He dropped. The other was already coming at me.

I ducked. His fist grazed my shoulder. I ran. Two steps. That was all I got. Then an arm around my throat.

I clawed. Kicked. Tried to twist. He lifted me clean off the ground. My scream was a garbled choke. My nails dug into skin. I caught his face. Ripped something. He slammed me against the car door. My vision blurred. The rag returned.

Pressed hard.

I held my breath. Twisted again. Slammed the back of my head into his face. Heard something crack. His grip slipped. I ran again. Made it to the sidewalk. I saw him.

Wolfe.

Just his silhouette. Lit by the streetlamp, coat unfastened, head tilted down as he moved toward the building like nothing had gone wrong. Like I was still inside. Like I hadn't already been stolen. I opened my mouth and screamed his name.

"WOLFE!"

My voice tore out of me like it was trying to break something. The man holding me tightened his grip.

I twisted.

Kicked.

"WOLFE!"

I screamed it again.

Louder. Ragged. Unhinged.

He didn't turn. He didn't hear.

I lunged. My feet scraped the pavement. My body pitched forward. I almost broke free.

Almost. The rag hit again. Cloth soaked through. Jammed against my mouth. Hands on my throat. I thrashed. Slammed my head back. Slammed my foot down.

"WOLFE!"

It was a sob now. A prayer. A scream that ripped from somewhere behind my ribs. He walked through the door.

Gone.

The last thing I felt before everything went dark was the edge of the trunk against my back.

And the sound of my name—not from Wolfe. But from the man who stuffed me inside.

"You're done running, girl."

Wolfe

I didn't hear her. That was the part that burned the deepest.

Not the silence. Not the stillness.

The absence.

I stepped out of the car without thinking. My hand brushed the roof as I shut the door behind me. The engine ticked in the quiet, a lazy heat curling out from under the hood as I crossed the pavement.

The streetlight flickered overhead.

No wind. No warning.

Just that still hum that comes right before something detonates.

I checked my watch. Three minutes. She said one. I told myself it didn't matter. She was just grabbing something. Just picking up a piece of memory. A page from the past we could use to rebuild the future. I told myself she was fine. She had to be. I couldn't take anything else being stolen.

I walked toward the building. Didn't rush. Didn't scan the street.

I let my mind drift back to Camille's journal, to the notes I'd made in the margins, to the way Barron's jaw had gone tight when he realized the final page wasn't about inheritance. It was about a contract.

She had signed something. I didn't know what yet. But I would. *Soon.*

I reached the door. It stuck slightly when I pulled it open. My fingers tightened around the frame.

Inside, the air was stale. Not unusual. Old buildings always smelled like this. Like concrete and regret.

I took the stairs instead of the elevator.

Habit.

My footsteps echoed. Second floor. The light above the stairwell buzzed.

Her apartment door was ajar. My pulse didn't spike. Not yet. She was in a hurry. That's all. She didn't close it all the way.

I stepped inside. The cold hit me first. Then the silence. It was too still. Like a pause that had waited too long for the next note.

I scanned the room. Slow. Deliberate. Floor vent open. Dust scattered around it. A chair tipped over. That was the first shift. The first crack in my ribs.

She wouldn't have left that. She was messy, yes. Chaotic, sometimes. But not careless. Not here. Not in this.

I moved farther inside. The mattress was untouched. But something in the air had changed.

I bent down, picked up the chair. And saw the wrench beneath it. Blood on the handle. Not a lot. Just enough. My lungs turned to ice.

I stood. Fast.

Checked the bathroom. Empty.

The closet. *Empty.*

Her scent still lingered in the air. Faint. Cedar. Smoke. Fear.

I pulled out my phone.

No messages.

No calls.

My fingers flew.

Texted her.

Where are you?

Delivered.

No read.

I turned—

But something pulled me back.

A shape on the floor.

Still. Off.

Faint glow from the corner near the mattress.

Her phone. Facedown. Left behind.

I crossed the room. Heart tight. Every step slower than the last.

Crouched low, knees biting against the cold floorboards. Flipped the phone over. Screen lit. My message waiting.

No reply.

Not read.

And then—

I saw it.

Not the phone.

Not the message.

The vent.

Metal cover askew. Like it had been closed in a rush. Or by someone who didn't have time to finish hiding what mattered.

I reached forward. Fingers steady. Pulled the grate aside.

Camille's journal.

Tucked deep.

Edges worn. Familiar.

I didn't move for a second. Just stared.

The last time she touched this, she was still mine. And now? Now it was buried like evidence. Hidden like it was meant to be found too late.

I slid it out. Stood fast. Journal and drive in one hand. Phone in my other. No hesitation. Just motion. I was down the stairs in seconds. She never would've left this unless she meant to come back. Unless something stopped her. And I was going to find out what. And make sure it never fucking touched her again. Boots like thunder against the thin carpet.

Out into the street. There was only silence. The kind that was crushing. I turned in a slow circle. Too slow.

My hand shook when I pulled the phone again. I hit redial. Once. Twice. On the third, it rang.

An unknown number.

I answered. Didn't speak. The line hissed.

Then a voice. Low. Tired. Pleased.

"Now it's your turn to crawl."

Click.

Silence.

I didn't drop the phone.

I didn't shout.

I just stood there, alone in the street, breathing in the last place she had been. And realized I had never known true stillness until I couldn't hear her breathing anymore.

And the silence didn't sound like absence. It sounded like worship torn from my chest. Like the echo of a prayer I never deserved to have answered. And I would kill them all for taking it.

32

———

CLOE

The first thing I felt was pressure.

Not pain. Not even weight.

Just the hum of something tight around my wrists, the ache in my ankles where the rope pulled skin raw. A thread of fire where circulation had stopped. The pulse in my temple beat slow and heavy, like my body was counting down from something I couldn't name.

The second thing was the smell. Not blood—not yet. But everything else.

The stench of mold crawling through concrete. Rust in the air. Old sweat soaked into fabric. A damp, sour rot I couldn't place until I breathed too deep and nearly choked.

Urine.

Not fresh.

The kind that lingered.

The kind that clung to walls and skin. I kept my eyes closed for a moment longer. Tried to piece myself back together one breath at a time.

Where was I?

Where was he?

Wolfe.

Flickers came back to me. I saw him before the dark. His back turned. His coat catching in the wind. The moment he stepped into the building, and the light swallowed him.

I had screamed his name. *And he hadn't heard me.* That was the sound still echoing in my ribs. Not the scream—the silence that followed it.

I opened my eyes. It was hard to tell what was real.

The room was dim, the only light a low orange coil from a bulb hanging half-dead above my head. It swung slightly, casting long shadows that bent the corners of the room into things they weren't.

The walls were concrete. Stained. No windows. No clock. Just a single metal door to my left, rust bleeding down its hinges.

I tried to move. Tried to lift my arm. The rope bit deeper. They'd tied me to a chair.

Metal legs. One wobbled. My back screamed against the posture. My thighs were cold, sticky with dried sweat. My mouth was stuffed with a rag so tight I couldn't even close my lips around it.

I breathed through my nose. The air was sharp. Rank. I swallowed around the gag. My tongue scraped cotton. My jaw ached.

I turned my head slowly. Pain bloomed at the base of my skull. The bastard had hit me harder than I thought. My scalp pulsed where it met the chair.

The door stayed closed. But I wasn't alone. I could feel it. Someone watching.

I tested my bindings. Quietly. My left wrist was raw, but the knot wasn't perfect. Too low. If I bent my hand just right, I might get enough leverage to loosen it. But not yet. Not while I was being watched.

I let my eyes fall half-shut. Tried to make my body go slack. Let them think I was still out.

My heart beat louder than it should have. Not fast. But hard. Like it was trying to stay loud enough for someone to find.

Wolfe.

He would come. He would be tearing apart the city already. But even knowing that didn't make the silence safer.

The door creaked. Just slightly. Then footsteps. Slow. Heavy. *Like the man attached to them had never once needed to run.*

I didn't move. Not yet. A chair scraped across the floor. Closer. Boots. Steel-toed. Scuffed.

He sat down in front of me. I could feel the air shift when he leaned forward. I opened my eyes. He wasn't the one from before. This one was worse. Neater. Buttoned shirt. Sleeves rolled. A leather watch too clean for the rest of him.

He smiled when I looked up. Not kind. Not cruel. Just— curious.

Like he was trying to understand how someone like me ended up here. Like I was a new puzzle and he already had the first piece.

He leaned forward.

"You awake, sweetheart?"

I didn't answer. Couldn't.

But the way I held his gaze made something shift in his expression. Respect, maybe. Or interest. He reached into his jacket. Pulled out a small knife.

I flinched. He didn't open it. Just set it on the ground beside him, like a promise.

"I'm not here to hurt you. Not yet."

His voice was soft. Clean. Too clean.

He reached up and untied the gag. Slow. Careful. It fell from my mouth like a curse. My lips were cracked. Blood dried in the corners.

He held out a bottle of water. The kind you get from a vending machine.

I didn't take it. So he did it for me. Tilted the bottle. Held it to my mouth. Water sluiced down my chin.

I drank. Because I had to. Because my throat was fire. He pulled it back before I got more than a mouthful. I wanted to spit in his face. But I needed the next sip.

He chuckled.

"See? Cooperation."

I stared at the knife.

He followed my gaze.

"Don't worry about that. It's not for you. *Not unless you make it for you.*"

He stood. Walked around the chair slowly.

"You made a lot of noise on the street, Cloe."

The way he said my name made my stomach twist. Like he owned it. Like it was something bought. He stopped behind me. His hands ghosted above my shoulders. Not touching. Just hovering.

I went still.

"Men like me don't get second chances. But you gave me one. Your debts became my profit."

His breath hit my neck. I bit the inside of my cheek.

"You should feel proud," he said. "You're worth more now than you were on your back. That's rare. That's something."

I didn't flinch. Because I refused. Because the one thing Wolfe taught me was how to bleed without fear.

He stepped back around the chair. Crouched. Met my eyes.

"Now we wait," he said. "They'll come. They always come."

He stood again. Grabbed the knife. Slipped it back into his pocket.

"You be good, and I'll keep you pretty."

Then he left. And the lock clicked behind him. And I started planning how to kill him.

Wolfe

I didn't take the stairs two at a time. I didn't run. I walked. Every step was deliberate. Every breath a calculation. My boots hit the tile of the apartment hallway like they had something to prove. If I let myself run—if I let myself feel—I wouldn't make it to the war room. *I'd rip the city in half before I knew where she was.*

The door was open. Someone had left it that way. Loyal, maybe. Royal. Didn't matter.

I stepped inside. Barron looked up from the floor plans. Loyal sat on the edge of the sofa, laptop balanced on his knees. Royal leaned against the kitchen island, eating something from a tin like we weren't all seconds from setting the world on fire.

No one spoke. Not until I closed the door. It clicked. Louder than it should have. Louder than anything else had sounded since I'd walked into that apartment and found the vent open.

My coat hit the ground before I was even across the room. Barron's eyes tracked me. Loyal paused the video feed on his screen. Royal stopped chewing.

I walked to the cabinet. Pulled out the scotch. Poured a glass.

My hand didn't shake. I wanted it to. I wanted something to break the stillness. But I wasn't allowed that. Not yet.

I drank half the glass in one pull. The burn hit the back of my throat. Sharp. Clean. It didn't help.

"They took her," I said.

No one moved. Loyal was the first to exhale. Royal dropped his fork into the tin.

Barron stood.

"How?" he asked.

I looked at him. Not with fury. With certainty.

"I let her go."

I watched the words land. Watched Royal flinch, barely. Watched Loyal go cold. Watched Barron take one step toward me like he might try to stop what was coming next. He didn't. Because he knew better.

I walked to the table. Set down the glass. Flattened my palms against the wood.

"She said one minute."

The phrase cracked something in me.

I said it again.

"One fucking minute."

Loyal closed the laptop. Royal pushed off the counter. I didn't look at them.

"They were watching us," I said. "They knew the second I left her alone. They waited for her to say it. One minute. Like it was a countdown."

I closed my eyes. And saw her. The last glimpse I had. Her back disappearing up the stairs. The shape of her hand waving me off.

Trust.

It had tasted like mercy at the time. Now it tasted like blood.

I opened my eyes. Royal stood across from me now. Quiet. Focused.

"What do we know?"

Loyal spoke.

"The burner that called you last pinged twice. Once near her building. Once outside the old train depot in the southern sector."

Barron pulled a folded map from his coat pocket. Unrolled it across the table. The ink was already smudged from his hands. Mine added more.

"She's not in a safehouse," he said. "Not cartel. Not Selene's people. This is older. Dirtier. The kind of men who don't need her alive to make their point."

I smiled. It was the kind of smile that didn't reach the surface. The kind that lived in bone. I turned. Walked down the hall.

My room was dark. The way I left it. The closet door hung open. I stepped inside. Pulled the blade from the box under my bed. Matte black. Handle worn to the shape of my grip. I strapped it to my thigh. Then I opened the drawer beside the nightstand.

Cloe's collar still sat inside. I looked at it for a long time. I didn't touch it. Not yet.

When I stepped back into the room, Loyal was already loading gear. Barron on the phone. Royal pressing something into a duffel bag. They didn't ask. They didn't wait. They just moved. I poured another drink. Held it up.

"They think she's alone," I said.

I looked at each of them.

"They think she's something they can keep."

I finished the drink. Set the glass down.

"We make sure they never forget who she belongs to."

No one toasted. No one smiled. Barron nodded once. Loyal

zipped the duffel. Royal rolled his sleeves. And I turned to the door.

Because the next breath I took would be on the road. And the next time I spoke her name—

It would be the last thing they heard before they died.

Cloe

I counted the seconds.

Not because I thought it would help. Not because I believed Wolfe would come bursting through the door like he did in my nightmares—too late to stop the bleeding, always too late. No, I counted because it was the only thing I had.

The ache in my wrists had turned sharp. My ankles throbbed with each shallow breath. My skin felt too tight. My thoughts, too loud.

And still—

I waited.

Because there was nothing else to do.

Because I had nothing else to give.

The room didn't get darker, but it felt like it did. Every breath pressed heavier. The air went thick, humid, metallic. I could taste rust in the back of my throat and didn't know if it was blood or memory.

The door opened. Not a slam. Not the loud, angry kind of violence I could brace for. Just a click. And a shift in the air. Footsteps, slow. Controlled. He wasn't in a rush. That was the worst part.

The man who stepped into the room didn't wear sweat-stained cotton or stink of fear. He didn't carry the weight of violence in his fists.

He was clean. Pressed slacks. White shirt. Rolled cuffs that had never been used to wipe blood from a lip. Leather shoes that squeaked slightly against the cracked tile. His hair was combed. His face unlined. A man who walked through filth but refused to let it cling to him.

And he smiled when he saw me. Not because he liked what he saw. Because he knew what came next.

He pulled a chair from the wall. Turned it around. Sat in it backwards, arms folded over the top like we were about to have a friendly conversation.

I didn't speak. He didn't expect me to.

"Cloe," he said, like he was greeting someone at a dinner party.

I blinked. The sound of my name in his mouth made my stomach twist. He didn't say it the way Wolfe did. He didn't breathe it like a promise. He held it like a leash.

"You're awake. That's good."

He reached into his pocket. Pulled out a small notepad. Flipped it open.

"We're just going to have a quick talk, you and me."

He looked up. Tilted his head slightly, as if studying me.

"You're quieter than I expected. That's rare."

I met his stare. Because I knew better than to look away. He smiled wider.

"You're not scared of me yet. I like that."

He reached into his jacket again. Pulled out a flask. Uncapped it. The scent hit first. Not alcohol. Something sweeter. Thicker. My throat went dry. He took a sip. Offered it to me.

"No?"

I shook my head once. He shrugged.

"Suit yourself."

He set the flask on the floor between us.

"I'm not here to hurt you. You understand that, right?"

I said nothing. He leaned forward. His voice dropped lower.

"But *they* will."

I held his stare. He laughed. Soft. Easy.

"You think he'll come. Wolfe. *Right?*"

My breath caught. I didn't move. But something in my chest cracked. He saw it.

"You think you matter to him. That you're some sacred thing he won't trade for the bigger game."

He reached for the flask again. Took another sip.

"You're not."

I smiled. Not because I believed him. But because he was wrong. So fucking wrong. He paused.

"You don't believe me."

I didn't answer. But I didn't have to. He stood. Walked a slow circle around me.

"You cost a lot of men a lot of money, Cloe."

His voice was sharper now. Not angry. Disappointed.

"Do you know how many of them paid for your silence? How many bet on your obedience? Your shame?"

He stopped behind me.

"And you ran."

I didn't turn. Couldn't. But I listened. Because every word was a thread. And I needed to know where he'd fray.

"You ran to Wolfe Lawlor. You begged him to leash you, thinking it would make you untouchable."

His hand touched my shoulder. I flinched. He chuckled.

"But now you're right back where you started. Only this time, there's no one to pawn your skin to. No way out but the one we give you."

He moved back in front of me. Bent. Met my eyes.

"So here's the offer."

He pulled a small phone from his pocket. Laid it on my lap.

"You call him. You tell him where to find you. Alone. No brothers. No plan."

He smiled.

"And we let you go."

I stared at the phone. Then back at him. And I spat in his face. The glob of blood and spit hit his cheekbone. Traced a line down to his jaw. He froze. Just for a second. Then he wiped it with the cuff of his sleeve. Slow. Deliberate. And smiled.

"That's alright."

He leaned in again. Closer this time. Too close. His breath was warm. *His voice a whisper.*

"We don't need you to be clean."

He pulled the phone off my lap. Slipped it back into his jacket.

"We just need you to bleed."

Then he turned. And left me sitting there. Tied. Cold. Heart slamming against my ribs like it could break the ropes. And I knew something I hadn't known before. They weren't waiting for Wolfe. They were feeding me to him.

Wolfe

I didn't know how long I stood in front of the window.

The glass was cold against my fingertips. The skyline bled orange and gray. The sun hadn't fully risen, and the city still slept like it didn't know it had swallowed something holy and tried to keep it.

My breath fogged the pane. Every inhale shallower than the one before. Every exhale too slow.

Loyal paced behind me. I heard him. The shift of weight.

The light tap of his knuckle against the edge of the counter every five steps.

Royal had stopped pretending to be calm. He leaned against the wall, arms crossed, eyes on the floor like he was watching someone bleed there. Barron stood by the door. Still. Waiting for orders I hadn't given yet. Not because he needed them. Because he wanted to hear the way I'd say it.

I blinked. The image of her back—disappearing up those stairs, braid swinging, her fingers brushing the doorframe like she was promising to come back—played in my head like a loop.

I hadn't looked up from my phone. I'd barely heard her say "one minute".

I had believed her. I had fucking believed her. I turned. The room froze. I walked toward the war table. My boots echoed across the wood.

I didn't sit. I placed both hands on the table, leaned forward, and looked at each of them. Loyal was first. His jaw tightened. His laptop open beside him, maps pinned to the screen. Royal straightened. Barron nodded once. No words. Just steel in his spine.

"They moved her by car," I said.

Loyal tapped the trackpad.

"Confirmed."

He rotated the laptop.

Security footage. Grainy. A dark sedan pulling away from the curb. Timestamped thirty seconds before I walked into that building.

"They had eyes," I muttered.

"Everywhere," Loyal added.

Royal shoved a knife into the sheath on his belt.

"You want me to follow the car?"

"No," I said. "I want you to follow the scent."

Royal grinned. Barron picked up his phone.

"I'll push pressure on the brokers. If Selene's tied to this, she won't see tomorrow."

"She didn't do this," I said.

Barron looked up.

"She would have if she thought it would hurt us."

I shook my head.

"She didn't want Cloe dead."

I stepped back. Walked to my room.

The others followed. Not because I asked. Because they knew something had changed. I opened the closet. Pulled the blade from the vault beneath the floorboard. Laid it on the dresser. It wasn't ceremonial. It was familiar.

I strapped it to my thigh. Pulled the gun from the drawer. Checked the clip. Full.

Loyal entered behind me.

"You have a location?"

He nodded.

"Last ping was east side. Near the docks. Warehouse complex. No recent shipping activity. Not cartel. Not syndicate. Independent."

"Loan shark," Barron said from behind him.

I closed the drawer.

"Which one?"

Royal answered.

"The one who took a cut from Callum. The one Camille warned us about."

The words landed hard.

Camille.

Always *Camille.*

I pulled on my jacket. Grabbed the collar from the edge of the desk. Not to leash her. To show them what they tried to steal. Barron handed me his phone.

"This is the man who pulled her. The one who knocked."

The screen showed a face. Pocked skin. Crooked nose. Dead eyes.

I memorized it. Then I handed it back.

"He dies last."

Barron nodded.

Loyal spoke again.

"We go quiet or loud?"

I looked at him. I didn't answer. Because they already knew. I walked to the door. Royal opened it. Loyal followed. Barron behind him. I was the last one out.

I needed one more second. To stand in the apartment that still smelled like her skin. To feel the weight of everything I didn't say.

I touched the doorframe. Then I whispered her name. And walked into war.

Cloe

I knew they thought I wouldn't last.

That I'd sit there in that rusted metal chair, hands tied, mouth broken open from hours of forced stillness, and eventually give in to the weight of it.

But I'd lived too long in silence to believe it could undo me. It wasn't silence that hurt. It was what came after.

The door had stayed closed for what felt like hours. No sound except the soft hum of something electric in the walls. Maybe a cooler. Maybe a wire running to a camera they hadn't told me about. Maybe nothing. But it was there. Buzzing. Waiting.

I worked my wrists against the ropes. Slow. Measured.

Pain sparked along the inside of my forearms, skin splitting in quiet tears as I twisted, pulled, flexed. Blood slicked the edge of the knot.

I kept going. Because pain was the only language I still trusted. My breath came ragged now. Not from fear. From effort. The right rope was loosening.

I shifted again. Legs shaking, thighs locked, my ankles still bound tight to the chair legs. Every movement sent a scrape of steel across concrete. I froze after each sound, ears tuned for footsteps. None came.

I bit my tongue. Tasted blood. Good. The rope gave. A flicker. Enough.

I didn't move yet. I didn't celebrate. Because one wrong twitch and they'd come back before I was ready.

I waited. Let my hand fall limp again. Let the numbness drain. When the door finally opened, it took everything not to jolt.

I closed my eyes. Listened. Not the clean-shoes man this time. Heavy footfalls. Broader frame. Thicker breath. The original one. The one with the rag. His boots thudded closer. I opened my eyes. He grinned.

"Still tied up, sweetheart?"

He reached out. Fingers brushed my cheek. I didn't flinch. I waited until he stepped behind me. Until I felt the shift in his weight. Until I smelled the sweat on his neck.

And then I moved. My hand snapped free. Fast. *Faster than he expected.*

I grabbed the broken edge of the chair. Slammed it back. He cursed. Lunged. Too late.

I twisted. The chair cracked. Wood splintered as I wrenched my ankle free. He reached for my hair. I drove the jagged chair leg into his thigh. He screamed. High. Sharp. Ugly.

I wrenched the wood free. Blood sprayed. He staggered. I stood. *Unsteady.* Legs shaking. Hands slick.

I grabbed the knife from his belt. Small. Dull. Didn't matter. I raised it. He hesitated. Only for a breath.

And in that second, I screamed. Not a cry. Not a name. A roar. Louder than the walls. Louder than the pain. My voice ripped out of my throat, raw and broken, soaked in fury.

"WOLFE!"

The name hit the ceiling.

Echoed.

The man lunged. I ducked. Swung the knife. Caught his shoulder. He screamed again. And I ran. Not far. Just enough. Just to the hallway. Just to the cold. I screamed again.

"WOLFE!"

I didn't scream for rescue. I screamed for vengeance. Wolfe wasn't coming to save me. He was coming to end them. Until it didn't sound like a name anymore. Until it sounded like a war cry. Until I knew he would hear it. I wasn't asking to be saved. I was calling him to kill.

33

WOLFE

I LEFT the door open when I came in.

It didn't matter. Nothing could get in that hadn't already taken her. The lock clicked anyway. Old habits. I let it. The air was cold. Not from the windows. Not from the outside. From the absence.

The lights were still on in the hallway. The living room bathed in soft amber. Someone had dimmed the sconces. Probably Loyal. Or Barron. They didn't want me walking into darkness.

They didn't understand that darkness was the only thing left that felt familiar.

I walked in slow. Boots quiet against the floorboards. My coat heavy around my shoulders.

I'd barely spoken since the warehouse. Since the screaming. Since her voice. They'd played the footage over and over. Pixelated. Warped. Echoing off those concrete walls like it was a warning.

But I'd know it anywhere. That wasn't a cry for help. It was a goddamn weapon. She screamed for me.

She called me like she knew the city could hear it.

And I hadn't answered.

I stepped into the kitchen. Everything was exactly as she left it. Her mug on the counter. The one she never rinsed.

I picked it up. Felt the cold ceramic in my hand. The faint lip print along the rim. My jaw locked.

I set it down. Not gently. Let it scrape the marble. The hallway stretched in front of me like it had grown longer. I walked it anyway.

The first door I passed was the guest room. Empty. Cold. I didn't look in. The second was mine. The door was ajar. I stopped. Her scent was still there. Smoke. Cedar. Skin.

I closed my eyes. Breathed it in like a prayer. Then pushed the door open. The bed was made. She hadn't slept here. Not in days. Not since Barron. Not since I told her she was still mine.

My shirt was folded at the foot of the bed. The one she wore when she let me fuck her mouth like silence was the only language she trusted.

I ran my fingers across the edge. Felt the fabric pull. She always rolled the sleeves.

I turned. Walked to her room. Her real room. Not the dumping ground I put her in for the first few nights. The light was off. I didn't turn it on.

I opened the door and stood at the threshold. It felt like standing at the edge of something that could still hurt me.

The bed was unmade. Sheets tangled. Pillow dented.

The robe she wore the last time I saw her hung on the back of the door. Her shoes were lined up by the dresser.

I stepped inside. The air was different here. Like it remembered her.

I walked to the dresser. Opened the top drawer. Everything was folded. Too neat. Like she thought she'd come back to it.

Like she thought she'd wake up in this bed tomorrow. The bed called to me like a punishment.

I sat down. Hands on my knees. The leather of my gloves creaked as I flexed my fingers. They hadn't taken her from my arms. They'd taken her from my trust. That was worse. *That was what I wouldn't forgive.*

I leaned forward. Set my elbows on my knees. Then reached for the nightstand drawer. Opened it. Her other collar still sat inside. Polished. Untouched. Waiting.

I ran my thumb across the inside. The engraving I never let her read: *What you give me is breath.*

I closed my eyes. Let the silence echo. Let it sound like her. But it didn't. *Not anymore.*

Because her phone was here. It shouldn't have been. Not facedown. Not hidden.

It should've been in her coat. In her fucking hand. Not left like a forgotten truth under the sheets.

And the second that landed—the second it hit me—something inside me snapped. I didn't fold the sheets back. I *ripped* them.

Tore the bed apart like it had lied to me. Like it had *swallowed* her. I grabbed the mattress and *flipped* it.

Hard.

It slammed against the floorboards with a sound that didn't echo—

it *shook*. Feathers spilled from the pillow I'd crushed in one fist. My other hand punched the frame backward, sent it crashing against the wall.

Wood cracked. My knuckles split. I didn't stop. I kicked the nightstand so hard it bounced off the drywall and collapsed sideways. The drawer flew open. Empty.

Everything was fucking empty.

Except—beneath the mattress.

Tucked into the dark.

Half-concealed.

Like it was waiting.

Her phone.

Face down.

Cold.

Her phone.

I froze. Not the one I gave her. The old one. The one she stopped using weeks ago.

The screen was cracked in the corner. Still had the same lock screen background—Camille's photo, half-cropped, too bright. It shouldn't have been here.

I stared at it. The screen cracked at the corner. A line spiderwebbed down the side like a fracture in glass you can feel before you see.

I didn't breathe.

I picked it up slowly. Like it might hurt me. Like it already had. My thumb hovered over the power button. It was warm. Not from use. From memory.

I closed my hand around it. Carried it to the nightstand. Plugged it in. The cord trembled slightly as I pushed it into place. I watched the battery icon flicker to life. Twenty percent. Then thirty. Then the screen lit fully. She hadn't changed her wallpaper.

It was still the photo I'd taken of her in the passenger seat of my car. Hair a mess. Eyes laughing. Lips parted. It didn't look like a girl in love. *It looked like a girl who finally believed she was safe.*

The first notification flashed across the screen.

Missed call.

Missed call.

Missed call.

Then a message icon.

Not received.

Drafted.

I touched it. The text opened. Only one line. *I love you. I'm sorry I made you trust me.*

My knees gave before my rage did. I sat on the edge of the bed, phone in one hand, the other gripping the collar I hadn't put on her.

I stared at the words. I read them once. Twice. And then I let them echo. Because she hadn't sent it.

She hadn't given me the chance to reply. Because somewhere between loving me and leaving the room, she had decided it was her burden to carry. Her fault to own.

I rubbed my thumb across the screen. The words blurred. Not from the glass. From the water I didn't feel leave my eyes. I hadn't cried in years. Not since Camille.

Not since her fingers went cold in mine and I realized love was just another way to bury someone you weren't willing to let go. But now? Now the weight felt different.

It felt like someone had handed me her heart still beating and told me to keep it safe—and I hadn't even noticed when it stopped.

I looked down at the screen again. The message stared back. Not a question. Not a confession. A farewell.

I opened a new message. Typed her name. The cursor blinked.

I couldn't find the words. There weren't any left that she hadn't already given me. So I let it sit there. An unfinished answer to a message never sent.

I turned the phone over. Laid it face down on the bed. Stood. If they thought they could unmake her—they hadn't seen what I looked like when I remembered how to feel.

And now?

Now I was feeling everything.

The table wasn't meant to be a table. It was meant to be weight.

The kind of weight you gather in one place when the rest of the world has stopped listening. It sat in the center of the room like a reckoning, the same one we'd used to map Camille's murder, to erase enemies, to draw a line between empire and extinction.

Tonight it was bare. For now.

I dragged Camille's journal from my bedroom. My fingers didn't shake, but the space between my breaths did. I carried it like it was fragile. Like it had weight she left for me to break.

I set it down. The pages fluttered. A whisper. Like she was still breathing somewhere between the lines.

I opened it. The brothers were already arriving. Loyal first, silent as breath, laptop under one arm, his hair damp like he hadn't bothered to dry it.

Then Royal, shirt half-buttoned, cigarette tucked behind his ear, eyes sharp. Barron last. Always last. Always deliberate. He closed the door behind him. None of them asked what we were doing. They knew. They felt it in the floor.

I stood at the head of the table and flipped the journal open to the red-marked page. If I disappear, it wasn't an accident. Royal moved first. Took his seat. Crossed one leg over the other like this was a boardroom.

Loyal sat next, fingers already flying across keys. Barron stood. Didn't need to sit. He leaned one hand on the corner of the table and stared at Camille's handwriting like it might unwrite the last five years.

I traced my thumb across her ink. Her pen had bled at the edge. She must have written it fast. Maybe afraid. Maybe not. She was never the type to run. Only to kneel when she was ready to kill something.

"They knew about her long before we did," I said.

No one interrupted.

"She left this for us. Not just names. Not just accounts."

I flipped the page. There it was. A signature. Not Camille's. The name of a man we'd buried years ago. Or thought we had. Barron's voice was rough.

"That's the broker who handled our first offshore pivot."

Loyal nodded.

"He disappeared right after Camille."

Royal leaned forward.

"Guess he didn't disappear far enough."

I turned another page. It was a map. Sketched by hand. No street names. Just lines. Arrows. A warehouse circled twice in black.

"She was watching them," I said.

"And they found out," Loyal added.

I tapped the map.

"This is where they took her."

No one argued. Because we all felt it. In our chests. That pull. That fire. I closed the book. Not to end it. To contain it. Royal reached for a pen. Circled the warehouse with a red marker.

"I want the fucking floor plan," he said.

Loyal was already pulling it up. Barron stepped back. Crossed his arms. He didn't speak. Didn't have to. He looked at me. Like he was ready. Like he was asking if I was.

I met his stare. And I didn't blink. Because ready was a lie. I was made for this. Built in the dark.

Born in the silence between grief and revenge. Camille had handed me the end of something that never should have started. And Cloe?She had screamed for me.

So now I'd make sure no one could ever scream again without remembering what I sounded like when I answered.

I opened the cabinet like it was confession.

The key turned slow. The click echoed in my skull like a trigger pulled back but not released. The door creaked. Not from rust—from restraint. I hadn't opened it in years. Not since Camille. Not since we put the blades away and agreed to pretend we could build something clean.

The hinges held their breath. Inside was steel. Cold. Clean. Familiar. The first thing I touched was the knife.

Black hilt. Matte edge. No polish. No shine. A weapon meant for darkness. I picked it up and turned it in my palm. The balance hadn't changed. Neither had I. Not really.

I strapped it to my thigh. The weight felt right. The second was the pistol. Sleek. Heavy. My fingers curled around the grip like they remembered.

I popped the clip. Full. Of course it was. I kept it loaded for a reason. Not hope. Memory. Because someday, I knew I'd need to kill like Camille was still watching.

I holstered it. Loyal walked into the room. He didn't speak. He opened the second cabinet. Pulled out another case. Laid it on the bed.

A shotgun. Tactical. Beautiful. Royal came next. He picked the crowbar. No hesitation. Barron stood in the doorway. Still. Watching. Like he was trying to decide if this was us breaking or becoming something new.

I turned to him.

"You're not going to talk me out of this."

He nodded.

"Good," he said. "Because I wouldn't know how."

I slid the second blade into the sheath at my hip. One more across my back. Three. Always three. One for the throat. One for the ribs. *One for the man who thinks I won't go for the eyes.*

Royal set a duffel on the floor. Opened it. Ammo. Flash bangs. Zip cuffs.

"We going in clean or loud?" he asked.

I looked at him. And I smiled.

"Both."

Loyal snapped the case shut.

"She was screaming," he said. "In the footage. *She called your name.*"

I closed my eyes.

I heard it again.

WOLFE.

Not a plea. A command. A summons.

My body locked around it like it had never been unmade. Like my name belonged in her mouth more than oxygen.

I opened my eyes.

"Then we answer."

Barron crossed the room. Grabbed a blade of his own. It was his father's. Still sharp. Still bloodstained. He didn't flinch.

I walked to the table. Set the journal down. Camille's handwriting stared back at me. Names. Numbers. A time. I tapped the page.

"That's where she is."

Royal looked up. "How do you know."

I stared at the pages. "That's where I'd take her."

Loyal nodded. Royal cracked his knuckles. Barron pulled the slide on his pistol. The room went quiet. Not from fear. From reverence. My phone buzzed once.

A new message. No name. Just the initials: *MQ.*

Forget the warehouse. Tower rooftop. Forty minutes. It's real.

Mason.

I stared at it. Last I spoke to Mason, he was on recon. Watching the apartment. Watching her building. *He touched her. Find him.*

I hadn't needed to say more. Now this. If Mason said move—

I moved. I strapped the last piece across my chest. Barron caught the look in my eyes.

"What is it?"

"Mason says to meet at the tower."

Royal looked up. "Why?"

"I don't know."

Still, he'd never failed me before.

Loyal closed the laptop. "Then we go."

"All of us," Barron said.

"He's waiting," I muttered. "She's close."

34

————

WOLFE

THE CITY NEVER SLEEPS. But tonight, it held its breath. We parked two blocks from the tower. Didn't say a word. Didn't need to.

Barron walked like the weight of his father's name had settled across his spine again. Royal's hands never left the crowbar. Loyal didn't blink—his pulse a straight line, his jaw locked around unspoken math.

And me? I walked like I'd already buried myself. I wasn't here to talk. I was here to take her back.

The Lawlor Tower rose like a mausoleum—steel and glass stacked over secrets. The front doors glinted under the streetlights. Too quiet. Too clean. A corpse dressed in chrome. Something was off.

Even the city seemed to know. The hum of traffic a few blocks away, muffled. Lights on nearby towers flickered—not out, not blinking. Just... uncertain.

No security in the foyer. No desk staff. No lights on the lower floors.

The reflection in the front glass looked more like a funeral procession than a team of men. Barron noticed it first. He stopped halfway across the street, eyes narrowing.

"Where the fuck are the guards?"

I didn't answer. Didn't slow. Just kept walking.

The front doors opened before I touched them. Not with the usual buzz. Not with the usual click. Just silence. Like breath held in a lung that was never meant to release.

The air inside was wrong. Cold without source. Clean without scent.

The kind of sterile that didn't belong in buildings—it belonged in graves. This building raised me. I bled into its walls. I mapped out revenge in these rooms. Now it smelled like strangers.

Loyal's hand went to his sidearm. "We're exposed here."

Royal didn't speak. Just nodded once and tapped his heel against the marble floor.

"Too quiet," he muttered.

Barron's gaze swept the corners. "They want us upstairs."

"I'm not playing fetch," he added. But he still moved.

The lobby lights were dimmed low. Just enough to see by. The artwork on the walls cast long, distorted shadows. We walked past the oil painting of the Lawlor patriarch—his eyes seemed to follow us now, more than ever.

We reached the elevators. One stood open. Waiting. The light above it blinked. Not out of order. Not misfiring. Pulsing. It was *ready*.

Barron stepped in first. Then Loyal. Then Royal. I entered last.

As the doors slid closed, I turned to face them. And for a moment, we were trapped in glass and steel and the tension of everything we didn't say.

The elevator was too bright. The lighting buzzed faintly. It cast our shadows long on the mirrored interior. None of us looked like ourselves.

Barron's reflection seemed older. Angrier. Loyal's was still. Too still. Royal's gaze flicked, scanning for patterns in nothing. And mine? Mine stared straight ahead. Hollowed out. Fixed on a door that hadn't opened yet.

Each floor ticked by like a heartbeat.

Like a countdown.

Thirty-seven. Thirty-eight. Thirty-nine—

Forty.

The doors opened. Silence. The air hit like a slap. Stale. Warm in the wrong way. Processed. Recycled.

The lighting here was off—different bulbs, slightly blue. A single overhead fixture flickered like it was glitching out of reality. We stepped into the hallway. And the world turned colder.

To the right, a streak of something.

Dark. Wet. Reflective.

Blood.

Not dried. Not old. Loyal crouched. Touched it with ungloved fingers.

"Still warm."

The trail led forward. Dragged across the floor. Heavy, staggering lines like someone had been hauled or tried to crawl. We followed it.

It turned down the corridor to security. A second smear joined it—hand prints. One palm. Then another. Fingers bent at the wrong angle.

Then we saw him. Reynolds. Our night security. Slumped against the alarm panel. Blood pooled around him. One arm stretched toward the emergency trigger. His index finger was broken. Hanging by tendon. One inch from the switch.

"He tried," Royal said.

"Didn't make it," Barron replied.

No one moved.

Then I stepped forward. Closed Reynolds' eyes. His hand was shaking. Even dead, it hadn't let go. We moved on. The corridor narrowed. Sound deadened.

Our footfalls vanished into the carpet. Only the hum of the building beneath our boots remained. A subtle vibration.

Wrong.

The lights overhead flickered. Once. Then again. Royal paused at the office breakroom. Pushed the door open with the crowbar.

Inside—

Coffee on the counter. Still steaming. Someone had been here. Recently.

Barron checked the fridge. Nothing.

Loyal opened a cupboard. Empty. Whoever had been here had taken what mattered. Left the rest as a decoy.

I moved forward. Toward the executive wing. The glass doors to our suite were open. That never happened. The corridor breathed around us. Not with air. With *attention*.

Every motion sensor watched. Every light flicker whispered. This building didn't just contain us. It had been *waiting* for us. The lights in the office were wrong. Too bright. Too even. Every bulb replaced. Every panel humming.

Then I smelled it.

Copper.

Acid.

Decay.

Not just death.

Something *intentional*.

Then we saw Mason.

He wasn't slumped.

He was *nailed* to the back wall.

Arms stretched wide. Palms pierced. Feet together, bolt

through the ankle. His torso had been opened. Ribs cracked. Skin peeled back.

Words were carved into the meat of his chest:

TOO LATE.

His eyes—only one left—stared past us.

Wide open. Frozen.

His mouth had been torn open. Tongue missing. Cheeks cut into a forced smile. Royal cursed. Loud. Real. Loyal took a step back. "They staged him."

"This is a message," Barron growled.

"No," I said. "This is a monument."

Royal stepped back and slammed his fist into the glass. It spiderwebbed but didn't break.

Loyal turned his face away. Barron drew his gun—not to aim it. Just to *hold* something. No one said it, but we were all thinking it. If Mason could die here, *so could we.*

I walked forward. Took Mason's phone. The screen was still on. One draft. Unsent.

It's not her.

It's a—

Then nothing. Glitched characters. A blank line. The signal cut. I looked back. The hallway behind us was dark now. Lights out. Doors sealed.

"Move," I said.

We entered the main suite. I stepped into the boardroom and rested my hand on the table. It was warm. Not ambient. *Wired.* I looked down and saw it then—

The edge of a cable. Taped to the underside. Painted black.

Hidden in plain sight.

That's when we saw them. Wires. Everywhere. Taped to the ceiling. Run along the floorboards. Hidden beneath the rug. Connected to a black box under the boardroom table.

Red lights blinking.

If I disappear, it wasn't an accident.

Camille's voice.

Ours now.

"Fuck," Loyal breathed.

He ran forward. Opened the box. Inside: enough explosives to level the tower. Thermal charges. Shaped. Timed.

"This is military grade."

Barron reached into his coat. "Disable it."

"I can't," Loyal said. "Not in time."

I looked at him.

Dead calm.

"How much time?"

He didn't answer. There was no timer. Just a signal. Waiting. Trip wire. Motion. Maybe remote.

"Back," I ordered, panic rising like a wave. *"GET THE FUCK BACK!"*

Loyal's voice cracked.

"We were never meant to walk out."

But it was too late.

A flicker in my head.

Camille—standing in this room years ago, laughing, alive.

Then Camille—*bleeding*.

Then Cloe. *Screaming*.

Then—

Darkness.

The lights died. The door behind us locked. And the room screamed. High-pitched. Metal shriek. Not from the bomb. From the speakers. Feedback. A final warning.

I reached for the collar.

Held it tight.

Pressed it to my lips like communion.

Like prayer.

Like the last breath I'd ever take would taste of her.

Barron raised his gun. Royal clenched the crowbar. Loyal didn't move. Just stared. Then the floor vibrated. One long pulse. The air thinned. Collapsed. Bled.

And as the world went white—

As the room erupted into light and heat and end—

I swear I heard her voice. Not begging. Not afraid. Just saying my name.

Once. Like salvation. Like damnation. Like the only thing that ever mattered.

Then

nothing.

3 5

———

CLOE

THEY STRAPPED me tighter this time.

No more rope. No more half-knots that left room to twist or slide.

This time it was leather. Thick. Stiff. Fastened with buckles that groaned when tightened. My arms pulled behind me until my shoulders screamed. Ankles shackled to the legs of the chair so wide it felt deliberate, like the posture itself was meant to humiliate.

My skin stung where they'd cleaned the blood too roughly. Salt water, maybe. Something meant to disinfect. Or punish.

My hair stuck to the side of my face. My lip was split again. I could taste the iron every time I tried to swallow.

They didn't gag me this time. Not because they were giving me kindness. Because they were waiting for the scream. I didn't give it to them.

The room was lit from above now. Harsh. Fluorescent. Artificial to the point of cruelty. It made the concrete gleam. Made the cracks in the floor pulse like veins. Made the shadows longer than they should have been.

There were no windows. No clock. No sense of time except the way my body ached in cycles.

The light flickered.

I flinched.

Not from fear.

From instinct.

The hum of the bulb buzzed in the walls. It echoed in my skull. A white noise that filled every breath I didn't take properly. I counted between the flickers. Between the soft scrapes of movement I heard behind the walls. Between my own shallow inhales.

Someone was watching. I knew it. I could feel it in my spine. The same way I used to feel Wolfe watching me from across the room, back when I thought his silence was the scariest thing in the world.

I would have traded this for his silence in a heartbeat. This wasn't silence. *This was theater.*

The room had been cleaned. The floor scrubbed. The smell of bleach not strong enough to erase the metallic tang that lived in the corners. The chair bolted to the floor now. A camera mounted high in the corner—I only saw it because the lens caught a glint when the light above it blinked.

They weren't hiding me anymore. They were *staging me.*

My chest rose and fell in slow, even breaths. I made it do that. I made myself inhale when I wanted to choke. Exhale when I wanted to sob. Every controlled breath was another second they hadn't taken from me.

The wound on my hip throbbed. I didn't know if it was infected. I didn't care. Pain was familiar. Pain I understood. Pain was the thread I followed back to myself.

My fingers were going numb. The leather bit into the nerves at my wrist. I tried to move. Just a twitch. Enough to keep blood moving. A mistake. A speaker clicked on overhead. Static. Then silence. They were listening.

I blinked up at the camera. Didn't flinch. Let them watch. Let them see what I looked like after Wolfe put a collar around my throat and taught me to kneel. Let them see who they took.Because I wasn't prey. Not anymore.

The door didn't open. Not yet.

But I heard the lock turn.

The air shifted.

I inhaled.

Held it.

Let the war start with breath. They didn't rush. That was the first thing I noticed. No one rushed in this place. Everything was done slow. Calculated. Like they were trying to teach me what helplessness looked like when it wore confidence.

The door opened with the same calm it always did. Just a click of the lock, a gentle push, the metal swinging wide like it had nothing to fear.

The man who entered wasn't one I recognized. Not from before. Not from the others. He was clean-cut. Suit crisp. Black-on-black. Like he thought the sharpness of his appearance made him more civilized. Like the shine on his shoes made him less monstrous.

But I knew better. I'd learned that kind of polish before. I'd kissed it. Served it. Let it use my mouth until I forgot my own name. And still I knew Wolfe was something else. This man didn't hold power. He wore it like it could be washed off.

He didn't speak at first. Just set a black case down on the table beside the chair. Flipped the latches open. One by one. The clicks echoed too loud in the cement room. Sharp. Precise.

I kept my eyes on him. He didn't look at me. Not yet.

Inside the case was a camera. Not a handheld. A mounted

one. High-end. Professional. With a wireless feed and a red light that blinked slow and steady like a heartbeat.

He lifted it carefully. Set it on a tripod. Turned it toward me. That's when he looked up. And smiled.

It was a practiced smile. The kind people give to news anchors and politicians. Empty. Meant to distract.

"We'll be live in five," he said.

Live.

The word hit harder than his stare.

I clenched my jaw. Didn't speak. He didn't seem to mind. He adjusted the lens. Zoomed in. Tilted the frame. He took his time. My chest rose and fell slowly.

I could feel every bruise stretch with each inhale. Every cut throb beneath the bandages they wrapped too tightly. My wrists were already bleeding again. I could feel the drip tracing down the side of my palm.

He stepped back. Nodded once.

"You're going to be the proof."

I said nothing.

"That the Lawlors bleed like anyone else."

The screen mounted behind him flickered to life.

A feed.

Live.

The Lawlor building. Wide shot. Pulled from street level. A cameraman's vantage. Cars passing. People walking. A normal day. Then the timer appeared in the top left corner.

Red.

Counting down from fifteen seconds.

I stared.

The seconds fell like teeth.

Twelve.

Ten.

Eight.

Something moved in the window.

Third floor.

The office I used to stand outside when Wolfe wouldn't let me in.

Five.

Four.

A flash.

Not fire.

Light.

Then the glass exploded outward.

A bloom of orange and black erupted through the facade. The windows shattered. People screamed. The camera jolted. Refocused. Smoke poured out of the hole in the building like the structure was exhaling its secrets.

I didn't blink. The man beside me didn't move. He just adjusted the volume. The screams got louder. Sirens in the distance. The feed switched angles. Another camera.

Closer.

The fire crawled across the frame like it had hands.

And then I saw him. Not Wolfe. Royal. Stumbling out of the smoke. Shirt torn. Blood streaking down one arm. His mouth moved, shouting something I couldn't hear.

The audio lagged. Then it caught up.

"WOLFE!"

His voice cracked through the speaker like it had teeth. My body jolted like he'd screamed it into me. The name hit harder than anything they'd done to my skin.

It wasn't just pain. It was a vow. And I knew—if Wolfe was still a name being shouted, then Wolfe was still alive. Then Wolfe was still *alive.*

He dropped to his knees in front of the building. Grabbed at the dirt. Dragged himself forward. Then the screen cut to black.

The man beside me turned the camera toward me. I stared into the lens. Not at him. Not at the feed. But at what they thought they were doing.

They thought they were making a statement. I was the proof. But I was also the weapon. Because they hadn't buried me yet. And Wolfe? He would set the world on fire to drag me out of this room.

They changed the feed. No warning. One second I was staring at Royal—bloodied, staggering, clawing his way toward the front of the Lawlor building like he could pull it back from collapse with his bare hands.

The next?

Wolfe's apartment filled the screen.

Not from the inside. Not the way I remembered it. Not the warmth of the kitchen under low lights. Not the smell of cedar and espresso in the morning. Not the way the bedroom looked when I stripped for him in silence.

This was outside. Street-level. Distant. A wide shot of the building's face. The windows all mirrored black. Still. Untouched. Until they weren't.

The camera zoomed in just as the second window blew out. Third floor. His bedroom.

The fire wasn't loud on screen. It rolled out of the frame like it had been waiting to breathe. Smoke thick and crawling. Glass rained from the frame. Pieces scattered across the sidewalk like broken promises. I knew that window. I knew that room. I knew the shape of the sheets he'd made me bleed into. And I knew he hadn't been in that bed since I left.

But still—

"*Oh.*"

Agony ripped through me, like a rib cracked open. That building held more than his name. It held the last place I felt chosen. The last place I felt real.

This wasn't about killing him. This was about burning the *last place I had been real*. The place I had curled against his chest and slept like I wasn't made of teeth. They weren't trying to destroy him. They were trying to *erase* me. The man beside me chuckled.

"No one was home," he said. "Shame. But you get the point, right?"

"You were his home," he said, too casual. "So we burned it."

I didn't blink.

Because I knew what came next.

If they thought that house held him—

They never understood what it meant to be Wolfe's.

I didn't answer. I'd already seen the point. And soon, Wolfe would too.

The screen flickered. Went black again. Silence pulsed in its place. I stared into it like it could stare back. And I realized—

They weren't just trying to hurt him. They were trying to unmake him. By taking me. By burning every space I had ever touched. By showing me exactly what it looked like to be erased. But I wasn't gone yet.

And Wolfe? Wolfe was still breathing. Which meant they'd made their final mistake. I didn't speak. I didn't move. Not even when the screen went black.

I closed my eyes. Squeezing them tight. I wanted to scream again. I wanted to tear at the leather straps cutting into my wrists, wanted to claw through the chair, the wall, the fucking city. But I stayed still. Because stillness was the only weapon I had left.

The door opened behind me. No sound, no warning. The only sign was the shift in the air, the subtle shift of pressure, like the room itself knew who had walked in and was already bracing for impact.

I didn't turn. I couldn't. But I felt him. The clean one. The man with shoes that didn't touch dust. The one who set the cameras, controlled the angles, directed the grief.

I opened my eyes. He circled slowly. Not because he needed to. Because he wanted me to feel it. The calm of a predator with nowhere else to be.

When he came into view again, I didn't look away. His hands were clasped behind his back. His eyes scanned my face with a precision that made my stomach twist. He didn't smile. Not this time.

"I think you misunderstand your role here," he said.

I didn't answer.

He crouched, folded his body with a grace that didn't match the room, didn't match the stink of old blood under the bleach, didn't belong in a place where people like me were made to bleed.

"You think this is about you," he said. "But it's not."

He leaned in closer. His voice dropped.

"It was *never* about you."

I felt my jaw tighten. Not from fear. From clarity.

"Camille," I whispered.

He nodded.

Slow.

"Smart girl."

He reached into his coat. Pulled something folded. Laid it across my lap.

A photo. I stared at it. Her face. Camille. But not how I remembered her. Not laughing. Not smirking. Cold. Still. Dead.

There was blood smeared across her mouth. Her eyes were half-open. Like she died seeing who did it. I wondered if she smiled when she saw it coming. If she knew we would carry her name like armor.

My breath caught. He dropped another. *Me.* From the corner of the room. Tied. Slumped. Bruised. Now.

"You're just a placeholder," he said.

I met his eyes. And smiled. Because Wolfe taught me to breathe through death. Because Barron taught me to kneel without breaking. Because Camille died screaming in silence— and I was still breathing.

He stood.

"Your scream won't matter," he said.

He stepped closer.

I didn't flinch.

"You think someone's coming?"

He leaned down. So close his breath brushed my cheek.

"No one survives this."

I turned my face slightly.

Let my mouth hover near his ear.

And I whispered: "He does." He froze. Just for a second.

And it was enough. I saw it. The crack. The fracture. The fear. Then he turned. Left the photos on my lap. And walked out.

The door shut. The lock clicked. And I stared down at Camille's dead eyes. And made a vow. *You won't forget us. You won't bury us. And I won't be the one they mourn.*

The sound of money has a rhythm. Soft, slick, like pages in a book being thumbed too fast. Not a shuffle. A hiss. Like breath caught in a chest.

That was the first thing I heard when the door opened again. Not boots. Not shouting. Not pain. Just cash. Counted slow. Fingers wet from sweat pressing each bill down with care. He was humming. Low. Off-key. The tune didn't matter. The ease did.

I didn't look up. I didn't have to. I knew who it was by the way the air changed. The room went heavier. More personal. Like the walls leaned in.

He walked past the camera. Past the chair he'd once strapped me to. He didn't glance at the screen still blinking quietly in the corner. The images of smoke and flame were old news now.

He sat on the crate to my right. Set the money down beside him. Stacks. Hundreds. Bound tight. Clean. *Too clean.*

My wrists ached from their bindings. My skin was slick with sweat, blood, adrenaline that never crested. My throat was raw. But I still had breath. And that meant I still had Wolfe.

He stared at the money for a while. Didn't speak. Just admired it. Ran his finger along the edge of each bundle like he couldn't decide whether to count it again or just fuck it.

He exhaled through his nose.

"It's funny," he said. "When you think about it. All this for one girl."

I didn't answer. My voice was gone. Not from screaming. From holding it back. Because they didn't deserve to hear me. Not until Wolfe was there to silence them. He looked over at me finally. Eyes small. Pale. Cold.

"You cost a lot of men a lot of debt."

He leaned forward. His elbows rested on his knees. He smelled like salt and cigarettes and power that never learned to whisper.

"You know," he said, "I was supposed to get shot four months ago. Back of the head. Strip club in Southwood. But you?"

He chuckled.

"You bought me time."

His hand reached out. Slow. Gentle. It brushed a strand of hair from my face. I didn't flinch. I didn't blink. He leaned in close.

"That's the thing about whores who think they're saints," he whispered. "You always get used."

I let him touch me. I wanted his fingerprints on my skin. He would see them. And Wolfe wouldn't carve. He would *ruin.*

The shark sat back. He picked up a cigarette. Lit it. Took one long drag. Blew the smoke toward the ceiling like the air above me didn't matter.

"Guess it was a stroke of luck I grabbed you when I did," he said.

He gestured to the TV. The image was looping now. The Lawlor building crumbling again and again like the footage refused to end.

He turned to me.

"So," he said, voice almost bored, "what are we gonna do about the money you owe me?"

He stood. Stepped in front of me. The smoke curled around his head. His shirt clung to his back. He reached down. Took my chin in his fingers.

"You gonna work it off? Is that it?"

He smiled.

"Or maybe we cut our losses. Make a new video. Send it to your boyfriend. Let him hear what it sounds like when someone else ruins you."

I stared into his eyes. And smiled. I didn't need to fight him. I just needed him to breathe. So Wolfe would know where to strike.

I heard it. Outside. Distant. A crack. Not thunder. Gunfire.

Another.

Closer.

The shark didn't hear it.

Not yet. But I did.

Because I was *his* leash.

And he was coming to drag me back.

36

WOLFE

Darkness wasn't quiet.

It cracked. Hissed. Hummed like bones remembering how to scream. I opened my eyes into black. But I didn't see the dark. I *felt* it. It pressed against my ribs. Tasted like concrete and fire. Buzzed in my teeth like the aftershock of a scream I hadn't heard yet.

Something was on my chest. Heavy. Sharp. Dust choked the air. My lungs seized. Coughed. Pain followed. Real. Immediate. Alive. I tried to move. My right hand shifted. The left didn't.

Pinned. I didn't panic. I reached across my body, fingers shaking, and pushed. Concrete gave way. Barely. The air tasted like wires burning. Like the Lawlor name finally dying.

I shifted again.

Grunted.

And then—

A groan. A voice.

Close.

"Fuck... Wolfe?"

Royal.

I turned my head. Pain spiderwebbed down my spine.

Fragments before the explosion came back.

Baron aiming his gun at the glass walls.

Royal driving the crowbar through the glass for us to escape.

We did. Somehow we made it to the stairwell door.

I found him now. Royal. Slumped against the wall, face covered in blood, one eye swollen shut. Still breathing. Barron was a few feet from him. On his knees. Hand pressed to his scalp. Blood soaked through his shirt. His voice was shredded.

"Go," he croaked.

"Save her."

I pushed off the wall. Staggered forward. My boots slid against the rubble. Everything tilted. My breath hitched. Then warmth. Running down my side. I looked down. Red. Too red.

I found it. Embedded. Metal. Long. Jagged. Stuck just above my hip, angling deep beneath the ribs.

I gritted my teeth.

Gripped the shaft.

The jagged edges dug into my palm.

Tore the skin.

I pulled. Pain hit like a lightning bolt. White. Radiating. Consuming. But I didn't scream. I *never* screamed.

The metal came free with a sick, wet hiss. My vision doubled. Then tripled. Blood ran into my eye. Or maybe it was sweat. Or memory.

For a second I thought I heard Camille's voice—

But it wasn't her. It was the hum. Low. Distant. Real.

I dropped it. Let it clatter to the floor. Blood poured down my side. Warm. Relentless.

I staggered to my feet. Legs trembling. The stairwell had held—barely. Everything else hadn't.

Loyal was buried under debris. I saw the movement of his chest. Shallow. Alive. Royal pushed to his feet, using the wall.

"You good?"

"No," I said.

"Let's go."

We moved. Or limped. Or dragged what was left of us.

The hallway above us was caved in. The floor below cracked open. There was no ceiling anymore—just the night sky. Just smoke. Just the sound of sirens from too far away.

But I still had it.

The collar.

My fist clenched around it so hard the leather creaked. It smelled like ash and her skin.

I pressed it to my mouth. Not like prayer. Like a fucking promise. My hand was bleeding, but it held. Tight. Like a life-line. Barron leaned against the wall. Nodded once. Eyes clear.

"Get her back."

I nodded. Turned. And crawled. My knees dragged across shattered glass. My palms tore open on broken tile. One nail bent back. Snapped.

I didn't stop. I didn't look back. I moved like a man who knew where God lived—and meant to kill him for taking her.

Through the smoke. Through the ash. Through the ruin of everything they thought would stop me.

I wasn't crawling toward survival. I was crawling toward her voice. And every breath I took was one they wouldn't.

37

CLOE

I woke to white.

Not light.

White.

Bleached walls. Bleached air. Bleached silence. Even the ceiling was wrong—too smooth, too clean, like it had never belonged to anyone.

The floor beneath me wasn't cold. It was indifferent.

A slab of concrete dressed in perfection, humming with fluorescent lights that didn't flicker. There were no shadows here. No edges. Just brightness. Just exposure.

And I was alone.

The gag was tight. Fabric soaked in something chemical. My tongue tasted metal. My lips were cracked. No chains. No ropes. Just absence. They'd taken everything. The collar. My shirt. My sound. And given me back silence.

I moved slowly. Sat up. My muscles ached. My stomach burned. Not like pain. Like consumption.

The hunger was sharp already. Coiled. Alive. Not the dull gnaw of missed meals. This was deeper. This was cellular.

I tried to remember when I last ate.

Soup.

Wolfe's kitchen. Kneeling on the floor. Devouring survival like it could anchor me.

I swallowed around the gag. Air rasped down my throat. The room had no corners. I crawled to the nearest wall. Pressed my hand to it. It didn't give.

There was a mirror on the far side. But not mine. A window. One-way. I couldn't see who watched. But I felt them.

The weight of it settled on my skin like breath that didn't belong to me. I sat back. Pulled my knees to my chest. The hunger shifted. Deepened. Every organ inside me turned on the others.

My body was already devouring itself. But they didn't come. They didn't feed me. They didn't speak.

I rocked once. Twice. The silence never broke. I pressed my forehead to my knees. Inhaled the scent of my own sweat, my own fear, my own unfinished screams. And I waited. That was the game. That was the point. To let me listen to the sound of my own body failing. To teach me what power sounded like when it wore silence.

My throat clenched. I couldn't swallow. The gag was too tight. But I didn't cry. I didn't whimper. I didn't beg. I breathed. And in the white light of that windowless room, I became something new. Not clean. Not broken. Just waiting. Breath was all I had. And it was still mine.

The lights never turned off. They didn't flicker. Didn't hum. Didn't shift from harsh to soft like they had any intention of pretending to care. They just burned overhead with that surgical, all-knowing glow. Flat. Cold. Constant. Like time didn't pass here. Like it wasn't supposed to.

There were no clocks. Just the weight of my own body

reminding me that I hadn't eaten. That I hadn't stood. That I hadn't been touched in hours. Maybe longer.

I'd stopped counting. Or maybe I never started. Because time only matters when someone might come. And no one came. Not yet.

The mirror on the far wall stared back at me. But it wasn't a mirror. Not really. It was a sheet of glass dressed in distance. A barrier designed to remind me that I wasn't alone—just invisible. My reflection was there if I shifted the angle. Just barely. Ghost-like. A smear of skin and bruises and collarbone and breath.

I sat with my back against the opposite wall. Legs folded. Spine bowed. Not because I was tired—though I was. But because the posture felt familiar. Felt safe. Felt mine.

The gag scraped the corners of my mouth. Dried spit flaked off every time I moved my jaw. My tongue was heavy. My stomach had stopped growling. It just curled in on itself now.

I stared at the mirror. I knew they were there. Someone was always watching. The feeling was too loud not to be real.

My skin itched from the awareness. Like eyes were peeling me back, layer by layer, documenting the erosion. Not looking for surrender. Looking for the moment before.

The moment just before I cracked.

The speaker crackled.

Just once.

Then silence.

It came again. Louder. Like someone tapping a microphone. Like they wanted me to flinch. I didn't. Then the voice came. Low. Smooth. Familiar.

Ellis.

"Let's see how long loyalty lasts without food."

That was all he said. Nothing else. No gloating. No warning. No name.

The speaker clicked off. And I was alone again. Only I wasn't. Because now it wasn't just about watching. It was about listening. They wanted to hear me fall apart. They wanted to record the breath before I begged.

But I didn't give them anything. Not the tremor in my spine. Not the pressure building behind my eyes. Not the twitch in my fingers that started every time my stomach twisted on itself like it was trying to devour whatever I had left.

I pressed my forehead to the floor. It was cold. Real. It grounded me. The tile didn't care if I survived. It would hold my body either way. But I did. I cared. I kept breathing. That was the only sound I still owned. And I made it loud enough for them to hear.

I smelled the food before I saw him. Not grease. Not rot. Not the sour staleness of whatever they kept hidden in sealed bags for other girls, other cells.

Real food. Warm. Bread. Meat. Steam.

I hated that my mouth watered. My body betrayed me before he even walked in. I tasted it behind the gag, like shame.

The door opened with the same click as before, the same hiss of hydraulic weight releasing, but this time it was slower. Staged. Like someone wanted me to feel it in my chest before they even stepped through.

Ellis Ward didn't walk in like a man with power. He walked in like a man who never had to reach for it.

He wore black. Tailored. His shoes caught no dust. His sleeves were rolled precisely one fold. The kind of perfection that made it look like none of this touched him. That I was just a smudge he planned to wipe off the glass.

He carried the tray with one hand. Balanced. Casual. The way Wolfe carried weapons. He didn't look at me right away. He set the tray on the floor. Too far to reach. Close enough to smell. Then he crouched. Not beside me. Across the room. Folded his arms over his knees. Watched me.

I didn't look at the tray again. I looked at him. Because I knew that's what he wanted. Because I wasn't here to crawl.

His mouth twitched like he wanted to smile.

"You're holding up well," he said. "All things considered."

I didn't respond. Couldn't. But my breath stayed even.

His eyes dropped to the floor between us.

"Camille begged by day three."

My body went still.

He saw it.

"She thought we were bluffing. Thought if she stayed quiet, if she stayed clever, we'd let her go."

He leaned forward.

"We did."

My heart stuttered.

He smiled now. Soft. Cruel.

"Thought maybe she'd forget what she saw. That if we gave her a window and a way out, she'd bury it herself."

He shrugged.

"But it didn't matter, did it, Cloe?"

My breath caught against the gag.

"No," he said, standing slowly, smoothing his sleeves. "We won't be making the same mistake with you."

He walked to the tray. Picked up the bread. Held it like it offended him. Then tossed it back onto the tray.

The sound was louder than it should've been. He didn't look at me again. He didn't have to. Because I wasn't supposed to fight. I was supposed to starve. I was supposed to fade. But I didn't.

I closed my eyes. And I bit down on the gag. Hard. Pain kept me present. And I wasn't Camille.

They wouldn't let me go. But I wouldn't leave anything

behind to clean. It didn't happen all at once. That was the cruelty of it. The slowness. The erosion.

My body didn't scream anymore. It whispered. Little things. The twist in my gut. The way my eyes pulsed every time I blinked. The low throb in the back of my skull that made light feel like needles.

My mouth was too dry to swallow. The gag rubbed every time I breathed, and now even breath had turned to friction.

I lay on my side. The tray was still on the floor. The food cold now. Forgotten. A performance that ended when he walked out. A script he didn't need to finish. He left it there so I could fail in front of it. I didn't. But I was close.

My thighs shook. My ribs stung with every inhale. I felt the sweat between my shoulder blades go cold, then dry, then return again. I didn't know how long I'd been like this. But I knew I was slipping.

The light overhead buzzed. My eyes fluttered. And then I wasn't in the room anymore. Not fully. The white walls softened. Warped. The mirror melted into shadow. The floor no longer pressed cold into my cheek. Something else did. Fabric.

I blinked again. The shadows shifted. A woman sat across from me. She wasn't real. But she was there.

Camille.

Not in the dress they buried her in. Not in the photo Barron kept on his desk. But in a plain blouse, sleeves rolled. Blood dried on the collar. Her lip split.

Her eyes didn't blink.

You're quieter than I was, she said.

My throat ached around the gag.

She tilted her head.

They hate that.

The lights flickered. I looked away. She was still there. Kneeling now.

You think you're here because you matter, she whispered. You're here because you remind them they're not God.

The floor shuddered beneath me. I couldn't move. My fingers curled into fists. Camille touched my shoulder. Or maybe I imagined it. It didn't matter. The voice stayed.

Let them watch. Let them count your bones. Let them measure your breath. But don't let them make you ask for it.

I stared at the ceiling. The light burned my retinas. Tears slipped down my temples. I wasn't crying. My body just didn't know what else to give. Camille's voice faded.

My vision blurred. But my mind sharpened. And I whispered her name inside my head. Not because I needed her. Because I wanted them to remember who they buried. And what rose up in her place. It started low. A vibration. Not in the room. In me.

In the hollowed space between my ribs where breath used to sit. In the curve of my throat where Wolfe had once fastened a collar and taught me how stillness could become worship. In the marrow of bones that hadn't broken but felt like they should have.

It didn't come from memory.

It came from refusal.

My lips cracked when I moved them. The corners split. The skin there had turned dry from the gag, from dehydration, from silence weaponized into obedience. But I moved them anyway.

My breath stuttered through the gag. Raspy. Raw.

And I hummed.

Just one note.

Low.

Ugly.

Broken.

It scratched the walls of my throat. Vibrated through my teeth.

And I held it.

The sound didn't travel far. The gag muted it. Muffled it. Made it small. But it was mine. It belonged to no one else. Not Ellis. Not the shark. Not the men behind the mirrored glass who watched me like I was a product waiting to be priced.

It was breath pulled from the part of me that hadn't given up. The part that refused to be quiet even when quiet was safer. Even when quiet was expected.

I hummed again. Higher this time. A little longer. My lungs burned. My head spun. But the sound held.

The light overhead didn't flicker. The tray of cold food still sat untouched in the corner. The mirror still stared back with nothing. But the hum filled the space between. Between me and them. Between what they thought they took and what I knew they couldn't have.

Wolfe would hear it. Not with his ears. But with the leash. The one we never needed to speak about. The one tied to breath. To blood. To every broken piece of me he hadn't tried to fix, only owned.

He would feel the pull. The vibration. The hum. And when he came, it wouldn't be to rescue me. It would be to end the silence. The hum wasn't a signal. It was war. And I was the anthem.

And Wolfe didn't need to hear it. He just needed to feel me still breathing—so he could decide who to kill first.

38

WOLFE

The engine cut but I didn't move. Blood soaked the waistband of my jeans. Sticky. Hot. Slowing now, but not gone.

I pulled open the glovebox. No gauze. No bandage. Just a roll of duct tape and a black cotton T-shirt she used to sleep in. I grabbed both. Pressed the fabric hard to my side. The cotton turned dark in seconds.

I wrapped the tape tight. Around my ribs. Around the shirt. A tourniquet made of memory and spite. My hands shook. Not from pain. From focus. This wasn't about surviving. It was about arriving. Alive enough to make him scream. And I still had the knife.

I reached into the trunk. Pulled the blades from their place beneath the mat. Strapped them one by one. Thigh. Ribs. Spine. Every sheath a breath. Every buckle a vow.

The city didn't slow. Cars passed. Headlights washed across my face. No one stopped. Just a man bleeding through his shirt, gripping steel, walking like death had given him a deadline.

I crossed the street. Down the alley. Past the graffiti that never faded. Toward the place they thought they could hide him.

He was waiting in the room at the end. Tied to a chair. Not scared. Not shaking. Just still. Like he thought being calm would make it better. Like he didn't know I was already walking toward him with Camille's name in my throat and a blade in my hand.

The door creaked as I opened it. Loud enough for him to flinch. Not enough to make me stop. The hallway smelled like bleach and piss. The light was yellow and low. Buzzing.

There was no mirror here. No observation glass. Just a man, a chair, a pipe bolted into the wall. And the kind of quiet that waited for someone to scream.

He looked up when I entered. Met my eyes like a man trying to measure risk. He saw it too late. There was no risk left. Only consequence.

I stepped forward. My boots left prints in the bleach-stained floor. My knife hung loose at my side. He didn't speak. Not yet.

He let me circle him once. Twice. Tracked me with his eyes like he could still talk his way out of it.

He couldn't. I stopped behind him.

"You were there," I said.

My voice didn't rise. Didn't crack. It just filled the room like breath.

"You were in the room when they brought Camille in."

He exhaled. Slow.

"I didn't touch her," he said. "I wasn't involved."

I stepped closer. The blade kissed the back of his neck. He froze.

"You didn't need to be involved. You watched."

He swallowed. I heard it.

"I signed a clearance order. I didn't know what it meant."

I pressed the tip harder.

He hissed.

"She died screaming," I said.

He flinched.

"No," he whispered.

I moved around to face him.

"That's right," I said. "Camille didn't scream. You know that, don't you?"

He looked away.

I crouched.

Close. Closer.

"She stayed silent. Even when you made her bleed. Even when you showed her the fire."

He shook his head. "I didn't touch her."

"You didn't stop it either."

I reached for his wrist. He tried to pull back. I didn't let him. The knife carved a line from his palm to the crook of his elbow. He screamed. Not loud. Not enough. I stood.

"But Cloe," I said. "Cloe screamed."

He whimpered. His head hung low. Then he lifted it. Just a little.

"She didn't scream," he said, voice shaking. "She—she hummed."

I froze. My grip on the knife tightened. He looked up. Terrified now. But honest.

"She hummed like it was the only thing she had left," he whispered. "Like it was the only way to keep from begging."

The room stopped breathing. I turned my head. Just slightly. And I felt it. The collar, still warm in my coat. The echo of her hum in my chest like it had never stopped.

I stepped forward. Knelt beside him again.

"*She hummed,*" I said.

Now I believed it. Now it lived in my ribs like a second

heartbeat. He tried to speak. I didn't let him. I leaned in, voice low.

"That was the only sound she had left."

Then I drove the blade into his side. Slow. Measured.

He didn't scream. Not at first. But when he did, I didn't stop. Breath was all she had. And now it was mine to take.

Barron

I stood in front of the wreckage of the Lawlor building.

Red and blue lights painted everything in emergency.

Sirens wailed in the distance. The sky hung low, heavy with smoke and the taste of blood in the back of my throat.

Emergency crews rushed in and out through the broken glass and steel, voices shouting names, demands, vitals. But I didn't move.

Loyal was propped against an ambulance, oxygen mask forgotten in his lap, face pale but eyes still tracking every shadow.

And beside me—

Royal. His coat was torn. Blood soaked through the left side. But he stood tall. Not a word between us. Not at first. Because there wasn't anything to say when your empire crumbled around your feet.

Camille's ledger felt heavier than it should have. I opened it with shaking hands. Page sixty-seven. Halfway down. Marked with a small star in red ink. *Continuity.*

That was all it said. One word. No amount. No recipient. But I knew what it meant. Continuity meant insurance. Legacy. The idea that what was built wouldn't end even if the people who built it did. Camille wrote that word like it was a curse.

I felt Royal glance over at the page. He didn't ask. Didn't need to.

"I found one more," I said quietly.

"Devane Holdings. Near the docks. Camille marked it."

Royal spit blood to the side. Nodded.

"Then that's where we go."

I didn't look at him.

"Wolfe?"

He ran a hand through his hair. It came back streaked with ash.

"He's already moving."

I closed the ledger. Blood had dried on the back cover. I didn't know if it was mine. Didn't care. Because Camille left the map. But Cloe was writing the ending.

And tonight?

We stood in the ashes. And said nothing.

Grief didn't make noise. Retribution did. And Wolfe was already on the way to deliver it.

Wolfe

We didn't start at the warehouse. We started with the men who led us to it. Not because I needed them alive. But because I needed to hear the hum again.

The gravel cracked beneath my boots. No voices. No orders. No countdown. Just breath. Just the weight of steel. Just the memory of a girl tied to silence and calling out without a word. The air in the safehouse was chemical—*false clean.*

London was already inside. Blood on his sleeve. Split knuckle. Collar torn like he'd just finished burying someone who didn't stay down.

He didn't greet me. Didn't smile. Just handed me a keycard

with fingers still streaked in red and eyes that looked carved from vengeance. Like this was the version of London they built when diplomacy failed.

"Downstairs," he said.

"Third door on the left."

I didn't thank him. Didn't speak. He didn't need that. And I was bleeding again.

The tape at my side had started to slip, crimson soaking through the cotton beneath my jacket. But I walked like pain was the currency I planned to spend.

I entered first. The corridor reeked of iron and silence. Blood splattered across the nearest wall. A trail smeared toward one of the open doors. Another body lay halfway in the hall, neck bent wrong, mouth frozen in something that might've been a scream if London had left him enough throat to finish it.

The floor was streaked with red. Violence painted like intention. London's kind of art.

The corridor was silent. A long row of numbered doors. No cameras. No echo. Door 3 waited. Closed. No lock. I opened it.

Inside—

a console.

a man.

a speaker still glowing.

The hum was playing. Faint. Warped. The last breath of her resistance caught in the air like a ghost that hadn't let go.

The man turned. Too slow. I grabbed him by the collar and slammed him into the chair. One hand held him still. The other hovered the blade just beneath his jaw. The speaker glowed behind us, the hum rising like it recognized me.

"You heard her," I said.

The man stammered.

"Please—I just ran the tech, I didn't—"

I pressed the blade tighter.

"Don't lie."

"I didn't know who she was—"

"You knew she was alive."

"I—I was ordered—"

"She hummed," I said.

"Because you didn't let her scream."

Then I pressed the blade in. Just enough to draw breath. Just enough to cut memory.

He broke.

"There's a second signal," he gasped.

I froze.

"Where?"

"Storage hub near the docks. Devane Holdings."

I pulled the blade away. Walked to the console. Brought up the signal. It matched. Pinged clean.

I turned to him.

"You were the last person to hear her hum."

His eyes went wide.

"No—please—"

My voice was steady.

"I want you to hear it one more time."

I pressed the speaker against his chest. Turned the volume up. Let the hum rise like smoke.

"You turned her hum into currency," I said. "Let's see how much you're worth when it's your blood on the signal."

Then I drove the knife into his thigh. He shrieked. I didn't stop. I sliced through the abdomen—deliberate. Watched him twist. Watched the meat split. Then lower. A tendon behind the knee. Heard the *pop*.

"You want to beg?" I asked. "Use your spine."

I tore the speaker cord from the console. Wrapped it around his neck. Tight. I carved a line just above his collarbone. Where Cloe wore hers.

"Now you know what it means," I said.

"To be owned."

"You recorded her pain like it was data," I said.

"You sold her voice to men who watched it on loop while she bled."

His body thrashed. He begged. He choked.

I twisted the blade. Then pulled it free. Then used it again. Not once. Not twice. Until the chair beneath him was red. Until the floor was painted in the truth.

You'd be proud of that one, Camille.

I made it last.

I didn't speak. I didn't breathe. She wasn't screaming. She was surviving. And now? I was vengeance. And Devane was next.

Cloe

I WOKE TO WATER.

Not gentle. Not clean.

Cold like punishment. Sharp like teeth. It slid down the inside of my thigh and soaked the floor beneath me.

Rough fabric. No soap. Just chill and friction. Someone wiped my neck. My chest. Down between my legs. Not fast. Not careful. Not curious. Just functional. Like they were cleaning a statue. A body they didn't want to rot before the show.

I didn't move. My wrists were loose but numb. My feet flat against the floor, slick with cold. The gag was gone. Replaced with nothing. Not silence. Just exposure.

I blinked once. A woman stood in front of me. Late forties. Gloves on. Face neutral. She didn't meet my eyes. If she had, she might have seen it. The rage. The breath. The echo of the hum still thrumming in my chest.

She didn't meet my eyes. But her hand shook—just once—when it passed over my ribs. Maybe she thought I didn't feel it. But I did. Fear recognizes itself.

They dressed me in white. Thin cotton. The kind that clung when wet. No bra. No underwear. No warmth. A dress designed to disappear under light.

She stepped back. Another figure entered. Man. Silent. He shackled my wrists. Ankles. Quick. Mechanical. I didn't fight. Not from fear—from readiness. Stillness was the only rebellion they still feared. He didn't speak. Didn't touch anything he didn't need to.

They didn't want me real. They wanted me clean. Polished. Framed. When they were done, they left me standing.Naked beneath white. Hands bound. Mouth dry. And breath still mine.

The door opened. Light poured in from above. And I knew the next part wasn't for me. It was for them. They dragged me by the wrists. The chains bit into skin that was already raw, already torn. My knees scraped the ground when I stumbled, and they didn't stop. Didn't pause. Didn't let me walk. They wanted the picture of resistance. Wanted to show me being pulled. Not carried. Not guided. Dragged.

The door opened. And the wind hit. Not fresh. *Sharp.* City air spiked with exhaust and ozone and the kind of salt that lives on rooftops. It cut through the thin cotton of the shift like it was looking for something soft to ruin. My skin pulled tight around bone.

They didn't give me shoes. The rooftop stretched in long strips of tile, bleached and heat-scarred. A single metal pole rose from the center like an altar.

Lights flared from every side—too white. Too clean. Not for

truth. For erasure. This wasn't a platform. *It was a fucking auction block.*

Glass towers blinking with the lives of people who didn't know what was about to happen. Who wouldn't care even if they did. No screams reached this high. No prayers, either. They shackled me to the post. Wrists high. Ankles wide.

The chain stretched my arms until my ribs ached. I was forced to stand. To stay upright. My weight dragged my shoulders down.

But I didn't collapse. I held it. I wasn't here to perform for them. I was here to remind them what a girl looks like when you try to erase her and fail. The lights came on. Blinding. They caught the cotton shift and turned it sheer. The outline of my thighs visible. My chest. My ribs.

I didn't move. Didn't flinch. Let them look. Let them see what they made. Let them see what Wolfe would destroy for. A door opened at the far end of the roof.

Ellis stepped out first. The man beside him followed. They didn't rush. Their footsteps were too soft. Too timed. Like they'd rehearsed this. Like they'd sold girls like me before.

He didn't look at me. He looked at the money in his hand. And I smiled. Not wide. Not kind. Just enough to bleed. No one ever looks up. But Wolfe always did.

The wind caught the edge of my shift. It lifted it just enough to remind me that I didn't belong to myself anymore—not in their eyes. It clung to my thighs, my ribs, transparent under the white light bleeding down from above. A spotlight designed not to show, but to strip.

They didn't ask for a scream. They asked for stillness. And I gave it to them. Because stillness was mine.

The chain tightened when I shifted. My wrists tugged high, shoulders aching from the weight. I had to stay upright. I had to let the posture be the punishment. But I wasn't collapsing. Not for them. Not for this.

Ellis didn't look at me when he stepped forward. His coat cut sharp across his frame, black on black, like he wanted to vanish into the city behind him. His eyes flicked to the floor. To the papers in his hand. To the man walking beside him.

The buyer.

I knew he was a buyer. Not by the suit or the money or the way his face didn't twitch when he looked at my body and then looked away. Not by the quiet he carried like it belonged to him. But by the fact that he never once saw me. Not really. Just the outline. The price. The potential return. He held the envelope like it weighed more than I did. Ellis accepted it without comment. Their hands brushed. Business. Clean.

Camille used to say the most dangerous men were the ones who never had to get their hands dirty. The ones who could sell you with a signature and still sleep after. She was right. Ellis turned to me. Smiled.

"Do you want to know what she said?"

His voice was smooth. Measured. Polished like everything else he wore.

I didn't answer. Didn't blink. He stepped closer. The light shifted. Cast him in shadow. Let me pretend I couldn't see the truth behind his mouth.

"Camille died thinking her voice mattered."

The words hit my chest like a second chain.

"You're not going to make that mistake, are you, Cloe?"

He reached forward. Tucked something into the waistband of my dress. A folded slip of paper. His fingers brushed my stomach.

I didn't move.

"You're not inventory," he said.

His mouth hovered just beside my ear now.

"You're the echo."

I didn't flinch. Echoes don't beg. They *warn*. And Wolfe? Wolfe doesn't answer with sound. He answers with smoke.

He stepped back. And I smiled.

I was never the silence. I was what came after.

And when Wolfe answered—it wouldn't be with mercy. It would be with fire.

39

WOLFE

Devane Holdings looked abandoned from the outside.

Rust-stained siding. Shattered windows. A fence chained shut with a lock that had long since been broken. The kind of place no one questioned. The kind of place where silence was stored like inventory.

I scaled the fence. Dropped down hard. Fell to one knee. Pressed my palm to the concrete to steady myself. My side screamed. The wound pulsed beneath the tape. Fresh blood bloomed under my shirt. The world tilted. Not from blood loss. From *rage*.

I bit down. Hard. Against the scream clawing up my throat. I was too close. Too fucking close to lose now. I got up. Step by step. Toward the door. No guards. No resistance.

The inside of Devane was colder than it should've been. Not chilled. Vacuumed. Like the building had exhaled everything human and replaced it with rot and power. A long corridor led me forward. One light flickered above. Every door was closed. Except one. At the end.

I stepped inside. There were no cages. No girls. No buyers. Just one chair. Facing a wall of screens.

The chair was leather. Black. Reclined slightly. Waiting. And the screens? Lit up. Twelve of them. Each displaying a different angle. The rooftop. The pole. The chains. *Cloe.*

She was standing. Strapped in place. Dress whipping in the wind. Hair stuck to her mouth. Eyes closed.

The camera zoomed in. High resolution. HD clarity. The shift clung to every line of her. The collar was gone. But her name was still there. Carved into the posture. Into the breath she still hadn't given them.

The ocean moved behind her. Waves crashing. Salt in the wind. It wasn't close. It wasn't Devane. It was *far.* Far enough that I knew, even before I looked for coordinates—

I couldn't reach her in time. *They knew that.* A speaker clicked on above me. Static. Then voice. Ellis.

"She's beautiful when she breaks, isn't she?"

I didn't respond. The screen shifted. Another angle. A buyer walked into frame. Took out a pen. Signed a form.

Cloe didn't move. But her eyes opened. And I knew she felt me watching. Knew I was there. And couldn't stop it.

The hum returned. Looped through the speakers. Soft. Weak. Survival noise.

I stepped forward. Grabbed the chair. Flipped it. Let it crash to the floor. The screens stayed on. Cloe blinked once. Then again. Her lips parted. She didn't scream. She hummed.

And I screamed for her. Not with voice. With the sound of a monitor shattering as it hit the wall. With the console crushed beneath the heel of my boot. With the blade I drove into the speaker that dared echo her breath.

They wanted me to see it. They wanted me to watch. They wanted me to know I was too late. And I was. But they were wrong about one thing. This wasn't the end. This was the moment I stopped hunting them. And started *erasing* them.

Cloe

He walked away like he hadn't left a grave behind. The paper was still tucked into the waistband of the shift. I could feel it pressing against my stomach with every breath. Not large. Not thick. Just heavy.

Like proof.

Like a receipt.

I stood there. Arms chained. Ankles tight. Body shivering—not from fear. From wind. From exhaustion. From the slow unraveling of hours that weren't counted anymore.

The man who'd offered the money didn't linger. He never touched me. Didn't need to. Because Ellis had already done that. He didn't leave bruises. He left permanence.

I stared ahead. Not at the skyline. Not at the building behind it. At the space between things. The air just above the lights where no one ever looked.

Ellis paused before he reached the door. Turned his head. Not enough to face me. Just enough to speak.

"Tell him what she signed."

Then he left. The door shut behind him. The chain swayed slightly in the wind.

The light from the city shimmered off the polished roof tiles. It hit my eyes and turned the edges of the world into a blur. I blinked, slow. Let the tears form. Let them dry without falling.

Because I wouldn't give them water. I shifted my wrists. The shackles scraped bone. The paper bent slightly. Pressed harder against my skin. I reached for it with my breath.

I remembered what Wolfe said once—about breath being

proof. About silence being a leash. About the collar meaning more when it wasn't visible.

They'd stripped me of everything. But they'd given me this. Camille's signature. A death warrant she didn't know she was writing. And now it was pressed to my skin like a brand. I didn't need to open it. I already knew what it said.

It said: *This is what power looks like when it thinks no one is watching.*

It said: *We let her go so we could kill her quietly.*

It said: *You're next.*

And I smiled. Because they thought I was an echo.

But I was a storm they hadn't named yet. I stopped asking for rescue the moment they showed me what was left of Camille. They didn't need to touch me after that. Not really.

Ellis's voice lingered louder than fingers ever could. His breath still lived in the space between my shoulder blades, where he hadn't touched—but made me feel it anyway. His words hadn't just planted fear. They rooted something else. Resolve.

The chain shifted when I adjusted my stance. My arms were numb. My toes curled against tile so cold it felt alive. The thin dress whipped against my thighs in the wind, pressing to every hollow like fabric could finish what silence hadn't.

I was still gagged by absence. Still tied by performance. But the paper in my waistband didn't move.

Camille's signature stayed warm against my skin, like it knew I was still listening. Like it wasn't ink, but memory. A final confession. Or a prayer so sharp it had to be folded just to be hidden.

If I had spoken then, it would have been to her. But I didn't. Because this wasn't a moment for voice. It was a moment for breath.

I inhaled. Slow. Deep. Felt the pain ripple through my ribs. Let it settle in the pit of my stomach like something sacred.

Then I hummed. One note. Low. Wrecked. It scraped up my throat like it had claws.

I closed my eyes. Let it vibrate against the chain. Let it touch the collar that wasn't there. Let it pulse through the city air that didn't care if I lived.

Then I did it again. And again. Each time softer. Each time stronger.

Because this wasn't a scream. *This was survival rewritten.* This was my leash snapping back into his hands. Because I knew what Wolfe would do when he heard it.

He wouldn't call my name. He wouldn't kick down the door. He would walk. And each step would be a sentence. Each breath a vow. I didn't beg. But I prayed.

"If you're going to break me," I whispered to no one, "don't do it in silence."

The wind caught the words and carried them nowhere. But I didn't need them to reach God. Only Wolfe.

And I knew he was already listening.

Wolfe

I stood in front of the screens. Shards of glass littered the floor. Blood dripped from my hand—I hadn't felt the cut. Didn't care. Her breath still lingered in the air like incense, like sin. Like a fucking sacrifice.

The feed stuttered. Flickered. Then shifted.New angles. New men.

Not around her. Behind me. At first, I thought it was another camera trick. Another torment. A trick of light in the corner of the frame.

But then the shadows on screen moved...*and the sound came from the room.* Footsteps. Measured. Controlled. Like a countdown ticking in flesh.

I turned just as they stepped forward—*three men in black. Blades drawn. Gloves tight.*

No masks. No orders shouted. They didn't need any. They weren't here to threaten. They were here to end it. The screen behind me still played.

Her knees hitting stone. Her body dragged. Her throat forced open by reverent, bloodstained hands.

They wanted me to see it. And now they wanted me dead with it. Not just a witness. A burial. But they were late.

I was already gone. What stood in that room wasn't a man. It was the answer to a vow. A wrath their gods couldn't swallow. A silence sharper than steel. I didn't scream. *I moved.*

And this time, the only thing that got hollowed...was them. Behind them, mounted to the wall of a derelict building, a massive screen flickered to life.

Cloe.

Spotlit. Shackled. Shown like proof of ownership. Her hum looped once—soft, fractured—then cut.

The first man lunged. I let him come. Dropped to one knee, let the weight of my blood pull me low—then drove my remaining blade into his thigh, twisted, ripped upward through the groin. He fell without a sound.

The second one came with precision—military-trained, elbow first, knee second. He caught my side. My wound split. I tasted copper.

He grinned—just for a second. Then I headbutted him. Twice. His nose broke. Cartilage *crunched.* I took his blade from his belt before he hit the ground. Drove it into his throat while he was still blinking from the stars.

The third ran. I chased. Blood in my boots, rage in my lungs, collar pressed to my ribs like a compass made of pain.

He rounded the corner. I tackled him into the pavement so hard his head bounced twice. I took my time with that one.

Didn't speak. Didn't scream. Just made him understand what it meant to breathe in a world where *she* had been silenced. When it was done, I stood. Covered in blood that wasn't mine.

The screen still glowed behind me. Cloe's image flickering. Looping. A lie made to sell the ending of a girl who hadn't broken. I looked up at it. Raised the knife. And threw. The blade spun once. Twice. Buried itself in the center of the display. Dead center of her throat.

The screen cracked. Flickered. *Died.*

I pulled the second blade from my boot. And kept walking. Because they thought that was the end of her. But it was just the last mistake they'd ever make. I left Devane on foot. Blood in my boots. One knife gone. One hand shaking.

The collar in my pocket felt heavier than steel. They had shown her to me. Dressed her in white. Lit her in spotlights. Sold her in high resolution while I watched. And I hadn't stopped it. The warehouse door slammed behind me. The night air hit like punishment. Cold. Dirty. Real.

I made it three blocks before I collapsed. My side tore open again. The tape gave. I staggered into an alley. Braced against the wall. I didn't cry. Didn't scream. I vomited. Blood. Rage. Breath. Then I stood. Wiped my mouth. Reached into my jacket. Pulled the burner. Dialed Royal. He picked up fast.

"Wolfe?"

"Tonight," I said. "No shadows. No clean exits."

He exhaled.

"Good," he said. "I'm tired of being clever."

I hung up. Dialed Barron next. No delay.

"You ready?" he asked.

"We kill everything that watched her hum."

"You still wearing the watch?"

I looked down. The second hand ticked.

"Every second," I said.

Hung up. Loyal was last. He didn't speak. Didn't have to. "Load it all."

Click.

The city kept breathing around me. Cars passed. Sirens screamed somewhere they didn't matter. But I was done answering to time. Now time answered to me.

I didn't bring flowers. Camille would've hated that. She didn't believe in soft things beside graves. I brought the knife instead. The one I used at Devane. The one still warm when I cut the man who looped her breath through speakers like it was ambiance.

The dirt was dry. The grass clipped. Loyal had come. Not Royal. Not Barron. But Loyal—Loyal never missed. Camille Lawlor. No epigraph. Just stone.

I crouched. Drew the blade. Not to sharpen it. To mark something permanent.

I carved it into the holster strapped to my thigh. Letter by letter. My thumb split on the third. I didn't stop.

C
A
M
I
L
L
E

Blood welled. I let it fall. Into the grass. Into the dirt. Into memory.

"You weren't the warning," I said.

The wind moved. Not soft. Sharp.

"You were the blueprint."

I didn't close my eyes. Didn't flinch. Camille never asked to be saved. She built the war she knew we'd have to finish. And now we would. Not from readiness—from being too late.

I stood. Blood on my hands. Her name cut into leather. The collar in my coat. The vault waiting.

It didn't creak when I opened it. It welcomed me. Air cold. Still. Holy. Like every silence inside had been waiting for a reason to echo again.

I stepped in. Steel. Leather. Blade. I didn't inventory. I didn't sort. I *chose.*

Knife. The one Camille carried. Second blade. Short. Balanced. Fast. Holster. Worn. Familiar. Pistol. Loaded. One in the chamber. Everything strapped into place. Tight. Final. Then the drawer. The collar. Not the one I took off. The one she earned.

I didn't buckle it. Didn't touch it. Just folded it. Slipped it into my coat. It would go back where it belonged.

After. The vault sealed behind me. Not locked. Entombed. I walked to the mirror. Didn't see myself. Didn't need to.

Camille's initials were carved into the sheath at my spine. Cloe's collar was pressed to my ribs. And my name? Didn't matter. Hers did.

I stood in the center of the apartment. Phone in hand. The war table clear. Camille's ledger open. One name circled in red. *Continuity.*

They thought Cloe was a variable. They didn't know she was the answer. I looked at the blade on the table. The one I'd use last.

Then I whispered:

"Tomorrow, you don't walk away."

And I made the call. Royal. Barron. Loyal. One by one. Each of them already awake. Already armed. We didn't say goodbye. We said nothing at all.

The last thing they would hear was breath. And then?
Nothing.

They think silence keeps her safe.

It doesn't.

It keeps me starving.

Selene dresses her up like discipline.

The Judge calls her a display.

Barron's gaze lingers too long.

And Loyal and Royal—they're not as still as they pretend to be.

But she isn't theirs.

Not really.

Every breath she holds, every tremor she hides—I feel it through the leash.

Mine. *Always mine.*

Selene whispers Camille's name like it's a blade.

She thinks secrets will break me.

But secrets don't break me.

They burn me alive.

And when I burn, I take everything with me.

They want her punished.

I'll show them punishment.

Chain. Fire. Silence turned into war.

Because she doesn't kneel for them.

She kneels for me.

THEIR PUNISHMENT is book three in the brutal dark mafia reverse harem romance Diamond Ties series. Savage, erotic, and merciless—this is a story of punishment twisted into desire, of brothers who war as

much as they worship, and of the girl who learns that penance was never about breaking her.

It was about binding her.